F   Jarrar, Randa
JAR

A Map of Home

A MAP
OF HOME

A MAP
OF HOME

a novel

RANDA JARRAR

OTHER PRESS

New York

Copyright © 2008 Randa Jarrar

Production Editor: Yvonne E. Cárdenas

Book design: Simon M. Sullivan

This book was set in Fournier by Alpha Design &
Composition of Pittsfield, New Hampshire.

Kafka epigraph on page vii translated from the
German by Ernst Kaiser and Eithne Wilkins,
revised by Arthur S. Wensinger. Habiby epigraph
on page 1 translated from the Arabic by Salma
Khadra Jayyusi. Cavafy epigraph on page 145
translated from the Greek by Edmund Keeley and
Philip Sherrard.

10 9 8 7 6 5 4 3 2 1

LIBRARY OF CONGRESS CATALOGING-
IN-PUBLICATION DATA
Jarrar, Randa.
A map of home / Randa Jarrar.
p. cm.
ISBN-13: 978-1-59051-272-2
1. Arab American women—Fiction.
2. Immigrants—Fiction.
3. Domestic fiction. I. Title.
PS3610.A77M37 2008
813'.6—dc22
2007050094

PUBLISHER'S NOTE:
This is a work of fiction. Names, characters, places,
and incidents either are the product of the author's
imagination or are used fictitiously, and any
resemblance to actual persons, living or dead,
events, or locales is entirely coincidental.

FOR MY PARENTS

Sometimes I imagine the map of the world
spread out and you stretched
diagonally across it.

—FRANZ KAFKA, in his letter to his father,
which he gave only to his mother

A MAP
OF HOME

I

In the so-called Age of Ignorance . . . our ances-
tors used to form their gods from dates and eat
them when in need. Who is more ignorant then,
dear sir: I, or those who ate their gods?

You might say: "It's better for people to eat their
gods than for the gods to eat them."

But I'd respond: "Yes, but their gods were made
of dates."

—EMILE HABIBY,
The Secret Life of Saeed, the Pessoptimist

ONE

OUR GIVEN NAMES

• • •

I DON'T REMEMBER HOW I CAME TO KNOW THIS STORY, AND I don't know how I can possibly still remember it. On August 2, the day I was born, my *baba* stood at the nurses' station of St. Elizabeth's Medical Center of Boston with a pen between his fingers and filled out my birth certificate. He had raced down the stairs seconds after my birth, as soon as the doctor had assured him that I was all right. I had almost died, survived, almost died again, and now I was going to live. While filling out my certificate, Baba realized that he didn't know my sex for sure but that didn't matter; he'd always known I was a boy, had spoken to me as a boy while I was tucked safely in Mama's uterus amid floating amniotic debris, and as he approached the box that contained the question, NAME OF CHILD, he wrote with a quivering hand and in his best English cursive, Nidal (strife; struggle). It was not my grandfather's name, and Baba, whose name is Waheed and who was known during his childhood as Said, was the only son of the family, so the onus of renaming a son after my grandfather fell squarely upon his shoulders. It was an onus he brushed off his then-solid shoulders unceremoniously, like a piece of lint or a flake of dandruff;

these are analogies my grandfather would the next day angrily pen in a letter sent from Jenin to Boston.

And why was my dear baba filling out my birth certificate so soon after my birth? Because before his birth, he'd had three brothers who had all evaporated like three faint shooting stars before anyone could write them a birth, let alone a death, certificate. His superstitions superseded his desire to hold me so soon after my emergence, and besides, he told himself now, we had the rest of our lives for that.

When he'd filled out the entire form, Baba regally relayed it to the black nurse, who he remembers was called Rhonda, and she stared at the name and sighed, "Damn." Then Baba, in flip-flops, turned around and raced up the white tiled hallway, by-passed the elevator, ran up the three floors to the maternity ward, and burst into the birthing room. Mama was nursing me and I was eagerly sucking the colostrums, now and then losing her nipple.

"How is my queen?" said Baba, caressing my mother's face.

"She's lovely," Mama said, thinking he meant me, "and eight whole pounds, the buffalo! No wonder my back was so . . ." Baba's brow furrowed, and Mama couldn't finish her complaint, because, eager to correct his mistake, Baba was already out the door and running down the white-tiled hallway, past new mothers and their red-faced babies, past hideous robes in uncalled-for patterns, bypassing the elevator, and sliding down the banister of the staircase, landing smack on his balls at the end of it. But he raced on, doubtlessly feared by the hospital's patients and nurses who saw an enormous mustache with limping legs, which, upon its arrival at its destination, was screaming for Rhonda, where is Rhonda, help me, Rhonda, an outcry that provided the staff with three weeks' worth of endless laughter and snickering.

Why had Baba assumed, no, hoped, that I was a boy? Because before his birth, his mother had had six daughters whose births all went uncelebrated. He'd watched his sisters grow up and go away, each one more miserable than the last, and didn't want to have to be a spectator to such misery ever again: to witness his own girl's growing and going.

Rhonda, who'd expected Baba to come back and try the naming thing again, emerged with the birth certificate already in hand, and Baba, who is not usually known for laziness, grabbed a pen and added at the end of my name a heavy, reflexive, feminizing, possessive, cursive, cursing "I."

Moments later, Mama, who had just been informed of my *nom de guerre*, and who was still torn up in the nether regions, got out of bed, flung me into a glass crib, and walked us to the elevator, the entire time ignoring my baba, who was screaming, "Nidali is a beautiful name, so unique, come on Ruz, don't be so rash, you mustn't be walking, your, your . . . *pussy*"— this in a whispered hush, and in Arabic, *kussik*—"needs to rest!"

"*Kussy? Kussy ya ibn ilsharmoota?*"—My pussy, you son of a whore? "Don't concern yourself with my pussy, you hear? No more of this pussy for you, you . . . ass!"

"Ruz, enough, have you gone mad cussing in public that way?"

"You think these people understand a word we're saying? You!" she shouted in Arabic, and pointed at a white woman nursing her child in the hallway, "your kid looks like a monkey's ass." The woman smiled at her in English. Mama looked at Baba again. "Aaah, there are surely hundreds of Arabs in Boston!"

"Actually, my love, this is where Arabs first arrived, in the 1800s, and called themselves Syrians."

Mama stared at him incredulously. Her brown IV-ed hand rested on her enormous hip, colostrum leaked into her night-shirt, and her large eyes, which were fixed at Baba as though poised to shoot death rays, were still lined with kohl.

"Impossible! You're giving me a lesson in history, you ass, and you named our daughter Nidali?"

"Yes, and another curious thing: the immigration officers would change the Arabs' names, so the Milhems would become the Williams, the Dawuds the Daywoods, the Jarrars the Gerards, and so on." Baba was trying to calm Mama down by distracting her.

"It's good that you are mentioning name changes, my dear; I'm changing the girl's name right this instant! First you give her a stock boy's name, as though she'll be raised in a refugee camp, as though she's ready to be a struggler or a diaper-warrior, then you add a letter and think it's goddamn unique." A nurse who had been following Mama presently gave up, and Mama continued. "No, brother, over my dead body and never again will you get pussy, I'm not forecasting this girl's future and calling her 'my struggle'! She'll be my treasure, my life, my tune, so don't tell me my pussy needs to rest!"

The elevator announced its arrival with a hushed DING, as though begging my parents to give up.

"Your tune?" Baba said, boarding the elevator with Mama. "Don't tell me, don't tell me: you wanted to call her Mazurka? Or Sonatina? Or Ballade? Or, or . . . Waltz?" Baba was giggling, amusing himself while angering Mama to unnamable extremes, a skill he was just beginning to master.

"There's nothing wrong with Sonatina!" Mama said, and the elevator made another DING, and she walked out.

Baba stood in the elevator still, pondering the idea of Sonatina Ammar, and finally he released a giant, expanding, white-tile-hallway-shaking laugh.

Mama must not have fought longer after Baba's laugh, or who knows: maybe she went to the nurses' station and talked to Rhonda, and maybe Rhonda told her that the birth certificate was already sent out—that Mama would have to go to the office of the City of Boston clerk and see the registrar of vital statistics, where they keep the birth *and* death certificates—and maybe Mama, who is the most superstitious of all humans (even more than Baba, and to that she'll attest) shuddered at the thought of taking me, a newborn, through the heat and the Boston traffic to a place where, she must've imagined, people went to fill out death certificates, and she must've further imagined that going on such a trip, to such a place, would surely bring about my death—because I still have my name.

MAMA LIKED TO say you could never judge how people might have turned out. For her—aforementioned superstitionist *par excellence*—if things hadn't happened exactly the way they'd happened, one out of three people involved would invariably be dead. "If we'd stayed in America the first time," she'd say, "maybe I would have believed that women's liberation thing and left your baba. Then we would have lived off my pitiful salary as a concert pianist at the local TGIF. Ah, no, no, this is a nightmare already, my daughter, no, things always turn out for the better in the end, Allah wills it so."

As Mama said this, I'd be fantasizing about growing up in Southside Boston with cool people, a giant, three-foot-long latchkey hanging around my neck. Only four years old, I'd come home from day care and pour myself a bowl of cereal. It could have been like the Bill Withers song, *"just . . . the . . . two of us"*: poor and Arab. People would have assumed that Mama, who has kinky black hair, brown skin, dark green eyes, and wears a lot of gold, was a Latina, and that I, a cracker-looking girl, was her daughter from a union with a gringo, and that would have been that.

But Mama is an Egyptian, her mother was a Greek, my father is a Palestinian, and my parents didn't stay in America, on account of my *yia yia* (my Greek grandma and the reason that I look sort of like a cracker) dying of a brain tumor at the old age of fifty-six. They didn't stay in Boston: they returned on an EgyptAir plane with me in Baba's lap, Mama curled up inside herself, and Yia Yia's ghost jammed in between them. They returned cheerless, in seventies polyester pants and straightened hair, to bury my yia yia at the Greek Cooperative Cemetery in Alexandria.

In Egypt, I played with a set of Russian dolls my dead yia yia once gave my mama. I pretended to be the smallest Russian doll, the empty-bellied one that goes in her mama, the mama that gets cradled in her mama and so on. I knew that the biggest doll, the biggest mama on the outside, was a Greek but that I was not a Greek. I noticed that all the dolls were split in half except me, even though I was split in half: I was Egyptian and Palestinian. I was Greek and American. My little blue passport, the one that looked nothing like Mama's medium green one or Baba's big brown one, said I was American. I didn't have to stand in a different line at airports yet, but soon I would. And Mama would stand in a different line, and Baba would stand in yet another line. It would make me feel all alone and different. It would make me believe that the world wanted to split up my family, so I'd pull to them even more.

After burying my grandma, we left Egypt and went to Kuwait, where Baba's new job awaited him. Kuwait, in the seventies, was a haven for Arab intellectuals and for people who wanted to live in apartments that did not resemble shelters.

In their first year of marriage, my parents had already moved twice. Baba said that moving was part of being Palestinian. "Our people carry the homeland in their souls," he would tell me at night as he tucked me in. This was my bedtime story when I was three, four. "You can go wherever you want, but you'll always have it in your heart." I'd think to myself: "That's such a heavy thing to carry." I'd visited this homeland once, noticed that there was a lot of grass, several rocks and mountains, and thousands of olive trees and donkeys. It helped to know this when I was little, forced me to have compassion for Baba who, obviously, had an extremely heavy soul to drag around inside such a skinny body.

WHENEVER I IMAGINED Baba running out just after my birth and sliding through hallways like a movie star, I knew he must have embellished. Baba liked to do that: tell stories that were impossible but true all at once, especially if those stories made him look like a rock star. This is because he used to be a writer and was now an architect. Our little apartment was filled with blue-prints and plastic models of houses instead of notebooks and poetry and ashtrays: a reality that filled him with great sadness. So Baba, a survivor, put that sadness into these stories.

Mama liked to expose him when he told such stories; she was his paparazzo, his story-cop. This was because she was the true rock star: a musician who no longer played music. Baba couldn't afford a piano yet, he claimed, though Mama always accused him of hating classical music and wanting her to be miserable. Our house was filled with Baba's blueprints and plastic models of houses and with my schoolwork and toys and dolls and a hundred half pairs of socks instead of a piano: a reality that filled her with great sadness, so she took it out on us. This was the core of our conflict as a family.

I knew from the beginning that home meant fighting, argu-ing, and embellishing, and that's why I loved school. School was where my parents were not. Teachers were there; they taught us facts based on reality. They weren't supposed to love us, and they didn't. They were English and cold and didn't resemble us at all. I liked this, that they did not hold a mirror up to me. Like some kids felt about play, school was my true escape.

AT SEVEN YEARS old, I attended The New English School in Jabriyya, Kuwait, a gray and blue brick and concrete monstros-ity made up of three large buildings. The first building was the secondary school, the second was the secondary school's sci-ence and art wing, and the third was our building: the primary school. We had our own playground and in the enclosed courtyard, behind glass, sat several taxidermied animals. This was scary for us since we were only seven years old and we didn't know why we were forced to stare into a fox's eerily real green eyes while eating a *za'tar* lunch sandwich. Even more disturbing was the peacock in the center of the scene. The peacock's feathers were long and gorgeous, but on its face was a look of horror. I was convinced of it. I tried to ask my best friend Linda if she thought so too, but she refused to look at the animals because she was the only girl in class whose parents were cool enough to have a dog. When we went back to our classroom and sat in our little chairs, my friend Tamer raised his hand.

"Yes?" Mrs. Caruthers answered wearily.

"Mrs. Caruthers, are the animals outside alive?"

"Right, I see. No, they're not. Anything else?"

"But . . . how do they look so real?"

"They're bloody stuffed, all right? They're killed off and then stuffed by some evil bastard called a taxidermist. Are we done?"

"Taxi drivers are not bastards. Some of them give me chewing gum."

I laughed at Tamer's defense of taxi drivers, but no one else did.

"Right. Smashing. Everyone open your books up to page 11. I want to hear you read, Nidali, since you're so vocal today."

I read a story about a girl who likes to ski on cold white snow, and every few sentences I'd wipe sweat off my brow. I was sweating because I was scared and because it was 104 degrees outside, but I kept reading about the girl who likes to ski. My pronunciation was awful and Mrs. Caruthers was obviously and irritably in need of a drink.

"Some of us simply *must* practice at home. Some of us are pronouncing our words as though they are pieces of stew stuck in our teeth. Some of us . . ."

"What's stew?" Tamer blurted out. Tamer had soft straight brown hair in a mop cut, a huge brown scar on his left cheek, and two enormous, gleaming black eyes. I kissed his scar once. His cheek smelled like round bread.

"All right, not stew: bloody kofta, is that better? Your pronunciation is the absolute worst, Mr. Tamer. Read the story on page 13, please."

Just then, the national emergency system sounded the alarm that made our ears ache for hours afterwards. The siren was emitted from a central city station at 11 A.M. on the first day of every month, and everyone at my school, which was in the southeast, could hear it as though the alarm were only a few feet away, and so could every other school and section of the country. Its melody was monotonous, a low beep that sounded like a "doy" followed by a higher beep, then a higher one, and then the highest, pause, then the highest again, lower, lower, and lowest beep with a five-second break in between sets: doy-Doy-DOY-*DOY: DOY*-DOY-Doy-doy. It went on for three minutes. During those minutes, Mrs. Caruthers went silent and reached in her desk drawer for her "water" flask. The class erupted, grateful to have these three minutes to gossip in our own language. When the alarm sounded its last beep we became mute, like a loud soccer game on TV that's been suddenly switched off, and we resumed our reading.

The silence made it seem as though the alarm never happened, as though there wasn't a ten-year war being waged over our little heads, between Iraq, the country just north of us, and

Iran, the country whose hills we could see across the Gulf's water on a clear, dustless day.

School let out, and we waited for our buses outside the gate and talked about Mrs. Caruthers's breath.

"It smells like my father's cologne," I said.

"It smells awful . . . like Tamer," Linda said.

"Shut up, Linda. You're going to hell because you're a Christian," Tamer said.

"It does smell like cologne. I drank cologne once. It made me drunk," I said. The yellow bus pulled up, #27. The driver's name was Varsoop, or something like that. He drove very poorly.

"I'm going to heaven because Jesus will save me, and you're going to hell because you pray without shoes," Linda said, sinking into a hot leather seat.

"I'm going to be allowed to fast Ramadan when I'm ten. Then when I go to heaven, I'll throw spit bombs on you, *if* you're in heaven," Tamer said.

"Who's Jesus?" I said.

"Jesus is the Son of God. He was crucified." Linda had a big smile.

"God has no son. He's all alone. My Baba made me memorize it," I told her.

"Don't bother, Nidali. She's a Christian. She's not going to believe you. Let her go to hell," said Tamer, flipping through an Egyptian comic called *Meeky*. But I didn't want Linda to go to hell. I knew that word: Christian. Baba and Mama said that my grandma was a Christian and that meant she was one of the people of the book, and people of the book go to heaven if they're good.

Ahmed, our bus monitor, sat in the front of the bus, his white teeth gleaming at a joke someone just told him. I asked around and found out that he was sixteen. I was only seven, but soon I would be sixteen and he would be sixteen and I could make him laugh too. But my hair was brown, and I didn't know any jokes. Baba told a lot of jokes whenever we went to my aunt's house. I would memorize them from now on, just like I memorized the *fateha* from the Koran.

The bus was yellow and hot. My thighs stuck to the leather seat and sounded like Scotch tape whenever I got up or moved. The girls on the bus chatted about music and asked if I saw the new *Thousand Nights and a Night* Ramadan special, and we talked about the actress Nelly and how she was so beautiful and blonde and Egyptian too. We sang the theme to *Alf Leila wa Leila*: "A story every night / a thousand nights and a night / a story every night."

We made one last stop before reaching my street, and Ahmed got off. His friend told a joke I didn't understand, and it made him laugh. I'd have to ask Mama why it was so funny. I wanted to make him laugh, wanted to see his bright white teeth standing on queue in his dark face.

The bus stopped at my gate. I saw Mama through the window, running toward the bus. I felt embarrassed at her breasts bouncing up and down underneath her white and beige dress. I walked down the steps of the bus and she hugged me tight. "I have a surprise for you," she said, but wouldn't tell me what it was just yet. She held my hand and we walked through the apartment complex's courtyard.

Our apartment complex was seventies-style beige and red brick, with two sides that faced each other, and in between, four sections that curved inward, so that the complex resembled a curvaceous woman, or an hourglass. The middle area, the would-be woman's waist, was a courtyard with long grass and plastic children's swings that were bought by the lower-middle-class parents in a co-op style agreement. In the center of the courtyard stood a three-foot T-shaped water pipe, which I personally never saw water spout from. The pipe was useful for tying up robbers when playing cops and robbers, banging one's head on when running while looking over one's shoulder, and sitting on to pose for photographs with an elder. I have such a photograph. My widower grandfather, my *geddo*, had been visiting us from Alexandria; he was standing behind me, cradling me, and I was sitting on the water pipe, narrowing my eyes to protect them from the strong afternoon sun. I can tell it must be around 5 P.M. in the photograph by our long, phantom-like shadows in the newly cut grass to our right.

Once we were home, Mama turned to me. "I have some good news. I'm pregnant," she said. "Mama's having a baby." She must have thought this was a funny thing because she was laughing and happy, so I was laughing and happy even though I hated this new baby. Where would it sleep? Who would take care of it? If Mama took care of it, who would take care of me?

Baba came home from work and exchanged his suit for a long white *dishdasha*, stretched his long legs on the coffee table, and lit a cigarette. I sat in his lap and looked at his stubble, imagining that there was a soccer game happening on his face: that the small black dots on his face were people and fans, and his mustache was a goal. I kissed his cheeks and asked him about the new baby. "Do you know how big this baby is?" he said. I shook my head no, and he said, "Your mama has a baby the size of an olive in her tummy!" This really worried me because now Baba had Mama putting olives and homelands inside her too. I wondered how this would change our lives.

Baba decided he wanted to fix up the apartment, remodel in anticipation of the new baby. My room was turned into a nursery, with my bed—big, brown, and awkward—tucked away into a corner. "The living room has to change too," he said. "I want to paint this wall, make it seem different, make the house look bigger." On Thursday, the first day of the weekend, he told me to wear old too-small clothes and help him paint the wall adjacent to the dining table. He tied my heavy long hair in a knot at the top of my head and we used a big brush to paint the wall a soft blue. It took a long part of the morning, and Mama made us bean dip and fried chickpea patties. While Baba and I ate, I understood the joke Ahmed had made on the bus. I laughed at the joke now and told it to Baba, who laughed as well. "Where did you hear that?" he said, and I told him that my boyfriend said it on the bus. I know that Ahmed isn't my boyfriend, I added, but I'd like him to be. "Nidali," he said, his face changing a bit, "we don't have boyfriends." "We?" I asked. "What do you mean?" "I mean," he said, "boyfriends are fiancés, and then you marry them. You are only seven. How can you get married now? So you see, my little moon, you cannot have a boyfriend yet!"

My stomach sank. This rule sounded stupid. Of course I couldn't get married now, but why couldn't I have a boyfriend? Soon I learned that every other girl understood this rule; why didn't I? I stared at the white wall ahead of me and avoided Baba's gaze. I felt as though I was not truly his daughter, that I must have come from elsewhere if I disagreed with his rules.

When we were done eating, Baba got up and said, "Do you want to know Baba's idea for this wall? You can help fill in the empty spots." He took his paintbrush and painted long, giant trees in our living room against the blue sky of the wall. The trees were slim and brown, with roots that showed and long, paper-thin branches. Baba let me paint small nests in the grooves between branches, and at the very bottom of the wall, right by the wooden floors, we painted grass. Low on green paint, we used a mixture of green and red. Because of this, the grass and the earth were violet in the forest—on the wall—inside our house.

SOME KIDS WENT to the pool, some kids went to the park, some kids—the boys—went to mosque. We went to the dessert shop by the Gulf: Mama's favorite hangout during her pregnancy. She always ordered the big chocolate ball, and I got gold chocolate coins. I liked unwrapping the thin golden covers and chewing on the circles. We sat in the sand and ate. It was a clear day, and the dust uprising stayed close to the ground so that we could see giant gray mountains across the Gulf water: we could see Iran. In the closer distance stood the water towers; there were three of them. The first was a spear with a ball in the middle, the second was just a spear, and the third was a spear with two spheres on top of each other. They looked like someone scooped ice cream onto the wrong end of an ice cream cone.

The spheres were blue and shiny like the Gulf's water, and Mama told me there was a restaurant in one if them that went round and round. I teased her and said that her stomach was as big as the blue sphere, the restaurant. She threw her head back and laughed a hearty laugh, the fillings in her teeth showing.

She told me those water towers were the reasons Baba wanted
to move to Kuwait. "They won the Agha Khan prize," she said.
"Aghawhat?" I said. She ran her fingers through my hair and
said I was the sweetest girl and that I looked like her mother.

"Do you miss your mama?" I asked.

"Yes. We will visit her grave the next time we go to Egypt,"
she said, and looked down, dusting sand off her long shiny skirt.

"How did she die?" I said, burying my gold wrappers in
the sand.

"She was disorganized. She put stuff in the wrong place, always put stuff in the wrong place. So she put a pomegranate in
her head and her brain crumbled." She said it the way she said
things when she volunteered at the museum: And here is the
Islamic arts section, and here is the science wing, and here is a
weird explanation of my mother's death. She'd never use the
scientific term: a tumor.

"Are you excited to have a son?" I said.

"Yes, but having a daughter has been just as exciting."

"Linda says God has a son. Isn't that crazy?"

Mama turned and looked at the Gulf. She took a deep breath,
then, "Some people believe that. Your yia yia believed it. She
was a Christian."

"But is it true?"

"*Habibti*, the truth is, different people believe different things."

I didn't understand how I could believe one thing when other
people believed something else. It made me feel as though there
was no way to really know the truth. But Mama told me that
this was precisely what the truth was: something too big for
everyone to agree on.

"For example, some people . . ." and she pointed across the

water, to the hills of Iran, "think that God exists in fire. Some people believe God had a son. And some people believe that after we die, we will be re-formed into other beings."

"Do you think people can be re-formed?"

"Possibly," she said, patting her belly. "Take the waves in the water at our feet. They aren't the same thousand waves, but they aren't completely different. Maybe people are like those waves, made of the same ocean of souls."

I patted her round tummy with her and thought about how she was once in her mama's tummy too.

She took a huge bite out of her chocolate ball and ran her tongue over her teeth so that the chocolate stuck to them, and then she smiled and pulled the curtains apart so that I could see the comedy on the stage of her mouth. She looked like someone had knocked her teeth out, so I laughed and laughed. She knew why I was laughing but pretended not to, repeating fake-angrily, "Eh? What's so funny? What?"

There were no other mamas like her. Most of my friends had mamas who prayed; Mama did not. Their mamas cooked and didn't play piano. Their mamas didn't say bad words and didn't yell at their husbands. Their mamas weren't Mama. I pondered this as I stared at her black front teeth, her huge pregnant belly, the sand surrounding her turning into gold flecks, the Gulf's waves crashing behind her, and I wondered whose soul my new brother would carry.

IN THE BLUE and white maternity ward I could hear my mother screaming. I stared at a clock that hung on the clean wall and noticed that the second hand didn't tick but moved in a fluid sweep. I wondered if this made time any different here, if this clock was a real clock, if Mama would still be Mama. The nurses kept giving me books to read and lollipops to suck on. The books were in Arabic and I loved to read from right to left. My eyes didn't hurt the way they did when I was at school reading from left to right. Writing stuff down off the blackboard was also from left to right, unless we had Arabic or religion class, which was only twice a day. In the beginning of the year, Linda took religion with us, but when the teacher asked her about Muhammad, she said she was Christian. The teacher, a short, bald-headed man with a comb-over, jumped out of his seat, his flesh jiggling, and yelled, "Why didn't you say anything? Christians and other non-Muslims aren't supposed to take re-ligion class. You are excused!" I felt bad for Linda, who wasn't going to memorize pretty words with us, or talk about the big ship with the animals on it. Then she told me that in her reli-gion there is a big ship with animals on it too. "But do your animals come in pairs?" I said. "Yes," she said. "You stole that story from us." "Who's you and who's us?" I said. She said Christians had the same stories we had. I asked about Adam and Eve, and she nodded. I asked about angels, and again she nodded. I asked about hell, which everyone called "the fire," and enthusiastically she nodded. I liked that Linda and I could be different but still believe in so many similar stories. There was a big Koran contest the following year, and I wanted to tell Baba about it. I knew I had to wait until after we took the baby home, if the baby would just hurry up and leave Mama's tummy.

The baby left Mama's tummy. He was red and blue and little. I kissed his little hand and rubbed his fat cheeks. "And now," Baba said, "you have a brother." I was glad Mama had a boy because I thought Baba would let me play and have fun now and be a girl. Just as I had this thought, Baba turned to me and said that since Mama would have to spend a lot of time taking care of the baby, I had to get my hair cut short.

My hair was long and Mama used to spend half an hour each afternoon brushing the tangles out of it, oiling it, and putting it in a ponytail. (Once, the teacher asked Mama to give me plaits for the school play and Mama gave me dishes because she had no idea what a plait was and neither did I.) So Baba took me to his barber, Sherif.

Sherif had a lisp and silly hair and wore a lot of rings and kept his shirt halfway unbuttoned. He told me he'd never cut a girl's hair before, and I told him, "Hair is hair," and Baba laughed. I laughed too, pretending not to hate that my hair was falling in clumps, like brown rain, onto the dirty tiles, that it now looked like boy's hair, that hair isn't hair.

"So how are you?" Baba asked Sherif.

"Like shit," Sherif said, then waved his scissors around, and yelled, "they think I'm a millionaire. My rent just went up. See that shit hanging outside?" He pointed with his long pinky nail.

"Lord almighty! You got a swirly barber shop sign?"

"I didn't just 'get it,' uncle, I fucking paid an ass cheek for it! The faggot charged me fifty dinars." He snipped a section of my hair, which he held between two fingers.

"He robbed you," Baba said, sipping a cup of Turkish coffee, a bitter look on his face. I'm sure he missed Mama's coffee. Mama, in the hospital, all alone.

"Robbed me? They raped me! What should I do? Walk out of my store like this?" He stopped cutting my hair and placed one hand in front of his pants and the other behind, over his bottom. "Because I had to sell my fucking underwear, Uncle. For a blue and red swirling piece of shit . . . but I need the business."

"Business. *Money, money, money, money . . . mo-ney!*" Baba sang this awful song he learned in America every time someone complained about money. Baba sang this song a lot.

Sherif brushed my hair and showed me the back in a small mirror. I could see my neck; it was bare. I could feel the wind from the fan tickling it. I felt naked and weak.

"I look like a boy!" I screamed, and Baba comforted me by saying, "You look like a princess. Now you can spend more time playing." I pictured myself outside perfecting my skating moves. Then I pictured myself perfecting them with short boy hair. "I'm gonna be the best boy," I spat out, and Baba gave me a frown. Whenever Baba frowned his forehead looked like a knot, and I wanted to put oil on it and spread it out.

After Sherif tried to blow dry all the loose hairs off my neck, Baba said we needed to go to the jeweler and get my new brother something. Once outside, Baba stopped in front of the shop and told Sherif, "It's the biggest barbershop swirl I've ever seen, if that's any consolation!" And Sherif yelled, waving his hand fiercely, "It does me no good to have such a big one when I have no underwear, *'Ami!*" and Baba laughed. I looked at what he was pointing at, and it was magic: a red swirl and a blue swirl dripping down, except they didn't drip onto the ground: they stayed in the glass cylinder that they were in. The glass cylinder didn't move at all. It's magic, I thought, and I wanted to be able to make magic too.

We walked past the fountain and down the steps of the shopping center, where the air conditioning made the back of my

They were drooping full of milk as she brushed the tangles and the curls out of her black hair. The hair dryer was on, and soon, as I sat reading in my room, I could smell the smoke, the smell of a burning house. I had to remind myself that it was just the smell of Mama's hair, and when I went to her room to check, I saw her arms raised, the brush in her hair, the dryer on it, and the white cloud of smoke above her naked body. She looked like a brown volcano. I went to my room and wrote her a short letter:

Mama,
I wish my hair was still long. I wish I could always do home-
work perfectly and Baba will never be angry with me again.

Then I stopped. I wanted to tell her that I wished she wouldn't sleep so much, wouldn't burn her hair, wouldn't let Baba scream at her or scream at me. I wanted to tell her I missed her. But I stopped, because I didn't want to upset her. Letter to Mama, second draft:

Dear Mummy,
I love you. I love Baba and my new brother.

I was lying—maybe not lying, but not telling her all the things I wanted to say because I didn't want her to be sad. It felt good to write a lie, to tell a small story. Mama called these white lies. Once, after dinner, Baba asked if she was making him his tea and she said yes, but when I looked over at the stove, there was no teapot on it. I asked her why she lied and she said it was a white lie, so it didn't count. I was comforted by this memory as I folded the paper with the white lies in it, licked a sticker onto it, and put it on her vanity table. She looked away from the mirror and, while blow-drying her hair, said something I couldn't hear. I pretended to and nodded, smiling.

It was Friday evening, the last day of the weekend, and Mama was ironing all our clothes, I think to make Baba happy. He'd been coming home with a briefcase heavier than my little brother, who he wanted to see more of. My little brother Gamal slept just before Baba came home. Mama didn't put him to sleep early on purpose but Baba was convinced she did.

So that weekend, Mama did all the ironing and had one shirt left: the shirt Baba got from England when he went there to visit his best friend from school who was now all grown up.

From the men's card game last week: "We were at Harrod's," Baba said. "I told him, you brother of a whore, don't pay for the shirt, and he said, *habibi*, you're here all the way from over there, and with two mouths to feed, so sit down and shut up, so I told him, listen, *habibi*, my dignity won't allow it, then he looked at me and said, brother, choose where you spend your dignity wisely, so I let the pimp buy it. It's the most beautiful shirt I own."

So Mama had that last shirt left to iron, and she'd abandoned it briefly to talk on the phone. I was playing with five rocks I'd painted red with Mama's polish and suddenly I smelled something burning. I looked over to the shirt and saw the smoke, so I went over to the ironing board and lifted up the iron. I lifted it up all wrong, I couldn't do anything right, and I burned my palm on the iron's corner. The searing heat hurt me, traveled all through my body, and I screamed. My scream brought Mama running into the room to check on Gamal in his crib, and when she saw that he was fine, she looked in my direction and realized that the shirt had burned through (but not that my poor hand was burned too). Baba came in and surveyed the scene, his eyes darting between the shirt and my palm. I saw it almost in slow motion: his thigh lifting his knee lifting his leg lifting his foot, his foot sweeping through the air, and the cleft in his brown shoe landing swiftly on Mama's bottom. Mama didn't seem shocked that he would do such a thing but she still let out a sob. Gamal woke up because of Mama's sob and cried; I screamed for Mama, for my hand, and for crying Gamal, and Baba yelled, "What kind of family is this, what kind of life!" went into his room, and slammed the door shut. I heard him locking it.

Mama went back to the phone, told her sister, who was calling from Alexandria with stories about her carefree bachelorette life, that my baba was an "insane curmudgeon," released a flutter of kisses into the receiver, and quickly hung up.

The house soon was dark. Gamal was back to sleep and it was time for me to sleep as well, but I felt sad and shaken. I asked Mama for a cup of water. She brought it to me. I asked her for a cheese sandwich, but instead I got an argument:

"You're not even hungry."

"I am!"

"No you're not, you just want me to work."

"No I don't, Mama, honestly I'm starving."

"Eat poison."

"Mama, just a sandwich."

"Do you swear?"

"I swear by the Lord almighty and the Ka'ba and the Prophet Muhammad, peace be upon him, just a sandwich."

She scratched her head and stomped to the kitchen, came back with the sandwich and no plate. I ate it in four and a half bites and then asked for more water.

"Drink your spit," she said, then took off her dress, slid it over her head in a swoop, put on a newly ironed *gallabiya*, and slipped into bed with me. I knew it was because Baba had locked the door, but I pretended that she just wanted to snuggle with me tonight.

"What's your most important possession?" she asked briskly, just as I was about to fall asleep.

I quickly answered, "my dignity," *karamti*, because Baba always said that.

She pinched my waist, told me I mustn't grow up to be so serious like Baba, and then said, "A sense of humor."

In the morning, I didn't want to get out of my cozy bed that was filled with Mama, her warm body and her smell, even though the crumbs from last night's sandwich were stabbing my side. She told me I'd miss the bus, so I put on my newly ironed uniform. I felt stiff in the starched shirt, like one of my paper dolls with a cardboard outfit on. I didn't dare ask Mama to pack me lunch. I just ran out to the bus stop as the bluish eagle stenciled onto the bus's side appeared. I got in and then realized that I never did my homework the night before. The assignment: draw two pictures of what you did this weekend. Linda got on and sat next to me. "Do you know what three times two is?" she said. "Five," I said, pulling out some paper and a pencil. "Wrong: six. I'm good at math, that's how I know these things."

I looked out of the window and wondered what I was good at, looked down at my burned palm and thought of what was on Mama's butt the moment before she'd put on her nightgown last night. Then I remembered what Mama said about having a sense of humor, and I drew two images, one of my palm with an iron imprint, and one of Mama's butt with a shoe imprint. I scribbled "My Weekend" and my name on the top of the sheet as the bus took a sharp turn onto Ring Road 5. A sense of humor—that's what I wanted to be good at.

TWO

COMFORT

. . .

BEFORE THEY MADE MY TWO HALVES, BEFORE I WAS IN THE
middle of them, Mama and Baba had been a happy couple for
five years. They were both twenty-five years old when I was
born, married less than a year. They'd met one early morning
while crossing the tram tracks in Alexandria, Egypt, eight years
before their marriage. Mama was in her lycée uniform, Baba in
his slacker uniform; she was on her way to high school, he on
his way home from a very late and drunken card game. Mama
would later claim that she snapped the elastic of her underwear
nonchalantly in a coquettish attempt at flirtation, but Baba
would refute this (of course, they could never agree on anything), saying that she didn't so much as look in his direction,
and that he, being a typical man, fell madly in love with her on
the spot.

"It's true I didn't look at you, because I'm legally *blind*, but
I did snap my underwear. You were too drunk to notice."

"I was not drunk. You did no such thing. I would not be
married to you now if you'd snapped your underwear at me,
so thank your almighty God that I didn't see you."

"No, I wish you had, because then you would have found me repulsive and not fallen in love with me on the spot, and I wouldn't be married to you now."

"Well, I guess it was meant to be that I didn't see you snapping your knickers at me; God willed it that way."

"Come on, do you think our Lord almighty was just sitting there in the sky, saw me snap my underwear, thought, 'Holy me, I can't let that handsome but prudish boy see that pretty girl snap her pink underwear, so I will blind him to it.' As if God were your secretary!"

"Your underwear was pink? You remember what color panties you were wearing? And you claim you didn't fall in love with me on the spot!"

"It was for the sake of humor in the story, man; I had to make it that God knew what color underwear I was wearing because 'God alone is omniscient, and takes cognizance of all things,' even young women's underwear." Mama had quoted *Luqman* 31:34, as though by repeating God's words she'd get Him on her side.

"Then He would have known that I would have fallen in love with you no matter what. You were done for."

Because Mama is legally blind, she and Baba technically did not fall in love at first sight. Because of their respective awkwardness and that of the world surrounding them, they spent the first two years of their acquaintance passing each other over tram tracks, inside trams, outside cafés, on street corners after a movie, at the Ma'moora beach in summers. Sometimes Baba, who wanted to impress Mama, would tell a short story in his loudest voice to the group of men he was with if he knew she would be standing in his vicinity for longer than a few seconds. Mama overheard these as intended and found them adorable in their desperation; through them Baba had told her everything he could about himself.

Alexandria, tram tracks, 1968: ". . . so then I told them that if I wanted to be a doctor, I'd be dissecting frogs, not the verses of al-Mutanabbi, or any of our great poets" (Baba's attempt at telling Mama he was a poet).

Meanwhile, ever a competitor, Mama thought she could relay a few things about herself through her piano playing, and when she realized that he would probably never see her play (unless she could manage playing a piano on wheels while crossing a tram track) she began taking her piano books out of her satchel and carrying them in her arms, making sure that the titles of the pieces always faced outwards. So, the sun would be shining on the old, pinkish-white, Parisian-style green-shuttered buildings, Baba would be standing at the corner of Saad Zaghlul Street, and Mama would pass by with her music book poking out under her breast, Frédéric Chopin, Ballade no. 3 in A-flat Major, op. 47. His face shone when he saw her, and she was pleased she'd impressed him. Little did she know that Baba knew jack shit about music (as far as he was concerned, Chopinian was the Armenian guy who sold chickens in the Ibrahimiya market) unless you played him something nationalistic or a tune he and his friends could *dabka* to, their arms linked in pretzels of defiance, their legs slamming the floor then flinging away from it.

Alexandria, tram, late 1969: ". . . and when I was born, my mother was exhausted from raising six daughters and losing three sons" (Baba telling Mama he was an only male child who needed a lot of attention).

She held her music theory books and her French literature on her lap, and when the tram jolted at the end of the line, Mama got off at the same stop as he, right at Alexandria University, signaling that she was no longer a high school girl, and the tram jerked away, students dispersing in different directions across the university grounds. It was on the tram that Baba finally noticed she was sending him signals through book covers, but it was his misfortune that the only foreign language he understood was English, and even that he read poorly. He'd go home to his Palestinian roommates and while they all played cards or smoked cheap cigarettes he'd argue with them about their schooling, saying all he remembered of English was a teacher who smacked his wrists and yelled, "Re-mem-ber—*Yata-thakk-ar*!"

"Fuck the English," his friends would say. "What do you want to learn English for anyway?"

"I don't. I want to learn French and Greek."

"Drink, drink, brother," they would say and offer him cigarettes.

Alexandria, outside Delice Café, 1970: ". . . I couldn't dream of a better marriage than the one between architecture and poetry; I love them both equally, and I can't imagine divorcing them from one another" (Baba letting Mama know he was still a poet but was very much interested in having food, and thus had chosen architecture as a day job).

Mama had stopped holding books to her breast and, although she was painfully shy, began yelling out information also, but not as suavely as Baba had, and to friends who were not as familiar with such schemes as his own friends had been.

Nefertiti Beach, Montazah, 1971: "My mother, who is a Greek, is designing a dress for my recital, which is on THURSDAY at the hall in the MUSIC BUILDING at FIVE in the EVENING, and my father, being an Egyptian and a Muslim, can't wait to come."

"*Ehl-'araf da ya* Ruz, stop screaming in my ear!" her friend Margot said.

"Yes, why are you giving us a history lesson in your genealogy?" her friend Salma said.

Mama ran her fingers through her hair, which was kinky as shit, and which she spent five pounds a week going to the salon to straighten, and then five hours a week in between salon visits ironing with her mother's iron on an actual ironing board.

Baba went to the recital and sat in the back row, awed that her fingers could move so fast for five whole minutes. He asked the gentleman sitting to his left what the song was named, but the man shrugged, and the man on his right whispered, Debussy's "Pour le Piano." Baba's mouth sagged, and a hairy "huh?" formed in his coiled brow. Next came a Bach suite. Baba shifted, feeling languid. In his mind, he was listing all the reasons he couldn't get into classical music: It was not for him; it wasn't *made* for a person like him, a guy from a mountain and a history of suffering; that was the way he felt about the Beatles too, and anything pop culture–related that his contemporaries, who seemed to lack his sense of guilt and baggage, enjoyed. It was Western and weird and elevated and condescending. He scratched his chin and pouted. Then Mama hooked him: she played a Chopin piece, his third ballade, and Baba was captivated by the opening melody, which made him recognize things he had no idea he felt. And then it disappeared, and the serrated dissonance that followed made him wish for the beginning melody. He longed for it . . . and it came back for a little while, only to disappear into dissonance again. And then it returned again. He was shocked at how much that melody moved him, at how much he yearned to go back to it. Quite simply, it reminded him of home.

Baba wrote down his feelings in his composition notebook as fodder for an unwritten poem, but couldn't work up the courage to introduce himself to Mama. So, later that night, Mama ate six éclairs, four *luqmat el qadi*s, a crème brûlée, and a pan of *basbusa*. She let her hair kink for the next two days while she moped around the house in soiled nighties and hugged a transistor radio, which was—like her Egyptian and Greek single self—permanently stuck between stations.

On Ma'moora Beach, Alexandria, in the summer of '71, Baba said: "Our reading will be spectacular. I can't wait to see the crowd and its reaction to our verses."

He was talking to his friend and fellow poet Ghazi, and didn't know that Mama was standing right behind him, wanting one of the flyers they were both handing out:

AUGUST 2, 1971

7 IN THE EVENING, IBRAHIMIYYA HALL, ALEXANDRIA UNIVERSITY

A NIGHT OF POETRY WITH THE YOUNG POETS

GHAZI AL-TAHER   WAHEED AMMAR   TAWFEEQ NABULSI

Mama thanked him for the flyer, didn't snap her panties, went to the reading a few nights later, heard him read, "When the kisses were sweeter than theft / When a single touch was bewitching / Would that the memories could be recalled / But can the heart return any purer?" and fell in love with him on the spot. This time, in the absence of her piano playing and his nervousness, Baba finally introduced himself to her. To his surprise, he introduced himself as Said. She felt stupid for saying nice to meet you—"*Fur-sa saida*"—because she'd feminized his name, and he felt stupid for introducing himself with a name he hadn't used since his boyhood. He spent the rest of the night trying to work it in that he was now named Waheed, pondering how he could pull this off without seeming a sociopathic fraud, and baffled at why he had introduced himself with that boyhood name to begin with.

They abandoned their poor attempts at courtship and made up for all those years by rendezvousing at *corniche*-side cafés and eventually in Cairo once a month, where Mama was enrolled half time in the musical *conservatoire*. They took the same train, sitting across from each other and talking, cherishing the privacy of those three hours. They actually talked. There was no arguing, no oral divorcing, no flying objects (except maybe clothing, but that, they claim, came only after marriage).

After the '73 war between Egypt and Israel, Baba wrote a poem that became famous in Alexandrian literary circles. It was entitled "Revolutionary," after Chopin, and although most people saw the poem's repeatedly addressed beloved as the Arab world, the beloved was really my mama. On one rendezvous in particular, the most important one of their lives, Baba brought with him an addendum to "Revolutionary" in which he asked for Mama's dark and lovely hand in marriage. That afternoon, Mama met Baba at a favorite spot: a cheap restaurant by the *corniche*; she had just returned from the *coiffeur*, and her long black hair was defiantly piled up in a chignon so exaggeratedly immense that it alarmed my father when she approached him.

"The bastard wanted to be artistic," Mama cried, pointing at her hair-tower of Pisa. She begged Baba not to notice it.

Baba immediately withdrew a piece of paper from his pocket and began reciting, and just as he was getting to the good part (he thought it was a good part) the devilish Alexandria wind blew so hard it knocked my mother's hair over and, according to Baba, sent pieces of it flying away into the Mediterranean.

"No!" Mama yelled at him later. "That didn't happen, you're such a storyteller. I never had a weave."

"And I never had a mustache! *Ya sheikha*—Come on lady, he put a weave into your hair to fatten up the chignon. Admit it!"

"Never!" Mama left the room.

"Admit it! *Your real hair / draped at your shoulders / while the weave / fell into the wave / and was banged against the beach's boulders!* Admit it!"

"Go to hell!"

Anyway, the proposal was not postponed, and Mama let Baba kiss her right there against the rusted railing by the sea.

Baba graduated with a degree in architecture, Mama a degree in music theory and composition, and soon, Baba, who didn't really know who he was or where he belonged, having been forbidden from re-entering Palestine after the 1967 war, proposed to my mama, who was so rooted she had been born and brought up in the same apartment. Baba asked her hand in marriage from my grandfather, the retired military man and ex-free officer who was less than pleased to give his eldest daughter to a Palestinian with no family in the country who was going to take her away, first to Boston where he'd secured a one-year internship with a lower-tier architecture firm, thanks to the Kuwaiti engineering firm that had hired him, and for which he was going to work upon their return and relocation to Kuwait. Mama, however, thought the match a perfect fit, and her mama, a tough, feisty woman, loved the idea of a poet joining her daughter in this journey of living and encouraged it no end, and since she was a strong and stubborn bitch, my grandpa had no real choice in the matter.

Baba worked long hours at the local branch of the Kuwaiti Architecture office in the months leading up to the wedding—long enough to afford tickets, from Palestine via Jordan, for his mother and father (they were thrilled at their only son's marriage to a beautiful girl who, because she was Egyptian, spoke like a movie star) and for only two of his sisters: his sister Kameela, whom he loved almost more than he loved my mother, and his eldest sister Samira, who had raised him until her own marriage sixteen years before, and whom he loved as much as he loved his own mother. They took taxis from Jenin early in the morning, passed through the Allenby bridge into Jordan, then took taxis to the airport in Amman, from which they boarded planes to Alexandria.

For years, Yia Yia, my grandmother, would always tell Mama not to eat out of the pot, which Mama still does to this day, but to get a plate out and eat like a human, or *zay elnas*, like people do. Mama disobeyed her and ate out of the pot, at the stove, standing up all the while, and Yia Yia told her not to eat too much, because *polla faya polla scata*—the more you eat the more you shit, and goddamn it, if she didn't stop eating out of the cursed pot it would rain on her wedding day, didn't she

know that? Mama always funneled another spoonful of mous-
saka and rice into her little mouth and told her mother there
was no connection between eating out of a pot and having it
rain at your wedding.

It rained at my mother and father's wedding in early October
of 1975, big rain that fell on the Fiat's windshield; they had borrowed it since they were carless, and my aunt Sonya had deco-
rated it with huge bunches of jasmine and wide yellow ribbon.
They drove along the *corniche*, through traffic and rain, and rain-
traffic, with a trail of cars behind them honking and cheering them
on all the way to Palestine Hotel, which was in the old royal park,
where the belly dancer was waiting, her hair kinked up because
of the humidity and the rain. Years later, I sat around Geddo's
and pored over these images for hours, of my mother in her white
tulle dress, her body close to my father's, in the white wedding
album Geddo kept on the shelf. Her mouth was slightly open in
one of the photographs, and I could see her crooked teeth, which
Baba said reminded him of the poor architecture of urban Egyptian buildings, and Baba had a serious five o'clock shadow, which
Mama says reminded her of musical notes.

MAMA AND BABA's stories had a very polished quality, and usually featured God being someone's secretary. Their fights were
about stories, and their fights and stories were like myths, told
and retold. In this way, Mama and Baba became my Gods.

I was just an eight-year-old, one who couldn't wrap her head
around the idea of a larger God, of souls, or infinite space, or
religion. Linda's Jesus, my Muhammad, Sherif the barber's
Marx . . . who were these people? What was going to happen

to all of us when we died? Why must I think about death, Mama asked. She didn't want to think about death. She wanted to forget her own mother.

Mama's idea that souls are like waves rang in my head like the notes of her songs. I told Tamer and Linda about it and they both laughed at me, and Tamer brought it up in religion class.

"Waves? Who told you such nonsense?" the teacher, Mr. Dawoud, asked Tamer. Tamer pointed at me.

"Is that true?" Mr. Dawoud asked me.

"No. I don't know if it's true, because no one knows what it's like after people die."

"God knows!" Mr. Dawoud thundered, "and He says that our souls return to God, not to others to be reused."

"Yes, sir." Please shut up.

"Our souls wait for the Hereafter, when we will all be judged."

I pictured our souls waiting in line at a supermarket.

Mr. Dawoud sat, running his hands through his combover after he'd regained his composure. "If you read the Koran, you will know all about this," he said. He adjusted his belt. "Those of you who memorize the Koran best will be allowed to enter a Koran contest. The contest will be held in Kuwait City Boys' School, and there will be three finalists, each of whom will win a gift certificate. But that is not the true reward. Those who win the contest," Mr. Dawoud eyed the boys in the first row, "will have proven that they understand the Koran best" (what I heard: "that they understand God best") "out of everyone in their age group."

I wanted to win this contest.

I ran off the bus because I wanted to tell Mama as soon as I got home. She was nursing Gamal and watching a *tamsiliyya*. The husband was about to divorce the heroine, so Mama shushed me. I rolled my eyes and put my hands on my hips, waited for him to utter the decree three times, "You are divorced! You are divorced!" The dramatic music swelled. "You . . ." "No, don't do it!" "Are . . ." "Don't, I beg of you!" "div . . ." "AAAAAAAAH!" Slow motion now: ". . . o r c e d!" Our heroine fainted. Mama turned to me.

"Huh? What is it?" And I told her about how the religion teacher didn't believe in Mama's ocean-of-souls theory and that there was a Koran contest, which I would win. Mama was excited for me but urged me not to tell Baba about it yet. "It's more than two weeks away, this contest. Tell Abuki now and he'll have you practicing verses all weekend. So promise you won't mention it for a while?"

"I promise," I said.

"Good. Now go to your room, I got you something. It's on your desk."

Mama was feeling guilty about me lately, I could tell. Whenever I'd come home from school, she'd have something new for me. That day, it was a sticker collection featuring a girl superhero: Woman of Wonder. She had shorts with stars on them, a golden lasso, and a crown that she wore like a hat. That last detail bewitched me. How could someone wear a crown so nonchalantly?

"Her real name is Wonder Woman," Mama called to me from the living room, "but that's how they've translated it."

"How do you know?" I called back, carefully peeling off the stickers so their edges wouldn't tear, and posting them around the room.

"Because when I lived in America," Mama yelled, "they had a show about her. It was called *Wonder Woman*." Mama came running through my room, her arms extended, as though she was fighting evil.

"Mama, you look like her," I said, glancing again at the stickers.

"Really? You really think so? Let's put some on your head-board." Mama was so pretty, but she didn't think she was. She wore lipstick and went on diets. Whenever I told her she was pretty the way she was, her face glowed with happiness. Now I wanted to make her a hat-crown.

We put the rest of the stickers on the headboard and I sat on my bed and stared at Wonder Woman. I loved her wavy black hair, so black it was almost blue: black like Mama's hair, wavy like mine. I stared at the eagle on her top; it was golden and resembled the eagle on the Egyptian flag. I admired her lasso because it reminded me of the rope women in Palestine tie on buckets and around goats' necks. I searched for hair on her arms but they were smooth. And when I saw the stars on her shorts, I was reminded of my blue passport, of how I was born in America. I wondered if Wonder Woman was Egyptian and Palestinian and American, like me. I looked at the stickers for hours until my eyes crossed and I started seeing small women of wonder all over the house.

Baba came home from work, lifted me in his arms, kissed my cheeks, and then asked me to bring him my homework. This would be the first in a series of reading materials he would di-gest in the evening. After reading my homework and marking it for corrections, he read the bills. After that, he settled into the couch and read his newspaper, since he didn't have time to read it in the morning while he was at work.

I'd hear him reading on the couch before I went to sleep. Sometimes he'd read the *Sharq al Awsat,* sometimes *Al-Ahram.* I'd listen to him flip the pages, each page making a sound like a wave of paper, a fan. The sound would comfort me. He'd flip the pages and curse, in the following order:

1. "The hypocrisy of Arabs, dirty Arabs,"
2. "The Americans and their capitalism,"
3. "Zionists and their Zionism,"
4. "Socialist cartoonists and their unfunny socialist cartoons."

I perfected falling asleep somewhere between 1 and 2. On a bad night, I slept shortly before 3.

That night I woke up sweaty and dry-mouthed, fresh from a nightmare. I rocked a little in bed, and heard Baba turning the pages of his newspaper. I called out for water, but no one answered, so I got up and walked to the bathroom, poured myself a glass, and then, on my way out, noticed that there was no one in the living room, no one in their bedroom, no one on the patio.

Upon further investigation (kitchen, bathroom again, under dining room table, closets) it became clear that Mama and Baba had gone out and left me there alone with Gamal.

Scared, I ran to bed, got in, and wrapped the covers around me. How many times had they done this? An old feeling visited my heart, the feeling that I was a dupe. It made me wonder what else I was being deceived about. Did Mama and Baba really love me? Was I safe in the world? Who protected me? And from there, things got worse: Was the world real? Was God real? Was *I* real?

I shut my eyes tight and started rocking. I rocked furiously. I heard Baba's newspaper when I rocked. I lifted my head and realized that the newspaper rustling was the sound of my hair catching on the Woman of Wonder stickers. So I kept rocking, and pretended that the sound was my father reading the newspaper out on the dirty green couch, which would be upholstered three times before they'd decide to throw it away.

And I duped myself into thinking it was Baba, with his make-believe paper, and Woman of Wonder, with her lasso wrapped gently around my hair, who rocked me to sleep, even though it was just me, all me. In this way, I learned how not to give myself credit for something I'd done all by myself.

MY RELIGIOUS COUSIN Esam was coming to Kuwait on an airplane all the way from the West Bank. Well, it was really a plane from Jordan, since there were no airports in Jenin or anywhere in all the occupied territories, so he had to take buses and vans and cabs and pass bridges and rivers and checkpoints to use the one in Amman.

Esam was old, eighteen or something, and Mama and Baba laughed, joking that he might want to marry me. This sent scary electric buzzes through my eight-year-old stomach, and Baba said, seriously, his mustache big and dark like a cocoon, "Don't worry, there'll be no marriages for you until you want to. And you won't want to until you have a doctorate. That's that!" I laughed nervously then, glad that I wouldn't be marrying anyone.

Baba and I filled out the competition's application and he told me, as he thumbed through the Koran, that I needed to memorize a verse from it. I nodded my head and wondered which verse he'd choose. Not a long one, I hoped. Please God, I love what you've written, but I don't want to memorize a long verse.

Baba chose several small verses instead of one long verse. I didn't ask him why, but he explained to me that the last few verses of the Koran would be necessary for me to know in the future. "All your life you'll remember these verses. I don't want you to be prepared just for a contest. Life itself is a test. Knowing these verses by heart will help you pass it, and will bring you comfort."

I sat on the floor in front of him and each of us held a book. He read and I repeated; he read and I repeated. I thought of the prophet coming home from his cave the first time he encountered these words, his wife Khadijja covering him in blankets, comforting him.

Esam showed up the next evening, haggard and exhausted; he'd stopped in Saudi Arabia to do 'Umra, the mini-*hajj*, real quick before he came by.

"Wow, that's good, very good," Baba said, patting him on the shoulder.

"You need to do it too, Uncle," Esam said. Baba looked away and asked Mama to ready the table.

I helped Mama bring out cheeses, olive oil, *za'tar*, breads, yogurt, fruits, fruit jams, pickled beets, and peppers. We sat at the table and Esam ate hurriedly, dropping bread flakes into his immense beard that resembled a small plant.

"Ruza, love, will you turn on the news?" We watched the news in silence, with an occasional question from Baba regarding my aunt and Esam's sisters, and sporadic giggles from me because of the newsman's funny, rigid Arabic; news anchors always spoke in standard Arabic, which rendered everything they said so serious and grave. Then, when the weather forecast came on, Esam jumped off the dirty green couch, ran over to the television set, said, "God forgive you," and turned it off.

"What happened?" Baba said.

"The forecast is blasphemous," Esam said, out of breath. "Surely you are aware of that, Uncle."

Baba stirred his tea and shifted uneasily on the couch. "No, I was unaware of it, *'Amo*," Baba said, calling Esam "Uncle," a term of endearment, the way he sometimes called me Baba. I loved how adults always called their dependents by their own names, so that grandpas called their grandkids Geddo, mothers called their children Mama, and aunts called their nieces and nephews Auntie. This term of endearment had a calming effect on Esam; he retreated to the couch and resumed regular breathing, but the television was still off.

"I thought," Baba continued, lowering his tea demitasse to his knee, "that the God almighty equipped us with brains so we could discover these things for ourselves: the weather, chemistry, math, philosophy, physics—all these useful things. . . ."

"Predicting the weather," Esam shouted, "is predicting the future, something only God can do. Weathermen, they're like . . . they're magicians, and surely you remember Allah's words against magic?"

"Sit down and shut up," Baba said, for once to someone other than me. He reached over the side table and emerged with a cigarette—where he got this cigarette, I didn't know—and he lit it with matches reserved for lighting the stove. He had me fetch them for him from the kitchen, since smoking was something he rarely did. His bringing a cigarette out of nowhere, though, made him seem like a magician to me, and I worried about his place with God and whether he'd angered Him, and fetched him the matches without my usual protests and whines.

Before bedtime, Esam went to the kitchen, where I was doing my homework, and took out a jug of water from the fridge. He then faced the door, got down on one knee, and lifted the water jug high above his head. The water came down like a stream and gathered in his beautiful beard-framed mouth. I couldn't believe how ceremonial this was: the simple act of drinking water. Then, just as suddenly as he'd entered the kitchen, he left it. I looked over at Mama, who was stifling her giggles by covering her mouth with a serving spoon. She turned to face the sink.

"See? See the crazy family I've married into?" Mama whispered to her dirty dishes. I didn't know if it was crazy. I wouldn't mind marrying Esam now, the handsome man in the white robe.

DURING A VERSE-MEMORIZING break, my neighbor Zeinab and I played memory on the carpet. I was winning.

"Allah is the greatest," I heard Esam chant from the hallway, and leaned my head to watch him pray. He prostrated himself, lowering his forehead to the floor, where he stayed for a long time. Baba once told me that the wishes you make while your head is down on the floor count the most.

"Are you playing or what?" Zeinab said, and I went back to the incomplete pyramid. Five for seven. I'd forgotten where everything was.

"Let me see your watch," I asked Zeinab without taking my eyes off Esam.

"Why?" she said, slipping it off her wrist.

"I'm timing how long he's going to stay down there making wishes," I said, and began the timing. It was 5:32. I wondered what Esam was wishing for: a girl, a new home, a better way to come here from the West Bank, a new pair of slippers, a more comfortable bed, a better future, a good meal (Mama was just an OK cook). Did he want to be a kid again? Did he miss his family?

He looked up at 5:36 and said, "Allah is the Greatest . . . Please God pray for Muhammad, and the people of Muhammad, as you prayed for Ibrahim, and the people of Ibrahim, and bless Muhammad, and the people of Muhammad, as you've blessed Ibrahim, and the people of Ibrahim. . . ."

"Who are the people of Ibrahim?" I asked Zeinab.

"Give me my watch back," she said. I did. "The Ibrahims, it's a family that throws big barbeques during Eid. They have a lot of daughters and the daughters are nice. They put makeup on me and braid my hair. . . ."

"What? No way. Why would we mention them every time we pray? Why would we want to be like them?"

"I don't know," she huffed, and we were down to four cards. King for king, prince for prince. She won.

At school, Mr. Dawoud sat down, put his glasses on, and read from a sheet of paper. "Those of you who signed up for the contest, wait by the main buses tomorrow morning. We will take bus #13 to Kuwait City Boys' School, and will return by lunch. Girls," he said, looking in my direction, "must remember to cover their hair." My friend Riham was in the contest, too, but her hair was already covered. Her father was from Yemen and told her she had to. I asked her, when she first started covering, if she was mad at him and she said she was happy to cover her hair and hadn't spoken to me since.

Baba would have never let me cover my hair. He said it was for donkeys. "What? Don't even consider it," he told me that evening. "Forget those retarded idiots! You must be cleansed to read the Koran, but no one ever said you had to be covered."

Esam coughed from his post in the corner of the living room. "Pardon me, Uncle," he said. "But this talk is incorrect. God has decreed that women cover themselves."

"Pardon me, 'Amo," Baba said, "but shut up." I wanted to kiss his stubbly cheek. It was strange: usually when he said "shut up," I didn't like it because he was either talking to me or to Mama—but just then, I liked it.

"Now," Baba said, and turned to me, "let's practice."

I was nervous, and recited the verses poorly. Baba was understanding at first, then grew more and more impatient with each mistake I made. My tongue twisted into a knot I was powerless to break. After I pronounced every word of *surat ul-sharh*, the verse of "Comfort," incorrectly, he disappeared into the bedroom and re-emerged with a hanger.

Right. I didn't want to anger Baba further but he *was* standing in front of me with a hanger, and it was making me more nervous than before. So I tried the verse again but I got it all wrong. "It's not, 'have we not dreamed up your chest and relieved you of the minister!'" he said, making fun of my mistakes. "It's 'have we not lifted up your heart,'" he hit my chest for emphasis, "'and relieved you of the burden which weighed down your back?'" The hanger whipped my back. I was crying now, and I couldn't speak.

I didn't know what made me sadder, that Baba was hurting me or that he was hurting me in front of Esam.

"Pronounce the words correctly!" Baba said. I couldn't. I didn't want to. I was hungry and I needed to rest. I wished he wasn't so angry with me, that he hadn't become this monster. Why did this happen to him? How did he let it happen? He looked different when he was mad. Sometimes he'd do this to Mama, just drag her on the floor, and she'd cry and tell him to stop. But I couldn't tell him to stop; I was scared I'd say it wrong. Now I was out of breath from crying, sobbing little sighs out every other second. Baba stopped hitting me and told me to start over.

I stopped crying. I remembered the words *sadrak*, and *wizrak*, and *thahrak*, because those were the places that hurt me. So I said them right; the questions God once asked Muhammad. But my pronunciation and my recitation became most powerful when I recited: "With every hardship there is ease. With every hardship there is ease."

FIFTEEN BOYS AND two girls stood at the bus stop. The boys were wearing shorts and shirts: what they usually wore. Riham was wearing a white headscarf, a long dress, a shirt, and gloves: what she usually wore. I was disobeying my father, my hair covered in Mama's handkerchief that I filched from her drawer, and my calf-length skirt fastened around my hips so I could stretch it down to my ankles. Mr. Dawoud looked at me and smiled, shaking his head.

Dozens of buses arrived at the City Boys' School carrying mostly boys from other schools, and we all lined up in the courtyard. One by one, the students disappeared behind a door and emerged a few minutes later with a look of relief stretched across their faces. I closed my eyes and practiced the verses in my head.

My turn. I went into the room and sat in a chair in front of the imam. His face was dark and his hat was red. There were no lights in the room and the shades were drawn. I crossed my arms over my chest and recited the verses, keeping the "Comfort" verse last. I didn't make a single mistake; in fact, I felt almost as though I was singing:

*Have We not lifted up your heart and relieved you of the
burden which weighed down your back? Have We not
Given you high renown? For with every hardship there is
ease. With every hardship there is ease. When your prayers
are ended resume your toil, and seek your lord with
all fervor.*

When I was finished, the imam said, "Thank you, sister," and bowed his head. I left the room with a soaring heart and a feeling of comfort, pitying the many faces still in line.

The yellow bus pulled into the New English School's parking lot at sixty miles per hour like a rectangular ray of sunshine, and I readjusted my hair under the scarf. I walked into the playground like that, all covered up and proud. My girlfriends—Sunnis, Shi'as, Christians, Hindus, and Mai, whose parents were communists—made a circle around me and hurled out questions.

"All I know is . . ." I said, and stopped for a moment. I wanted to say I was proud of myself, that I was good. But I kept it all inside in case revealing it would make this feeling—or worse, my friends—go away, and instead I said, "The boys in that school are way cuter than the boys at NES!"

Alone at home, I went directly to my room, to my bed, stared at the ceiling, exhaled. I decided to take a nap. When I lowered my eyelids I saw dark and jagged geometrical shapes, then the Imam's head when he lowered it to thank me. I turned onto my side, and when the rustling of stickers didn't greet me, my head shot up. I surveyed my headboard and my walls and realized that my Woman of Wonder stickers were definitely gone.

I knew exactly who the culprit was. I walked over to my brother and squeezed his mouth open, but only his milk teeth and red tongue greeted me; there were no stickers. "Sorry," I said hesitantly. He'd been eating everything lately, stuffing his mouth with fried potatoes, paint chips, cockroach wings, and old letters. Because of him, Baba once screamed, the entire 1973–1974 Baba–Mama correspondence was lost.

Next, I asked Mama about the stickers, but she lifted up her hands and shook her head; *she* didn't do it.

My stickers were just gone. Disappeared, as though Woman of Wonder had evaporated or flown away to other places, other girls' headboards. As though God had come in and peeled her away from me.

As soon as I had that thought, I approached Esam and yelled, "Did *you* tear down my Woman of Wonder stickers?"

He paused for what seemed like an hour, then spoke. "You mean the pictures of the naked heathen that were on your bed?"

He adjusted the skullcap on his flat, ugly head. I no longer found Esam handsome; I saw his chin growing warts as he spoke. "Yes, I did," he said.

"She was not naked. She had shorts with stars and a falcon on her top like the falcon on the Egyptian flag! She wore a crown like a hat. She held a truth rope and had many powers!" Including making me feel like a normal girl and helping me get to sleep, but I didn't want to tell him that.

"She should not be the woman you admire," he said.

"Why not?" I said, now sobbing uncontrollably.

"Because," and he looked straight into my eight-year-old eyes, "she is a shameless prostitute."

I screamed out. I cried and my nose ran. I sprinted to my room and fell into my bed, thinking how cruel, how unjust! My heart beat into the sheets and I banged my fists against the soft mattress underneath. But I never asked Mama for a different set, nor did she offer to replace them. In the stickers' place white pieces of paper remained where the glue had refused to part with the wall, so it appeared as though there were Woman of Wonder ghosts all over my room, apparitions where she had once stood guard. For a long, long time after she vanished, these white spots were, to me, parts of God.

By the end of the week, Esam found a job and an apartment to share with other religious brothers like himself. He packed his clothes and books and waited at the bottom of the hourglass, outside the apartment complex's gate, for the van to come pick him up, and I stood next to him, half-sad to see him go. I kicked rocks with my foot and said, "I hope you've got an umbrella and some plastic covers for your things. It's going to rain." I don't know why I said this; thanks to Esam, I hadn't watched the weather report all week. I just saw the sand picking up and swirling in curls the way it does in the desert; I smelled water in the thick air.

"Only God knows the weather for sure," Esam spat out at me. "He controls all in His infinite power." He turned away.

Back in the apartment, I watched him from the front window. I watched and watched as the sky ripped open and the rain fell and fell onto his shoulders and into his boxes, making his books soggy, his hair a wet mop, drenching his leather slippered feet, and soaking his gallabiya so thoroughly I could see through it, see his underwear, and after a minute, through that too, to the line that ran along his backside. I remembered how a few years before I'd tried to see people's underwear in Mama's magazines by cutting their clothes out with a pair of scissors; instead, I would only see the next page. I had failed then, but just now, I felt like a woman of wonder.

THREE

THE HOUSE WILL HAVE MUSIC

• • •

THE WEEK AFTER THE CONTEST, I STAYED IN BED FEIGNING
the flu. Mama believed I was sick because it was monsoon season and the dust was kicking around the courtyard like jinnis
at a drunken party. I liked that I didn't have to leave my room,
that this fake illness allowed me to be alone and forbade anyone to be near me. I lay in bed and read Dickens, comics, and
detective books. I ate nothing but *za'tar* burgers and apple
wedges, and the apple wedges cut my gums so that I tasted my
own blood and thought about death. I thought and thought and
my forehead burned until the end of the week, when Mama
came home and announced that she was adopting a new "baby."

Mama announced the adoption loudly. She banged down the
door in her attempt to bring it home: a used baby grand. Gone
was her dependence on Baba to save money and buy a piano
for her; she'd found a way to scrape together enough to buy
one for herself.

She hauled it in with her friends Hujran and Paula; they
carried it by its sides with their dainty nail-lacquered fingers.
I was perched on the covered patio, my stomach howling with

hunger, my eyes following three women carrying a three-legged piece of furniture.

After several minutes of trying to get the piano to budge: "Go bring Mama your roller skates."

Oh, no. Destruction. I brought her my roller skates anyway and threw them on the floor by her friends' feet. They put one skate on the left foot of the piano, the other on the right, left its third leg barefoot, and rolled it into the house.

"Hujran, sweetie, push to the left!" Tante Hujran was asthmatic and not much help. Tante Paula was strong and tough; her arms were round and solid, and she rolled the piano into the house through the covered patio. I cried the whole time as my skates got stabbed and ripped by the three-legged monster.

Mama and I cooked an extra-special dinner to sedate Baba and soften him up to the idea of the piano. When the grape leaves were rolled into tight green cigarettes and swimming in tomato sauce in the pressure cooker, I looked at the piano and asked Mama, "Can I touch it?"

"Can you touch it?" Mama said, sitting down on the piano bench. She ran her finger across the chipped wood. "This is my life now, my instrument . . . through which I'll be expressing myself. I won't be in the bathroom cleaning or reading the paper anymore. Forget the paper. It's full of stupid people doing stupid things to ruin the world. I've got music. The house," she said, nodding to me, "will have music. You can touch the piano."

IT WAS SOON after the piano's arrival that the certificate appeared in the mail, already in a gilded silver frame with my name calligraphied on a dotted line. It said, "This certificate is awarded to the student Nidali Ammar in recognition of h—er winning the Koran contest. Signed, Headmaster of the City Boys' School, Kuwait." I was one of three finalists. Baba kept laughing his silly laugh that made him choke on hiccups, his drunken playing-cards-with-the-men laugh, and he pointed to where it said student, or *tilmith*—which indicated a male student. The judge had been forced to alter the word and add a feminizing *ha* to make the male student, the *tilmith*, a *tilmitha*. I asked Baba why it was so funny, and Mama came over from the piano and sat on his lap.

"Imagine the old imam," Mama said.

"OK," I said, closed my eyes, and pictured the dark-faced, red-hatted man from the Boys' School.

"He's not used to giving little girls certificates," she said.

"Now imagine him adjusting the certificate that's supposed to be for boys," Baba said, still laughing as he pointed at the places on the certificate where the corrections showed through.

I was happy I'd won . . . or at least come in as one of three finalists. But something told me Baba was happier. This truth upset me. His happiness didn't seem to stem from a place of pride, but rather from the source where feelings of accomplishment reside. It was almost as though *he'd* won. I watched him hiccup, almost in slow motion, as he held up the certificate to the light coming from the balcony. Mama was already at her piano, playing something she must have been making up as she went along. I knew she was proud too, but she was too preoccupied with creating something to invest all her energies in my success. With her back to me and her fingers arched over the black and white keys, I wanted to go over there and hug her, but I was scared of interrupting. I stood in place, between them both, and mulled over what my victory meant to me.

I WAS TEN years old, and on the weekends I'd wake up just as early as I did on school days, except I'd pretend to be asleep. In this way I was able to stay in bed, under the covers, and stare out the window or at my sheets, and daydream. Mama had bought my sheets years ago; they were English alphabet sheets, and for every letter, there was a word. I stared at the C, which was big and yellow, and at the word "CASTLE" beneath it. If you whisper the word castle to yourself over and over again while lying in bed and pretending to be asleep—castle, castle, castle, castle, castle, castle, castle, castle, castle, castle, castle, castle, castle, castle, castle, castle, castle, castle—it ceases to have any meaning at all. Your head will stop projecting the image of a castle and the word itself will disappear. I loved being in this place, where I could make things disappear from my head. I had a favorite trick that made my mind feel like it was slipping from me, floating out of the bathroom window and into the dirty *manuar*, with the birds. If I didn't stop the trick fast, my mind would likely unlatch the birds' cage and fly away, hitching a ride on their backs. The trick was done in the bathroom. I'd sit on the edge of the tub and look at the light bulb when it was turned off, or, if it was nighttime, at the walls' white and pink tiles. Then, I'd repeat a question to myself, "*ana ana, ana ana, ana ana?*—Am I am I am I am I am I am I?" over and over again. When I'd tricked my mind, it would float away, and I could see that I *am* just I. I'd see myself from outside my own mind: my life, my body, and I was not half something and half another, I was one whole, a circle. It would scare me so much I'd bring my mind back and shiver.

I'd stay in bed and stare at the word "castle" while Mama played piano in the living room, and I'd wonder if playing piano for her was like the mind trick was for me. I'd think and think, reside in my safe chimeric haven until Baba would tell Mama to keep down that racket and wake us all up so we could go visit his best friend and cousin in Fahaheel. We'd all protest until he'd threaten our lives, then pick Gamal and me both up in his arms and pretend we were flying. I'd put some clothes on and wait for everyone in our Oldsmobile, preparing for the twenty-minute ride to the country's Palestinian ghetto.

We took the highway through the desert, past huge A-shaped metal structures (electricity converters), past silver silos and a barren landscape, and arrived in a neighborhood full of shoddy white-gray buildings, small groceries, and gated schoolyards. Baba's cousin lived in a blocky building with a white concrete courtyard. We parked outside and walked through the courtyard to the elevators, which took us up to the apartment. Sometimes, I wondered why we didn't live in this neighborhood; later, I understood that Baba didn't want to live with his own because he never felt like he belonged with them.

Gamal and I sat in my second cousin Tamara's room with her little brother Hatim and we played Atari and told each other made-up stories. Tamara was four years my senior and was in love with George Michael and had WHAM! posters on her closet doors. We dressed up in pretend American clothes and danced to the music coming from her tiny boom box in the corner of the room. Tamara and I played the vixens in a WHAM! video, and Hatim did his best to be George Michael.

Unsatisfied with his impersonation, Tamara nominated Gamal for the job. She used her mother's eyeliner to paint sideburns on Gamal's face while he noisily protested. Exhausted and hungry after our little performances, we ran to the kitchen and made *ʒa'tar* burgers. Hatim forced Tamara to write out the secret recipe in green marker.

INGREDIENTS.

Sesame seed bun
Za'tar *(thyme, sesames, and spices, from Sido's farm in Palestine)*
Kraft Singles cheese slices (from Safeway)

First, turn on your sandwich toaster. Then put three slices of cheese on bun and top cheese with za'tar *(2–4 tbsp). Then close bun and stuff in toaster till melted. When the cheese melts outside of the sandwich and onto the toaster, you'll be a lucky son of a dog. You can scrape the cheese off with a knife and eat it, in fact, we highly recommend eating this hardened, baked cheese.*

We all sat in the bedroom eating our *ʒa'tar* burgers and imagining how cool it would be if our dads quit their boring jobs and opened a fast-food restaurant. We would call it *Za'tar Burger.* We made up a jingle for the would-be restaurant, and at night, after we heard the men slap their cards on the table, scream at each other, click their whiskey glasses, fart, and curse each other's religions, we went to the living room and presented them with the jingle. I was the dancer and lead singer. Mama and petite Auntie Naila sat in our fathers' laps and everyone clapped hands to the beat. Auntie Naila winked at me every time

I attempted a high note, and screamed *"Aiwa!"* when we did a complicated foot twirl. The jingle also involved a small rap sequence in English, which I penned all by myself since my cousins went to public schools and learned only Arabic (lucky bastards). When the jingle ended, we all bowed and curtsied, and the men threw cards at us in lieu of roses. Auntie yelled, "The girl can sing, brother, you should let her be a singer!" and I lingered on my tiptoes in the middle of a curtsey, waiting anxiously for my father's reaction to what Auntie had suggested. *"Atfoo,"* Baba said, feigning spit, *"Salli 'al nabi,* Nidali's going to be a famous professor. And she will write essays and articles by the dozens. Singer, she said. *Ya* Naila, you're a crazy donkey." When Auntie insisted, Baba said, "Why don't you quit your post as headmistress and open up a *Za'tar Burger?"*

At the end of the night, Baba and Mama bade my uncle's family farewell and we all dawdled in the stairwell of the apartment building by the elevator while the adults continued to chatter. I read the graffiti on the walls, and it made me blush. Bored and impatient, Tamara pulled me into the elevator and we rode it up and down several times while our parents' conversation continued endlessly, and in that elevator she told me stories about boys. The elevator went down three flights and she talked about Ali, then up seven flights and we were onto Salim. We were safe here in this traveling room, going up, going down, the numbers glowing orange. When my parents were ready to leave, my cousin and I were in the elevator on the first floor. We heard Baba yell, "God damn you girls, why is this elevator taking so long to come up?" and we rolled our eyes; adults always showed a strange impatience when it was least convenient for us.

Baba zigzagged home, and Gamal and I sat in the back and breathed in the scent of our velvety seats. Mama pushed a cassette into the car stereo's mouth; it was Abdel Halim Hafiz. I looked out the window and at the desert rushing past us, at the sand beginning to collect in the air: a dust storm, *toẓ*, preparing for a small uprising. The streetlights in the desert were small and high, and I crossed my eyes slightly to make the lamps resemble wider blobs of multi-colored light. On the radio, Ab-Halim sang:

I'll be yours
forever more
Stay and be mine.
Take my eye
and come see me
once in a while.
No, take them both,
And in exchange, just stay
Because I've been wide
awake since that very first day.

Romantic violins swayed in the song's background and then two guitars took turns playing, like lovers talking. One was classical and the other sounded more like a ukulele than an *'oud*. I thought my making this distinction would impress Mama but I didn't say anything, just looked out into the desert and at my own reflection in the window. I stared into my own eyes and pretended I was a boy singing to me, *Ana lak 'ala tool, khallik liyya*, and I thought about love. Eventually the sounds of my parents' giggling, the music, the car, and the desert storm brewing outside lulled me to sleep.

FOUR

A MAP OF HOME

• • •

MAMA LEFT. I WAS ASSIGNED THE DIRTY PINK BATHROOM, THE watering of plants that droop all over the apartment, and the *manuar*—a small roofless space in between the bathroom and my room (if you look up, you see the square-framed sky); the northwesterlies would soon bring dust all over the bicycles, the bird's cage, and any hanging laundry. The fight was the biggest they'd ever had. Baba told Mama he was sick of coming home and finding the house dirty, the kids dirty (ahem . . . I'm very clean and gorgeous, thank you very much), and the dinner uncooked. But it was the thing that brought them together in the first place that split them asunder.

"You're at that piano day and night . . . Goddamn you, Fairuza, can't you be a wife? A wife," a glass broke, "I married a wife, not a damn concert. And you have no regard for my feelings whatsoever. The men at work bring in lamb rice and lentil soup and what do I bring?" He slapped the table. "I bring a wilted chicken sandwich with a piece of lettuce from the era of Tutankhamen. You're letting go of your responsibilities here . . ." he waved his arm around the apartment, "in our house. Wake up! Wake up! All I have to do is say it three times!"

"*Kuss ummak*—Your mother's cunt, okay? Don't tell me what I'm not doing and what I am doing. Even the Prophet Himself said you have to please your wife. Where is my pleasure?"

"I don't please you, you selfish bitch?"

"God almighty, I'm not talking about you, man. I want to be left alone once in a while! In life, life! I want pleasure in my life!" She slammed her fist against her thigh.

"Let's go. I'll show you some pleasure in life." He turned to me. "Nidali, get your brother, we're going for a drive." Here we go. "Fairuza, get off your ass. I'm going to show you the pleasures in life. How good it is to be alone. *Yalla*, let's go!"

The car started to smoke halfway out to the desert. The yellowness stretched before us and behind us like a ramp leading into hell. We were surrounded by patches and patches of yellowness, of sand punctuated by long black power lines suspended from T-shaped black electrical structures that looked like giants guarding hell's gates. Mama sat in the front seat fussing with a piece of thread she'd ripped out of the upholstery. I sat in the back seat and showed my brother how to cross his eyes and look at the lights above the power lines.

"Mon-staws," he said, his breath sweet milk. I gently squeezed his cheek and kissed him.

Baba was driving faster than the lorries. Then, when he reached a place in the road that seemed suitable to him, he slammed on the brakes. The car made a screeching sound that brought my brother's chubby hands up to his ears. Baba reached over Mama's belly and opened her door.

"Out!"

"Fine. *Mish naqsa*—I don't need your insanity! Thanks for the lift." She jumped out of the car and slammed the door with great force, then started to walk away toward the power lines. I stuck my face on the glass and breathed hard against it. I waved my hand in case she turned around, but she never did.

"Nidali, in front!"

I hesitated.

"Now!" Baba's eyes were red. He popped in a cassette.

I swung my legs over the armrest and plopped into Mama's seat, in her place. It was still warm from her big butt. I watched Mama's butt and her back and her body and her hair get smaller and smaller in the passenger-side mirror.

The cassette was from an old concert of Umm Kulthum, singing about how someone was her age. Not her age, her life, Baba corrected me. Baba told me to memorize the song and start singing it. He drove around the desert until the sun set, until the earth beneath us looked like a big black hole, until I sang the stupid song flawlessly.

"Will you let me be a singer, then?" I asked, when he took both hands off the steering wheel and clapped.

"Never. Singing is not bad, but you can do better. You can be a doctor! A big professor of literature! Write poetry like I used to do. Write poetry and teach in England. Show those bastards the greatness of our literature. You can be whatever you want."

"Just not a singer?"

"Right. Or an architect."

"So I can't be like you."

"No, and you won't want to be. You'll see. You're still little."

We were heading home; I recognized the water tanks on the dim horizon. There were six of them, white with blue stripes, standing all in a row. They looked like martini glasses in pinstripe suits. I leaned my head on Baba's warm shoulder. I knew I couldn't talk about Mama or say that I was worried about her, in the desert all by herself. I wondered how Baba could want me to win a boy's contest and behave so cruelly to Mama, who's a girl, like me, and I wondered why Mama let him. Why did she leave the car and go into the desert's emptiness? She was probably dead, dead like her mama. I didn't want to think about it, so I asked Baba, "What did your poetry say?"

"It said things about our homeland, about Palestine. But I grew tired of writing about war. That's all we did, write about war, about how sad we were after '67, about our bad condition. So then my poetry said things about your *stupid* fucking *mother!*"

I wanted to steer the subject away from Mama, so I said, "What is '67?" Baba laughed and turned to look at me, but the look on my face must have betrayed that I honestly did not know.

"*What?* Goddamn your school! Goddamn the English, those pink pigs with their ugly history of atrocity and anguish! They've taught you nothing! Saturday, Saturday you'll start a new school—an Arab school, with Arab girls and an Arab teacher in the Arab world. With history classes. What do they teach you in history class in that shit school? What did you learn about yesterday?"

I shrugged. "The Vikings," I said. We were in the city now, our apartment a few blocks away. I turned west and looked at the dark, calm gulf.

"The fucking Vikings!" he screamed, and slammed on the brake pedals; the tires screeched in protest, and I remembered Mama again. The Olds stopped in the middle of the road, swerving to the right a bit. My brother giggled in the back seat;

this had been an amusement ride for him. Baba got out of the car and spilled out a harangue, facing the Arabian Gulf, facing the smoking engine, facing nothing at all. "Really, what did I expect from the people who fucked Ireland and South Africa and Palestine? May God's wrath burn the teachers in your school. Tonight! Tonight you will receive a lesson in your history. How will you ever be a minister or secretary of state or professor if you only read about the fucking barbarians? May the caves they lived in be their eternal dwellings! Sons of whores."

Great.

All I wanted to do was watch *Fatoota*—a show about this Egyptian comedian with a handlebar mustache, who is followed around by a three-foot-tall, blue-screen, miniature version of himself in a bright green suit, a huge tie, and really, really big clown shoes—and eat *za'tar* burgers. But *no*. Baba was going to end the lovely night of sacrificing my mother to the desert and plucking my vocal chords dry with a history lesson.

My math notebook, which was thick and filled with tiny squares, was out on the desk. Baba dictated history to me. I found out about the Suez canal (we rewound to '56 after he discovered I didn't know about that, either) and how my geddo was a fighter called a "Free Officer." Geddo is Mama's baba but Baba treated him like a historical figure so he wouldn't have to think about Mama. Geddo and dozens of other officers went to Egypt's King Farouk in 1952 with a huge battalion and told him to buzz off. Well, Baba said "fuck off" but I wasn't allowed to repeat it. So he told him to buzz off and put him on a ship called the *Mahroosa*, the Protected One, and sent him to the English. "You like zem so much, go live with zem," Baba imitated Geddo's

words. Then there was Nasser, who Baba had videos of. As
2 A.M. rolled around, Baba made me watch these. Nasser was
yelling and yelling and my eyes were drooping with sleep. I
almost nodded off, but Baba thrust his arm right under my chin
and told me to look at his arm hairs. "They're standing on
end!" I looked. They were. "The man was a saint. God have
mercy on his soul, may he rest in peace!" Baba told me about
'67. He showed me an old *Life* magazine he'd bought in
America that had all the Israeli pictures in it. I saw the map
with all the arrows pointing out of Palestine and into Egypt,
Syria, and Jordan. He told me to read the article and I did. I
was amazed by this Israel and its power, and I asked Baba if
we were Israeli since he is from Palestine which is the same
as Israel.

Explosion. Total Baba-led earthquake. Okay, so we're not
Israeli but we are Palestinians. At least he is. He told me to
go get a blue book from the bookshelf; PALESTINE IS MY
COUNTRY in big white letters on its side. I thought that was
funny because the Israeli flag is blue and white. Baba flipped to
a page with the real map of Palestine on it and made me trace
the map and draw it over and over again. The sun crept into
the living room and shone onto the forest Baba and I once
painted. The painted leaves shook and little droplets of morning dew began to dot the purple grass.

I hadn't slept all night.

Baba checked my last map, the map of home, he called it, and
let me go, saying I drew the Galilee perfectly, like the water
violin that it is. He retired to the kitchen and heated up some bread
and cheese squares, which my grandma sent us from Jenin. As

Seldom in Mama–Baba history had victory been so efficient so visibly decisive in so short a span of time. The matri-ch's insisting thrusts swept across the Baba's desert of no-resistance; air strikes—in the form of no dinner—hit d destroyed the opposition's bases. The stronghold fell on second day of fighting, when Baba, unwilling to just admit at he was afraid of losing Mama to the piano, declared that it s un-Islamic to bring pianos into the house and play music day.

"Oh," Mama glanced at her watch. "Abu Isa called a little iile ago about your new shipment of whiskey." Mama had ployed her naval vessels. "He said it'd be delayed until xt week."

"Next week, that brother of a whore! Goddamn, we're going have a dry card game!" Baba shouted.

"Yeah, the fucking piano is staying here," Mama said, and iba squatted in the sand, announcing the very welcome end the Mama–Baba sixty-hour battle.

But the war raged on.

he ate the white cheese his mama sent him he probably thought of my mama; he was red-eyed and sad and I knew he already missed her. I put on my uniform and hallucinated Mama coming home, sitting at the piano, and playing Chopin's Ballade no. 3 and Baba remembering how she was the first person to make him love music, and them falling in love all over again. But it was just a hallucination. I tied my shoelaces and went to wait for the bus, wondering which sand dune Mama was buried in now.

When the last bell rang, I waited for Mama to come and pick us up but she hadn't come home from the desert yet, so Baba picked us up instead, carrying a box of pizza he bought from Pizza Italia loaded with our favorite ingredients: olives and meat. We watched television all day and all night, ate our pizza at the coffee table, drank our Nescafé, and left the dirty cups and dishes littering the living room floor. Gamal sat on my back and pretended to drive a train, and Baba drank his illegal whiskey out of a small cup. We watched English and American shows the country had imported for the year. In these shows, every time two people's faces got close to each other and the music turned cheesy, the faces suddenly broke apart and the music abruptly stopped. I asked Baba, what just happened? and he explained that those people had kissed and their kiss had been censored.

"What's censor?"

"It's when you take the film and cut out the parts that offend you."

"So, there's a man who cuts out the kisses?"

"Yes," Baba said.

"I never realized that, that you could be a kiss-cutter when you grew up."

Baba laughed. "You have to be a real ass to have that job, right?"

Late that night in my bed I thought of kissing, of how the two people on the television might have kissed. I knew it was supposed to be wrong, what they were doing, but I didn't know why. I thought of how Mama and Baba used to kiss. I was worried that someday I'd kiss someone and then that same someone would deposit me in a desert. I decided I would never fall in love.

Just then, I worried about Mama and felt foolish that I hadn't been praying for her, that I'd been thinking about kissing instead.

I got up and did my ablutions as quietly as possible so as not to wake Baba. I slipped a towel on my head for a veil and faced the direction Baba faces when he prays once a week, on Fridays. I thought about Esam, who I hadn't thought of in a while. I wondered if he was back on the West Bank now, married, happy . . . kissing. I shook my head; I had to stop thinking about that! I wondered if I should perform my ablutions again since I'd had an impure thought but I decided I didn't have to, so I began my prayers for Mama. The entire time I was worried whether my prayers counted or not, and just as I was about to finish, I inadvertently let out a long fart. I knew I'd have to repeat both the ablutions and the prayers now but I didn't because I was too lazy, and I hoped God hadn't heard my fart, even though I now smelled it.

. . .

THE PHONE RANG while I was recovering in [her] the bathroom and the *manuar*. I was dreamin[g] lee, that I was a bird flying over it with rolle[r] I heard Baba yelling into the phone. "Hello, b[r] *ing here?* What for?"

Mama had hitchhiked to Auntie Naila's ho[use] sleeping in my cousin's bed. Mama was winn[ing]

"If you bring her here, make sure it is at [?] manded as he surveyed the sad state of the ap[artment]

At seven, Mama waltzed through the do[or] I could hear Chopin. She'd apparently be[en] with my uncle and just taken a cab. She didn[?] just looked at the apartment: at the smoke clin[g] ing, my brother naked and dirty, crayoning [?] fanning a burnt casserole dish, the cups an[d] ing out of the carpet like shrubs. We looke[d] standing as though nailed to the dirty floor, [?] early arrival.

This gave her a one-hour advantage ove[r] launching an attack much earlier than he'd expe[ct] erated his attempts at claiming the place as his [?] ing via taxi and not through the main entrance [?] would she took him completely by surprise. She [?] to the side and disappeared through the corrid[or] bath in the now-clean bathroom. I stood in th[e] boiled water for her tea, gripped a bunch of drie[d] angry. I wanted the piano to burn, along with B[aba] wanted Mama and Baba to get along.

SUMMER'S FABRIC

• • •

IN MY MIND, ALL MY SUMMERS ARE FOLDED UP LIKE A *MASHRAF*,
a dinner tablecloth, and put away, sauce stains and all, in the
drawer of the summer I turned eleven and my famously single
aunt turned into a bride. I flew to Egypt on an airplane with an
ancient Egyptian image decaled on the side of its wing. Mama
came too, and so did my little brother, but Baba couldn't come
because Mama said she didn't want to see his face. He pretended
not to care, said he had to work on a building. I imagined him
in a yellow hard hat, actually building, even though in reality
he was the guy in another building, drawing a picture of the
building the yellow hard-hatted men were going to have to
build. On the plane, I tried not to think of him sitting in the
silent apartment, his eyes sad and his heart lonely. I couldn't
help but think of him, though.

We landed in Cairo, and I heard the new Hanan song
"*Besma*"—"The Smile," and it cheered me up. I smiled instantly. The airport was much bigger than the one in Kuwait,
the ceilings were high and silver. I loved the indoor billboards,
the giant cola bottles with the gleaming fake dewdrops. Mama
put me in charge of spotting our luggage.

I found the four bags that held all our transportable earthly possessions and yelled to the skycap. He was brown and tall and had big black eyes in his thin face. Once the suitcases were piled up on the carts (two of them), Mama and I walked to the greeters' area. It wasn't long before Geddo spied us and yelled my brother's name. One day, I would understand that he always did this out of respect. "It's not right to yell out a woman's name in front of a bunch of people," he'd inform me. I ran over to Geddo and hugged him. He carried me and complained teasingly that I was too heavy, then kissed my cheeks. Geddo's cheeks were soft, and he had big jowls that hung like girlie purses. I loved the brown spots that dappled his skin, the smell of olive oil soap on his neck.

"You look like your grandmother!" he screamed, then put me back on my feet. My grandmother was dead, and I hoped I didn't look like a dead person, but I just smiled. Mama handed my little brother to Geddo, who lifted him high in the sky and said, "Welcome, thank God for your safety, my boy!"

"Where did you park, Baba?" Mama said, and Geddo directed us to the car. It was not the old Mercedes Geddo used to drive; he told us he sold that one for fifty Egyptian pounds. He said he didn't want any money for it but the woman who bought it insisted.

"No money?" Mama said, a sigh in her voice. "Why not, Baba?" She got into the new Fiat with my brother on her lap. Geddo gave the skycap a green note, and the man kissed it and touched it to his forehead.

"Yes, no money. Get in, my girl," he told me, and slammed my door. "No money, because that car was a joke. We got it with the revolution, your mother hated it, she almost ran over he ate the white cheese his mama sent him he probably thought of my mama; he was red-eyed and sad and I knew he already missed her. I put on my uniform and hallucinated Mama coming home, sitting at the piano, and playing Chopin's Ballade no. 3 and Baba remembering how she was the first person to make him love music, and them falling in love all over again. But it was just a hallucination. I tied my shoelaces and went to wait for the bus, wondering which sand dune Mama was buried in now.

When the last bell rang, I waited for Mama to come and pick us up but she hadn't come home from the desert yet, so Baba picked us up instead, carrying a box of pizza he bought from Pizza Italia loaded with our favorite ingredients: olives and meat. We watched television all day and all night, ate our pizza at the coffee table, drank our Nescafé, and left the dirty cups and dishes littering the living room floor. Gamal sat on my back and pretended to drive a train, and Baba drank his illegal whiskey out of a small cup. We watched English and American shows the country had imported for the year. In these shows, every time two people's faces got close to each other and the music turned cheesy, the faces suddenly broke apart and the music abruptly stopped. I asked Baba, what just happened? and he explained that those people had kissed and their kiss had been censored.

"What's censor?"

"It's when you take the film and cut out the parts that offend you."

"So, there's a man who cuts out the kisses?"

"Yes," Baba said.

"I never realized that, that you could be a kiss-cutter when you grew up."

Baba laughed. "You have to be a real ass to have that job, right?"

Late that night in my bed I thought of kissing, of how the two people on the television might have kissed. I knew it was supposed to be wrong, what they were doing, but I didn't know why. I thought of how Mama and Baba used to kiss. I was worried that someday I'd kiss someone and then that same someone would deposit me in a desert. I decided I would never fall in love.

Just then, I worried about Mama and felt foolish that I hadn't been praying for her, that I'd been thinking about kissing instead.

I got up and did my ablutions as quietly as possible so as not to wake Baba. I slipped a towel on my head for a veil and faced the direction Baba faces when he prays once a week, on Fridays. I thought about Esam, who I hadn't thought of in a while. I wondered if he was back on the West Bank now, married, happy . . . kissing. I shook my head; I had to stop thinking about that! I wondered if I should perform my ablutions again since I'd had an impure thought but I decided I didn't have to, so I began my prayers for Mama. The entire time I was worried whether my prayers counted or not, and just as I was about to finish, I inadvertently let out a long fart. I knew I'd have to repeat both the ablutions and the prayers now but I didn't because I was too lazy, and I hoped God hadn't heard my fart, even though I now smelled it.

. . .

THE PHONE RANG while I was recovering in bed after cleaning the bathroom and the *manuar*. I was dreaming about the Galilee, that I was a bird flying over it with roller skates on, when I heard Baba yelling into the phone. "Hello, brother. She's *coming here? What for?*"

Mama had hitchhiked to Auntie Naila's house and had been sleeping in my cousin's bed. Mama was winning the war.

"If you bring her here, make sure it is at eight," Baba demanded as he surveyed the sad state of the apartment.

At seven, Mama waltzed through the door and I swore I could hear Chopin. She'd apparently become impatient with my uncle and just taken a cab. She didn't say anything, just looked at the apartment: at the smoke clinging to the ceiling, my brother naked and dirty, crayoning the walls, Baba fanning a burnt casserole dish, the cups and dishes growing out of the carpet like shrubs. We looked like refugees, standing as though nailed to the dirty floor, stunned at her early arrival.

This gave her a one-hour advantage over Baba, and by launching an attack much earlier than he'd expected, she obliterated his attempts at claiming the place as his own. By arriving via taxi and not through the main entrance as she normally would she took him completely by surprise. She tilted her head to the side and disappeared through the corridor, then took a bath in the now-clean bathroom. I stood in the kitchen and boiled water for her tea, gripped a bunch of dried sage, and felt angry. I wanted the piano to burn, along with Baba's temper; I wanted Mama and Baba to get along.

Seldom in Mama–Baba history had victory been so efficient or so visibly decisive in so short a span of time. The matriarch's insisting thrusts swept across the Baba's desert of piano-resistance; air strikes—in the form of no dinner—hit and destroyed the opposition's bases. The stronghold fell on the second day of fighting, when Baba, unwilling to just admit that he was afraid of losing Mama to the piano, declared that it was un-Islamic to bring pianos into the house and play music all day.

"Oh," Mama glanced at her watch. "Abu Isa called a little while ago about your new shipment of whiskey." Mama had deployed her naval vessels. "He said it'd be delayed until next week."

"Next week, that brother of a whore! Goddamn, we're going to have a dry card game!" Baba shouted.

"Yeah, the fucking piano is staying here," Mama said, and Baba squatted in the sand, announcing the very welcome end of the Mama–Baba sixty-hour battle.

But the war raged on.

SUMMER'S FABRIC

• • •

IN MY MIND, ALL MY SUMMERS ARE FOLDED UP LIKE A *MASHRAF*, a dinner tablecloth, and put away, sauce stains and all, in the drawer of the summer I turned eleven and my famously single aunt turned into a bride. I flew to Egypt on an airplane with an ancient Egyptian image decaled on the side of its wing. Mama came too, and so did my little brother, but Baba couldn't come because Mama said she didn't want to see his face. He pretended not to care, said he had to work on a building. I imagined him in a yellow hard hat, actually building, even though in reality he was the guy in another building, drawing a picture of the building the yellow hard-hatted men were going to have to build. On the plane, I tried not to think of him sitting in the silent apartment, his eyes sad and his heart lonely. I couldn't help but think of him, though.

We landed in Cairo, and I heard the new Hanan song *"Besma"*—"The Smile," and it cheered me up. I smiled instantly. The airport was much bigger than the one in Kuwait, the ceilings were high and silver. I loved the indoor billboards, the giant cola bottles with the gleaming fake dewdrops. Mama put me in charge of spotting our luggage.

I found the four bags that held all our transportable earthly possessions and yelled to the skycap. He was brown and tall and had big black eyes in his thin face. Once the suitcases were piled up on the carts (two of them), Mama and I walked to the greeters' area. It wasn't long before Geddo spied us and yelled my brother's name. One day, I would understand that he always did this out of respect. "It's not right to yell out a woman's name in front of a bunch of people," he'd inform me. I ran over to Geddo and hugged him. He carried me and complained teasingly that I was too heavy, then kissed my cheeks. Geddo's cheeks were soft, and he had big jowls that hung like girlie purses. I loved the brown spots that dappled his skin, the smell of olive oil soap on his neck.

"You look like your grandmother!" he screamed, then put me back on my feet. My grandmother was dead, and I hoped I didn't look like a dead person, but I just smiled. Mama handed my little brother to Geddo, who lifted him high in the sky and said, "Welcome, thank God for your safety, my boy!"

"Where did you park, Baba?" Mama said, and Geddo directed us to the car. It was not the old Mercedes Geddo used to drive; he told us he sold that one for fifty Egyptian pounds. He said he didn't want any money for it but the woman who bought it insisted.

"No money?" Mama said, a sigh in her voice. "Why not, Baba?" She got into the new Fiat with my brother on her lap. Geddo gave the skycap a green note, and the man kissed it and touched it to his forehead.

"Yes, no money. Get in, my girl," he told me, and slammed my door. "No money, because that car was a joke. We got it with the revolution, your mother hated it, she almost ran over that milkman, remember? And none of you could ever drive it. The car was a waste, and good riddance! It took the bad and it went."

"Yes, Baba, but fifty pounds? You could have tucked it into a garage somewhere for fifteen or twenty years, then sold it for thousands. The car was an antique!" My brother started squirming.

"When did Tetta Yia Yia almost kill a milkman?" I said, excited.

"Fifteen or twenty years? Have you gone crazy, my daughter? Who knows if we have ten or twenty years, or if we'll even wake up tomorrow?"

"I guarantee you will wake up tomorrow, Baba! Your health . . . knock on wood . . ." Mama banged a closed fist against the dashboard, which was made of plastic—"I mean, you're in great health, God keep you! Fifty pounds, father! That car was our family history."

"*Atfoo*," Geddo spat out into the wind. The spit circled back into the car through my open window and landed two inches from my eye. I wiped it off with my sleeve. "Our family history is more than a black and ragged Mercedes which was a remnant from the revolution and . . ." he spat again, and again, it landed just west of my eye, "a piece of *junk*. How is Abu Gamal?" Geddo said, switching subjects to my father.

Mama fell silent, and on the car stereo, which had a radio but no cassette deck, Umm Kulthum sang sweetly, stretching her vowels when it suited her, shrinking her consonants when she felt most melancholy, so that Mama didn't need to answer her baba about my baba, because *Elsitt*, the Lady, was doing it for her:

Ya rayt ya rayt, ya rayt ya raayt yaa rayt, ya rayt . . .
I wish I wish, I wish I wiiish I-I-I wish,
I wish, I wish, I wish I wish,
I wish, I wish, I wish I wiiish, I-I-I wish . . .
I wish, I wish, I wish, I wi-ish I-I wish,
I wish, I wish, I wish, I wiiish,
I wish *I,*
I wish I'd,
I wish I'd never
fallen in love.

Umm Kulthum chanted the last line as though it represented both an afterthought and an inevitable fate.

The little beige Fiat made its way west. We were five hours away from Alexandria even though it should have taken only three hours to get there. In traffic, Geddo rolled down his window and asked a neighboring car about the soccer score. The Ahlawi team was beating the Zamalkawi team by two points. Geddo grinned and smacked his hands together. "We are Ahlawi," he told me, his blue eyes gleaming in the rearview mirror. I nodded, happy to belong to a soccer team association. And that it was winning. The guy driving on our left had somehow managed to get his television inside the car and glued onto the dashboard. He was watching the game and yelling loudly that the player who had just missed a chance to score was "a pimp who would sell his own sister's twat." My mother told me to roll up my window but I resisted and told her I was sweating. She relented, and my brother came and sat in the back with me.

The billboards in Cairo advertised plays and toilet paper and Fanta and new singers' albums; the Nile stretched out in the distance and provided no solace breezewise. Men pedaled dangerously past us; women with hair tied up in handkerchiefs whizzed by us on scooters and on foot. They all fell behind as the Fiat sped off onto the highway, and as time faded, the cement buildings did, too. Geddo's new Russian car had a bent antenna, so the radio station he had on blended Elsitt's singing with the game, and the wet air whipped through our window so my hair coiled up and expanded.

Soon, adobe huts appeared and night enveloped us. I could faintly make out birds perched on black rods sticking out of the huts by the side of the road. Stalks of vegetables rushed by us, and it started to smell like salt and shit. I stared at the stars and pretended they were the thousand lights of a skyscraper in the middle of the desert. I asked Mama how much longer, but she had given in to sleep. I slept too, and dreamed of Baba; in my dream he wore a yellow hard hat and slid down the hallways of St. Elizabeth in Boston, America.

By the time we reached Alexandria, the *corniche* was packed with people of all ages. Many were eating corn, or *tirmis*, or melon seeds and spitting out their seeds' coats on the road or the sidewalk. On our left, as we drove west to Ma'moora—Alexandria's beach town, where Mama had an apartment in her name—I watched the sea roll fat, foamy waves in our direction. Children, men, and women, some of whom were in their clothing, all bobbed in the waves or raced to the showers. I couldn't wait until morning when I'd pack a small bag, carry sand chairs, and walk to the beach with Geddo.

Geddo's little Fiat made its way through crowded Ma'moora, and within minutes we reached our street, the one with the small mosque at one end and the stagnant boat on the other. I squinted and tried to make out the boat's shape in the distance, and I could. It was almost as irremovable as the mosque. Geddo had to honk at a few kids who were playing soccer in the street; they moved aside and let us pass.

The car stopped in the middle of our street and signaled the arrival of long-gone ex-residents. 'Abdo, the *Bawab*—the super in charge of the building—his wife Ummu Madeeha, and their daughters Madeeha and 'Afaf, all came to greet us and laid dozens of kisses on my little brother's cheeks. He reveled in this attention, his little feet kicking. Soon, my aunt Sonya came down from her apartment, already charged with demands and anxieties; she kissed my brother hurriedly, scooped me up in her arms, and held my hand the four flights up to our apartments, the whole while talking rapidly to my mother like one of those auctioneers I'd seen on the cartoons Mama watched with me, clicking her tongue in a deriding tut-tut whenever a cartoon animal shot or maimed another. "And how are you, little moon? I missed you more than anything," Sonya finally spoke to me.

"I'm fine, thanks be to Allah, Tante Sonya," I said, and she covered my forehead with her palm.

"What? Did you call me *Tante*? What's the matter, you got a fever? Never call me Tante, just Sonya. I'm your friend!" Then she started the make-believe auction and said to Mama, "Okay, sister, I want to make sure you have all the fabrics, and you won't believe the design of the dress, the design! And the shoes, O eye, they're from London—Ibtisaam actually remembered to get them, that selfish buffalo, in any case, the man is still working things out with his mother in Damanhoor, can you believe the witch is actually thinking of not coming, Hhhhmh, let her, may the jinnis pop her one, and O heart, the hotel had a fire two days ago but it shouldn't affect our hall, and the belly dancer wants fifty pounds extra, the whore's gone mad with the syphilis she probably has and God I hope you'll like him, sister, he's *kalbooz*—a little fat, but he's got a big heart to go with it!" We reached the end of the staircase and she patted my head. "And you, you little monkey, you better not look prettier than me with those light curls of yours." She pinched my cheek. "I'll let you wear rouge. And nail polish!"

"No," my mother broke in, and lowered her big frames to her eyes. She looked like a fly. My brother was already chewing on an electrical wire and banging a table with an old tennis racquet.

"Yes, sister, yes, and yes, the girl will look pretty like a flower on her aunt's wedding day," Sonya said, and opened our door. The apartment looked spotless, just the way we left it.

"No, my father says no make-up until I'm eighteen," I said.

"Your father? Oh, you mean Mussolini . . . well, he won't be there, right? The girl's wearing rouge, sister," she addressed Mama, "and you're not wearing these," she commanded, and gently tapped a long red fingernail against my mother's glasses.

My aunt was eighteen when her mama—my yia yia—died. Yia Yia used to stay here, on this same street, years ago. She started to come here when my mama was little, like me, in the fifties. Soon, Mama would want to visit Yia Yia's grave, and we'd all dress like army personnel, act like army personnel, and drive downtown to the Greek Cooperative Cemetery. I wondered whether this would happen before or after I got to wear lipstick for the wedding.

Geddo came upstairs with 'Abdo, who was carrying two suit-cases, one on each shoulder. I wanted to sit on his shoulders and touch his white head wrap, let my fingers feel his sweat, and just as I was thinking this, he dropped the luggage and grabbed me, lifted me as though he were a forklift: "Beware of the winch!" he said. "Don't think I'll let you get away!" He took me to the balcony. "Should I drop you?" he teased, swinging me over the railings. "Fairuza, should I drop her?"

Mama chewed her nails absentmindedly, a habit she kept over the years like a jeweled heirloom. "*Aiwa*—Yes, 'Abdo. I've had enough of her."

He hung me over the railings, and my heart beat fast like the tablas we made out of old cans. I was not scared. I knew he'd never let me go. He hoisted me back up after I protested, and I landed safely on the balcony's white tiles that sound like glasses clinking together when Mama walked on them with high heels or when I walked on them with a small, sharp stone wedged in the soles of my sneakers.

I rested on the couch on the balcony after the men left, and after my brother fell asleep, it was just Mama and Sonya, and they began making Turkish coffee. I slapped mosquitoes on my thighs, but they'd already flown away and left behind their stamps: red circular marks. Mama and Sonya talked loudly about their old man and new man, respectively, about other men, about their cousins, new acquisitions of land (none) or cars (one) or bad hairstyles (at least forty-three), and about why some women couldn't stop being stupid. They chatted long into the night and I drifted in and out of sleep, their voices a lullaby that exhilarated and comforted me, my family's women talk-ing. When I was in that space that was halfway between sleep and consciousness, Mama banged a mosquito dead against the wall, then continued reading Sonya's coffee cup.

The last thing I heard was Mama and Sonya arguing playfully about the time they drank too much beer at the beach and got their asses kicked by their mama; they couldn't agree which boy bought the beer for them, and as their voices rose and fell, I drifted off into a sleep veiled with the smell of cardamom coffee, Cleopatra cigarettes, and future dreams.

A short inventory of the fabric Mama brought for Sonya's wedding: satin, silk, Egyptian cotton, crushed velvet, polyester, acrylic, mesh, nylon, and a see-through fabric that came in layers and layers so that it looked like a mille-feuille and made you hungry. The designs varied from floral, soft embroidery, and square patterns, to diamond stitches, eyelets, and flowers stitched with hanging fake opals. The colors were white, off-white, creamy white, gold, and silver, all for Sonya's gown; tangerine, grape purple, eggplant purple, and sumac purple for Mama's dress; soft pink and silver stars on pink for my dress; and cayenne red with a dash of thyme green around the edges for all the cousins' dresses.

We were in Mama and Sonya's old apartment in Chatby, downtown Alexandria, and when Mama opened the suitcases in her childhood bedroom, she turned the room into a small fabric market like the ones we saw in *ʒan'et el-sittaat*—the women's quarter. Two French doors swung open when we arrived, the wooden shutters behind them creaking as they parted ways to bring the sunlight in.

"Let God's light in!" Mama said as she scrambled around the apartment opening windows and balcony doors. The doorbell sounded a tired cuckoo and Sonya went to answer it, yelling, "Yeah, mother of 'Adel, I'm coming . . ." and let the seamstress in. The woman was dressed in black from head to toe, and I didn't know how a woman who looked so sad could sew dresses for a wedding without jumping off her balcony. After a few minutes of small talk, sweet-tea-making, mourning of Umm 'Adel's husband (father of 'Adel), and sweet-tea-drinking, the women turned to the suitcases, told Umm 'Adel, "Measure her," and pointed at me.

I lifted my arms up, lowered them, parted my legs a little, put my feet together, and the measuring tape ran all over my body like a lost and hurried white- and black-striped lizard. Umm 'Adel asked me, "And which do you like better, Kuwait or Egypt?" I answered, slapping my hands together the way Sonya sometimes did, "Yee, Egypt of course, my sister, there's no comparison!" This pleased her immensely, and she tilted her head back and laughed, showing off big gaps in her mouth.

"*Yalla*—come on, go play in the other rooms," Mama told me, and I was free. I ran to Mama's old room, the one she slept in as a little girl. I sat at her dresser and looked at all the photographs—hundreds of them—underneath the dresser's glass top. I saw a piece of yellowed paper:

AUGUST 2, 1971

IN THE EVENING, IBRAHIMIYYA HALL, ALEXANDRIA UNIVERSITY

A NIGHT OF POETRY WITH THE YOUNG POETS

GHAZI AL-TAHER   WAHEED AMMAR   TAWFEEQ NABULSI

Baba's name winked up at me. I ran away from it to the old piano room and sat on the creaky bench. I lifted the lid up and banged it against the piano, and dust flew up like tiny stars to greet me. I coughed and looked at the sheet in front of me, but the notes resembled black bumper cars with their antennae sometimes up, sometimes down. I couldn't make sense of this alphabet that Mama understood so fluently.

She must have heard me playing nonsense because she came to the room and sat at the piano, claiming her rightful throne. She lifted her hands, let her fingers droop, then began: Chopin. I stood at the edge of the piano and played a high note every now and then, pretending to be one who could play Chopin. Then I decided to dance instead, so I danced through the French doors to the balcony, which encircled the entire length of the apartment, while Mama pounded out Chopin on the ancient dusty piano, which sometimes ate a note here and there, and created a perfectly imperfect tune.

I danced back and forth and passed Sonya's window, and years later, I can still glimpse her through its frame, watch her while she gets fitted for her wedding dress. I remember imagining her life with her husband being just like the wedding dress, something she'd have to create with fabric and hope would fit her, something that looked beautiful from the outside but was actually quite uncomfortable. I wondered what she'd think if she heard my thoughts, and I wondered if thinking this way meant I would never be fitted for a wedding dress.

MAMA LET ME play in the street with my friend Lamia every evening after swimming, eating supper with Geddo and Sonya, and watching an old Egyptian movie. The movies were in black and white and had a beautiful girl who could sing and dance, and she sang and danced so suddenly in the middle of every scene. Sometimes I got up and sang and danced, too. One day, the movie was in color, and it was about ancient Egypt. All the actresses were in braids, the actors shirtless and in skirts. *Shhh!* I was so wrapped up in this scene: A pharaohess had to shun her lover, and she stood at the top of a thousand steps. I was watching her all the way from the bottom step. And just now she was making the declaration, but what was that? An airplane crossed the blue sky above her, just left of her head, went into her braids, through her head, and out the other end.

"They ruined the movie!" Sonya said, and threw her biscotti at the TV screen. "Why couldn't they reshoot it?" She was really distressed.

"They probably didn't have enough money to reshoot," Geddo said. Geddo defended all things Egyptian.

"Obviously not," Mama decided to get involved. "They couldn't even afford to buy good wigs. Look at that actress's braids. They're made of her real hair. The ancient Egyptians used wigs to fake how neat and thick their hair was."

"Ah, so you lived with the pharaohs? You were there yourself, a witness to Pharaoh hairstyles?" Geddo said, getting up.

"No, no," Sonya said, "look at that guy on the left. He's wearing a *fanella*—an undershirt."

"Maybe he's shy about his *bazabeez*," Mama said. I love this word "tits."

Bazabeez? Bazabeez!

"Maybe he braided his chest hair for the scene and then got too shy to show it off."

"That's enough," Geddo said, and walked toward the door.

"Take it easy, Baba," Mama said.

"You were in the military to defend Egyptian land, not Egyptian film," Sonya said.

"Egyptian cinema has a *morsel* of what Hollywood has, so it's incredible they can make movies this good," Geddo said.

"Yeah, with airplanes in Pharaoh movies," Sonya said.

"You know," Geddo said, "this was your mother's favorite movie."

Silence. Guilt descended like a fat mosquito and sucked out all our blood.

"Really?" Mama whispered.

Silence again.

"No," Geddo said, and we all pretended to throw biscotti at him.

"Traitor," Sonya said.

Geddo laughed and shielded himself from the biscotti assault and said, "But you wanted to believe . . ."

"*Dammak tiqil,*" Mama said. "You're not funny."

And Yia Yia's ghost stayed in the room, heavy like she once was.

Cemetery visit day. Mama woke me up earlier than usual and made me wear the only nice outfit I brought to Alexandria: a skirt, a shirt, and black patent leather shoes. She washed my hair and slicked it back, tore out the crust around my eyes. My brother wore something nice too, and we all got into Geddo's Fiat, but Geddo didn't come with us. He never would.

Mama drove through Alexandria traffic like Knight Rider, and I sat in the back and read all the ads on the buildings' walls: a giant Crush soda bottle six stories high, a new play in the Corniche Theatre (Adel Imam was in town), an opening for a coffee shop. With my window rolled down I could smell the fish as we drove by the Myami neighborhood, and boys crossed the street like we were turtles that could never run them over. I stared at the ocean to my right, at the old beach cabins parked in the sand. Mama drove quietly.

We stopped at a flower shop in St. Mark and Mama sent me inside, giving me a twenty-pound note.

"Listen, get her that long flower, the one with the white petals that come out like handkerchiefs; it's got a long, green stalk, you'll recognize it."

I stood there firmly and did not go. I didn't know how to buy things on my own.

"What's the matter? Go get the flowers for your grandma!"

The man in the store knew exactly what I wanted and wrapped the white flowers in cellophane, and I gave him the twenty and carried the flowers out to the car the way Mama carried Gamal, tightly to my chest.

When we arrived at the G. C. C.—the Greek Cooperative Cemetery—Mama parked the car at the gate. The dogs inside barked at us fiercely, and the guard greeted Mama like an old friend and directed us to the grave. Mama put on her sunglasses.

White crosses. Crosses like the ones that hung around my friend Linda's alabaster neck, except huge, enormous, and some of them had long stories written underneath them in Greek. Some of the graves were tiny; I never knew little kids could die. I was suddenly afraid for my brother.

"Those are the remains of men who fought in the war and didn't make it back in one piece," Mama said, as though she'd read my mind. I wondered what was worse: dying as a baby and not feeling it, or dying as a soldier, which Geddo once was; being torn to a thousand bits, so that you have to be buried in a box. "Actually," Mama said, "they're babies." Witch.

At Yia Yia's grave, I stood still and told her all the things I've been doing in my life. I told her I wished I'd known her, and then looked over to Mama, who was reciting a *sura* from the Koran. I looked down at the flowers; they were held together with a clear wrapper that had gathered tiny drops of dew. Like me, the flowers had grown hot and tired. I looked over at Mama and, under her sunglasses, I saw the same drop, like dew on her cheek, like glass. Baba told me once that glass begins as liquid, that he saw men in a cave once blowing into the liquid to make beautiful fluted cups. He promised he'd take me one day. Now I saw that Mama's tear was like glass.

Did Yia Yia understand it when we prayed for her soul, prayed Koranic verses? And most importantly, would we all be together after we died? I wanted to ask Mama, but she looked like a mean jailer just then. Mama liked to call people that— jailers—when they looked mean.

Mama gestured at the flowers. I took them out of the cellophane and put them in the cement vase that was attached to Yia Yia's grave, and I tried to read the words, but they were in French.

Mama held my hand and carried Gamal; we walked past the hushed dogs and the sparkling white tombs, and Mama drove home more cheerfully than before. We passed the chic Rushdi neighborhood and Mama threw her soda bottle on its pavement and turned the radio up. I looked at her profile and wondered if I would do this after I visited her grave one day. I looked at her hands and tried to memorize them because one day they would be in a box in a cemetery. But then she put her finger in her mouth and bit her nails. I wanted to ask her if it was hard for her to be my mother since she didn't have a mother, but she seemed to be in a good mood and I didn't want to ruin that for anything.

THE NIGHT OF Sonya's wedding at Hotel Palestine in the Montazah, the huge Alexandria park which was once King Farouk's palace, I waited with all the children at the foot of a stage where Sonya and her husband would sit, greet guests, eat sweets, and drink glasses of chilled hibiscus tea out of each other's hands. The dress fit me a little too snugly around the armpits, and I wanted to tear it off and dance like the half-naked dancer at the entrance of the hall. She wiggled her hips and shook her rump, and small shiny stars rested on her nipples. I was embarrassed by her a little, but I couldn't help watching her skin and feeling silly. I finally saw Sonya; she looked beautiful in her painstakingly sewed gown—I wondered where the seamstress was that night, why certain people of certain classes were not allowed to celebrate the things they helped create—and her new husband looked exactly as I'd expected him to: kind, short, lost. He was looking at the dancer the way I had looked at her earlier. Then he turned and watched Sonya's face tense and smile at her guests.

I took the flowers and spread them across the floor. Sonya stepped over them and sat on her poofy chair. She was ignoring me tonight and I complained to my cousin Layla about it.

"Shut up, it's her wedding."

"You shut up, I'm wearing this tight dress and these stupid shoes and I want to go home and watch the Ismail Yaseen movie."

"No, no, don't tell me there's an Ismail Yaseen movie on tonight."

"Yeah, and we're missing it."

"Let's sneak out," she said, tugging at her neat black braids. We pretended that we were going to get some hibiscus tea and escaped through the front door.

After a long and fruitless search, we discovered that the hotel had no televisions in the lobbies, so we went out through the ground floor's door and sat on the beach. I thought about how my parents got married in this same hotel, and swam at this beach afterwards.

"My parents got married here too," I told Layla, as we stuck our feet in the Mediterranean.

"They *slept* together here," she said, her foot making a circle in the sand.

"What do you mean . . . why are you saying it like that?" I said.

"I mean they *did* it, they were *naked* and your baba put his *thing* in your mama." She pointed between her legs.

"You're lying. People don't do that!" I covered my ears with my hands, completely horrified. I looked for the moon in the sky, but I couldn't see it, so I looked at a star and willed myself to it.

"Yes they do. I'm not trying to disgust you. They really do. That's how babies are made. You were probably made right here," she said, her hand waving at the ocean like a game show hostess waves at a prize. "Ask your mama. It's true."

I kept looking at the star, far away, and made myself believe that I was halfway there. Then I was jolted back onto the sand. What if it was true? "What do people do?" I asked her. "Do they have to be *completely* naked?"

She sat down next to me, glad that I was behaving like a willing pupil. "Yes and no. They can if they want to be. It's easier if you're naked, wouldn't you think? But the man's thing goes into the woman's thing and it hurts at first. You *bleed*. Then you don't bleed ever again." She started unbraiding her hair.

"Yes you do. My mama bleeds every month. She becomes a monster right before she does. One time, she threw a clock at me. It missed, and a bunch of batteries fell out of it. So she picked up the batteries—the huge batteries!—and threw them at me. I ducked under the bed."

"Don't switch subjects. That's her period. I have mine now. I got it when I turned twelve last year. The blood from doing it is different blood. Tante Sonya will bleed tonight . . . if she's a virgin." Layla's hair was completely unbraided and she was placing long pieces of seaweed into it. She found the longest piece of seaweed and wrapped it around her neck like a sea-boa.

"What's a virgin?" I asked.

"Baba told me we're like a match. Once we're lit, we can't be lit again. So, when your mama slept with your baba, she got lit. If Sonya's been lit before, she won't light up tonight, and he'll know she's not a virgin."

"Whatever," I said. "Sonya doesn't care about virgin or not virgin. I don't know what you're talking about. That guy, my new uncle, loves her. It doesn't matter," I said, getting up and facing the hotel. Its huge glass windows blinked at me.

"You really *don't* know what I'm talking about," Layla said, and walked back with me. "Hmmph. Ask your mother, then. She really needs to tell you these things. You're almost big enough to start your period too."

When we re-entered the wedding hall, we saw Sonya and her new husband dancing, holding their hibiscus tea up in cheers. Then he lost his grip and spilled it on Sonya. Mama rushed to her with a small towel, trying to wipe it off her wedding gown. I came up closer and heard Sonya say, "My new husband spilled *sharbaat* in my lap. Can this be any more awkward?" She waved her hand at the ceiling, at God. "A normal wedding, damn you! That's all I wanted! Did he have to spill that shit in my lap?" And when I saw the red stain in Sonya's lap I was sure what Layla said was true.

A week after the wedding, immediately following the *'asr* afternoon prayer, a black sedan pulled into the street. From our balcony, we could see that it was a stranger's new car, and the neighborhood kids ran after it as though it were an ice cream truck or their first and last chance to see a movie star. The car stopped in front of our building, its front door swung open, and a man's well-shoed foot emerged. Then the whole man stood up and a few seconds later I realized that it was my father. Mama registered something I could not. She slapped her face and screamed and cried.

I hadn't realized how badly she didn't want to see his face.

My brother, who was chewing on an ear of blackened corn, was nonchalant. Baba came upstairs and, weeping into her shoulder, said to my mother, "May God have mercy on his soul." He waved me over to where he and Mama were standing and hugged me into their embrace. "Sido died, my love," he said; his great, strong father was gone.

Mama gave me twenty-five piasters and her permission to go to the market and rent a bicycle by myself. I wanted to kiss her but she had no embraces to offer, so I tucked the money into my pocket and slipped out into the dark. I decided to walk to the market through the street that was nearest the sea so I could smell its ghost waves on the humid wind. I saw a poster for a play and I wished I could go; it was called *Rayya and Sakinna*, two evil murderesses who lived in Alexandria long before Mama or Yia Yia were born.

I arrived at the souk and twisted through the gaps between people's bodies, breathed deeply the smell of fried and honeyed dough. If Sido hadn't died I would have eaten the dough and not felt bad, but even looking at its speckled light brown crust made me think of dead flesh. The bicycle man wanted me to promise to return the bicycle—which I thought was so unworthy of being returned, with its tattered wheels, rusted and broken handlebars, half-torn seat—by the time the show *Dallas* ended. I didn't know how this crazy man with three teeth and hands black with bike grease expected me to know when *Dallas* would end, since I didn't have a fancy bike with a TV propped up on the handlebars, but I nodded and rode off. You must smoke that hashish stuff, I said under my breath, and I was impressed that I'd had this grown-up thought.

I pedaled down to the beach and watched couples buy jasmine necklaces from the jasmine-necklace man. I turned around and zoomed in and out of streets that were illuminated by people's televisions that had been brought out onto balconies for the evening. There were two channels: Channel One was reserved for boring news and Channel Two, it seemed, was reserved for *Dallas*. Every balcony TV watcher was tuned in to the show. When I looked up from the street I didn't see the stars; I saw hundreds of blue television screens dotting the skies. I made a ramp out of an old straw crate some woman had been fanning corn on a few hours earlier, and after at least twenty pathetic attempts at flight, the show's closing song came on, roaring through the streets louder than the Friday morning sermon, and I rushed over to the market to return the hashish-smoking bicycle man his bike.

I walked home through the main road and watched older girls get hassled by boys in cars; the boys shouted and whistled and the girls shouted and giggled. I walked down our street to the foot of my building, where I discovered that someone had tethered a small monkey and left him there, it seemed, for the sole purpose of terrorizing me. I didn't know how to go around this monkey, who'd been pooping all over the floor. All I wanted was to get around the thing and to the stairwell; if I could do that I'd be fine and I'd live. But the monkey had no intention of letting me pass; he flashed his dirty teeth at me, showed me his red ass, and jumped at me. I turned around, walked to the front of the building and shouted, "Baba!" but he didn't answer. Where could he be? Now I wanted to hug him and tell him I was sorry about his baba; I wanted to memorize his hands, too. "Go away," I told the monkey.

"Wi ah ah ah ah!" the monkey said.

"Yes, that's very true. Your political views couldn't be more on point!" I said.

"Wa oooh oooh wa ah!" he argued.

"I wouldn't say that out loud, you capitalist!" I yelled at him. This went on for a while, back and forth, until I heard the short sharp sound of Mama's heels in the stairwell. She walked out and waved her hand at the monkey.

"The neighbors, those sons of dogs and bitches. They think it's a zoo. What has the country come to?" Her hair was tangled and matted to one side as though she were in a comic book and her hair was a thought balloon hanging above her face. Her nightgown was on inside out. How strange my mama was sometimes.

"Capitalism!" I answered her question although I didn't really know what the word meant. She scooped me up in her arms and called me a monkey, and her chest smelled warm and salty, different. I told her the bike renter was on hash and she laughed for the first time that sad day.

BAREFOOT BRIDGE

• • •

TO GET TO PALESTINE, WHICH BABA CALLED THE BANK—
el-daffa—and bury my baba's baba, we had to fly to Jordan and
then drive to *el-daffa* and cross the Allenby bridge. On the airplane, I took out a map from the pocket in the seat in front of
me, and on it, Palestine was the country stuck to Egypt, so I
asked Baba, "Why can't we just drive there, or take a plane
straight there?" He told me to be quiet and fasten my seat belt
before the stewardess came to kick me off the plane. I wanted
to hold his hand like the times we walked along the beach next
to our apartment, the mud squishing and sucking at the bottom of our sandals, my small hand wrapped around his enormous hairy knuckle.

In Jordan, we took a taxi from the airport to the border.
Baba sat next to the driver and looked straight ahead and
Mama looked at Gamal. I looked all around me, at this new
place that looked nothing like sandy, flat Kuwait, or lush, flat
Egypt. I saw the rocks sticking out of the mountains that flew
past us and the sand and the green trees lining the road. We
drove down a mountain and my ears finally popped; I felt like
we were on a roller coaster, except we had windows.

I asked Mama for some paper and a pen and she fished them out of her bag. I wanted to draw everything I saw: the leather in the taxi, the cucumber sandwich my brother half-ate and then vomited, Baba's stubble, the dried skin around his eyes, Mama's lipstick-lined mouth, her face, the face of the rocks outside, the wind whipping in through the window. I realized I couldn't draw all these things but I wanted terribly to record them, to make order of my surroundings, so I made a list of them. I didn't write numbers or anything, just listed the things I saw. When I was done I gave Mama the sheet of paper and she folded it in half without looking at it. Now I wished the wind would whisk the list I made and place it in Baba's lap; then, he'd open it up and read it and he'd feel better. Mama brought out a brush from her giant purse, which held five years' worth of receipts and eyeliners, and she brushed my hair impatiently. I wanted to say, "Ouch! It's not my fault Baba's baba died," but I didn't. Mama's coral lips twitched as she brushed. The taxi carried us all the way down the mountain, and the wind rustled through the glass and whipped through my hair and messed it up again.

The car slowed down and everyone inside it got nervous. I looked ahead and saw yellow and black stripes on something that resembled a gate, where a soldier stood, dressed in green. My father gave him papers and the man let us out; we sat with several other families on benches by the road. Mama and Baba didn't talk, and I just looked at the soldier and his shiny rifle. We sat for a long time; then a bus pulled up next to us, and we were allowed to get on.

The bodies on the bus swayed back and forth, and from where I sat, I could barely see the people's faces. Their bodies looked like the dresses and T-shirts I'd seen just a few days earlier hung up on wires at the market. Two women started talking about what village they were from and then they smiled because they were distant relatives. The driver parked the bus at another yellow and black gate and stepped out for a moment. I followed him with my eyes and watched him get a cigarette from the soldier who was coming up the steps. The soldier inspected all our passports with a cigarette dangling out of his mouth. He never took it off his lips. I thought that was a neat trick but I was worried about the long piece of ash hanging precariously over people's heads.

When the soldier was done looking at papers, the bus driver got back into his seat and drove again. We approached a bridge and the driver told us we could get off. I asked Baba if this was *the* bridge and he nodded his head and patted my shoulder.

There were many soldiers, boy soldiers *and* girl soldiers, standing outside a gray building. I walked past a girl soldier and admired her long curly hair tied up in a ponytail; I'd never seen a girl soldier before. Inside, we stood in a line by our luggage, and after an hour they checked our bags, dumped their contents out onto the wooden counters, and asked us where we lived. Baba answered them and they zipped up the bags and kept them, telling us to sit down and await inspection. I asked Baba how long all this would take and he said, "All day," and looked over at the soldier. It seemed like he and the soldier were talking but they didn't say a word. I went over to Mama but she told me to hang out with Gamal so she could rest. I drew with Gamal and stared at the boy soldiers for a while. They were cute and I knew I wasn't supposed to think they were but I couldn't help it; they were tall and light-skinned and their eyes were hazel and their teeth shone when they joked with each other.

After a while, Mama, my brother, and I were separated from Baba; we had to go to an area off to the side of the building and take our shoes off. There were many other girls there and they had their shoes off as well. There were women in pretty dresses, women in jeans, women in veils, women in short skirts, women in traditional dresses with gold bracelets lining their arms and blue tattoos on their chins, women with big bug-eye sunglasses and big purple-tinted eyeglasses like Mama's, women in khaki shorts and tank tops, all women with no shoes on: all barefoot. It was hot, the sun was in the center of the sky, and the roof of the building was made of metal.

The girl soldiers told us to step into the makeshift corridors that separated into rooms that resembled fitting closets at a store. The rooms were sealed off with cream-colored fabric, and inside, I took my dress off and stood in my white underwear and my pink undershirt. I was almost naked, and barefoot. Mama took off her skirt and blouse and was left in tight underwear that was meant to tuck her tummy in, and a see-through bra: she was almost naked, and barefoot. The girl soldier, I noticed, looked like a boy, and I would have assumed she was a boy if it weren't for her chest. She ran a black machine over Mama's body, and I felt embarrassed for Mama, naked in front of this rough-handed stranger. As though she'd heard my thought, the stranger brought the black machine over to my armpits and ran it all over my body. It felt like a thick, black snake. Then Mama farted a huge silent fart that stunk up the fitting room and forced the soldier to leave for a few seconds.

We giggled, and Mama said *kaffik*, and I gave her five.

From the room next to ours we heard a girl soldier yell, "*Ma zeh?*"—What's this? and then another woman scream in Arabic.

Then our soldier peeked her head into the room, told us to put our clothes on, and went outside to see what was going on. I rushed my dress on, stepped outside the small room, and saw the two soldiers looking at a big gold chain and speaking a language that sounded a lot like Arabic.

"*Eyfo?*"—Where?

"*Ba* kotex *shela*! *Ken*!"—In her Kotex! Yeah!

The girl who'd hidden her gold chain in her Kotex stood next to them, her arms crossed over her chest. "I don't have money to pay the tax!" she told them in Arabic. Mama came out of the room and took my hand.

We went and looked for our shoes; they were in a huge laundry bin in the center of the bigger room. I asked Mama why they were there, and she said the soldiers took them and X-rayed them to make sure we weren't hiding anything in them.

"Like what?" I asked, dangling the top half of my body over the bin. I found cute flower sandals, brown shoes, and pretty red heels, but not my shoes.

"Like bombs," Mama said, inspecting her beige heels, "and grenades."

"But," I said, finding one shoe but not the other, "I thought grenades were bigger than a . . . shoe!" At last, I found the other shoe.

"Hhhhm!" exhaled a woman in jeans and skinny glasses, "the girl's got more sense than those blind ones!"

A few minutes later the entire bin was emptied, yet the woman in the jeans and the skinny glasses still hadn't found her shoes.

"You stole them!" she said, pointing at a pretty girl soldier with braces on her teeth. The soldier laughed. "You bitch! You can't take my shoes, you hear me? *Walek*, they're mine!"

"I didn't take your dirty shoes. Now get back in line and get out."

"Who took them then? I put them in your goddamn bin and now, poof!" she clicked her fingers. "Gone! Where are they?"

"Only *Hashem* knows, lady! Now get in line!"

"*Bala Hashem bala khara*! Don't give me that God shit! I want my shoes!"

The soldier gave her a blank stare.

"I'll stand here on hunger strike if I have to, woman, but I want my shoes back."

"Take them!" the soldier screamed, hurling the strappy sandals at her.

The girl lifted up her glasses and examined the heels. Apparently satisfied, she slipped them on and, once outside, said, "First my land, now my Guccis! Goddamn it."

We sat on a bench in the bright sun and searched for Baba. In a little while, he reappeared, and walked over to us with a bottle of water. I wanted to tell him stories about what just happened but he said we had to be quiet in case they called our name so we could collect our bags and go. Mama handed me some cookies, which I inhaled while black flies buzzed around my face and eyes. All around us there were people, people hungry and tired, people waiting. Mama tried to talk to a woman next to her, but Mama's Palestinian dialect was shabby and the woman was a peasant. Mama tried the Egyptian dialect, and another woman told her to keep talking "like a movie star." Mama was embarrassed and stopped talking altogether, which suited Baba just fine.

When the sun was halfway down in the sky, a soldier yelled out our name and Baba crossed the yard and got our bags from him. We then looked for a taxi to take us to Baba's village, Jenin, and found a van full of people who were going there too. I sat on Mama's lap this time and Baba took my sleeping brother. I watched the ponies, the olive trees, the almond trees; I noticed how neat the rows of trees were, the small sprinklers that shot water at them, the green army jeeps that zoomed past us, Baba's face, which resembled the sliced rocks in the mountains on our left. I was afraid and tired, and I didn't understand why we had just been treated so poorly for so long. I closed my eyes, smelled the lemony air, and buried my head in Mama's blouse.

THE NEXT DAY, I woke up in my grandma's house to the sound of the falafel and bread deliveryman on his bicycle. He rang his bell and Sitto opened the front gate to greet him; I heard the bell and the creak and rushed down to be with her. In the early afternoon, Sitto and I sat in the kitchen in the house that my baba built her and rolled cabbage leaves with rice and meat and cumin and salt inside. Sitto looked like Baba, exactly like my baba, except her hair was longer and she didn't scratch her omelets because she didn't have any. We rolled the red meat, rice, cumin, and oil mixture into triangles of boiled cabbage leaves, placed them in a big pot, and dropped whole cloves of garlic in. When I looked into the pot, the rolls and the cloves reminded me of dashes and commas. I wanted to tell Sitto this but I remembered that she couldn't read or write.

But she could tell stories. Sitto told one about two sisters, one poor and one rich. "The poor one goes to the rich one's house and the rich one's stuffing cabbage leaves. The poor one craves some but the rich one's a bitch and doesn't offer her any, so she goes home and makes her own. The mayor comes to visit the poor one's house for some reason so she offers him cabbage and he accepts, but while she's serving it she farts. She turns red and slaps her cheeks and wishes the earth would open up and swallow her, and it does. Underneath the earth she sees a nice town, people, and carriages. She walks and bemoans her fate out loud. Suddenly she sees her fart sitting at a café drinking coffee and dressed very posh. She tells him he's a bastard and why did he embarrass her so? He says he felt stuck inside her and wanted out. The people of the underground town harass him and tell him he needs to make it up to her, so he says, fine, every time you open your mouth gold will drip from it. She goes back up and the mayor is gone and her husband asks, where have you been, wife? And she starts to explain but gold drips out of her mouth, and she becomes rich and never wants for a thing again! And her rich bitch sister, she gets jealous and wants even more riches, so she emulates her sister and farts in front of the mayor when she has him over for stuffed cabbage and the earth swallows her up and she looks for her fart but everyone's a bum in her underworld, everyone's sad and impoverished, and when she finally finds her fart he starts cursing her and saying he felt so warm inside her why did she push him out? But she doesn't get it and she asks him for gold and he tells her to get lost, the villagers expel her and she goes back to her world where the mayor is gone and the husband yells where were you, no good wife? And she opens her mouth to explain but scorpions drop out of it and bite her all over until she dies." By the end of the tale all the cabbage rolls were stacked in the pot and Sitto put the pot on the flame and said, "*W-hay ihkayti haket-ha, w'aleki ramet-ha"*—And that's my tale, girl, I've told it, and to you, girl, I've thrown it.

Back home, in Kuwait, when Baba had gotten letters from his now-dead father, they would include a message from Sitto. Sido would write the message for her, and her signature would be a little circle with her name inside it. Baba explained to me that she used a ring to sign things, and I never understood this; I thought the ring was the same as her wedding ring. But that day, while we waited for the cabbage to cook, she asked me to write her daughter's husband a letter about the white cheese crop. She dictated it to me. When I gave her the paper so she could "sign" it, she took out her signing ring; it was not her wedding band at all. She dipped it in ink and then smashed it onto the paper dramatically and winked at me. It occurred to me that Sitto didn't care if she couldn't write: she told tales and winked and made cheese.

During the forty-day funeral (we only stayed for three days), the women sat in a circle and told stories about Sido, once in a while slapping their cheeks and rending their dresses. I slapped my cheeks and tried to rip my dress but Mama shot me laser looks and I stopped. I just wanted to be like everyone else.

When I was alone with Sitto again, I asked her how she met Sido, and she laughed and laughed, even though I didn't think my question was funny.

"He came to our house as a messenger for his father," she said. "You see, his father had come to visit us about the olive trees. I took his horse at the gate because the stable keeper was praying. Your great-grandfather was very taken with me because even though I don't have a lot of teeth now and I'm very fat, I was pretty in those days."

"You're still pretty, Sitto!"

"God send away the devil! You liar!" She pinched my cheek, hard. "Your great-grandfather sent your grandfather to come ask after me. He wanted to know if I was available for marriage. But when I saw your grandfather, I wanted to be *his* wife. Like that, I don't know why. He was very handsome in those days too, and not bald! Your grandfather asked if I was available for marriage and I answered, yes, I am available to marry him. And I winked! Your grandfather understood and forgot all about his father. He took me for himself. And after I gave birth to six girls, your father, God keep him, arrived!"

I liked sneaking over to Sitto so she could tell me more stories. The day before we left, she told me about the half-and-half boy who was half a human because his father ate half the pomegranate he was supposed to give his infertile wife to help her carry his child. I wondered if she told me this because she thought I was half a girl since I'm only half-Palestinian. But Sitto told me that the boy in the story was stronger and better than the kids that came from the whole pomegranate, and that when she called me "a half-and-half one," that's what she thought of me.

THAT LAST AFTERNOON on the bank, Baba took me to the cemetery plot. Sido's grave had a wooden plank with his name and a *sura* carved onto it. It was the opposite of Yia Yia's grave: it had a Muslim Man in it, instead of a Christian Woman. I stood with my hands folded over my chest and recited the *fateha*, wondering if my baba's baba was comfortable under all that dirt. I then recited, in my head, all the verses I'd learned, like a showoff, because I wanted Sido to know I was good. We took a short walk past the cemetery and the shrub-dotted land to a tiny house on a hill. Baba opened its gates and showed me the big room inside.

"This is where I grew up," he said. "Here, with my sisters. And whenever a brother would die, since three of them did, they buried them in that lot over there."

"Where we just were," I gasped, scared by the thought that Baba's little brothers were buried already. Where would Gamal be buried? Would we all be buried separately, far away from each other the way Mama and Baba's families are?

"And we went to the bathroom outside." He looked around at the room and bit his inner cheeks. He didn't look sad. Mama would always say that Baba was the kind of man who was happy being sad. Maybe she was right. I looked around the room and tried to picture nine bodies sleeping on the wooden floor, six girls with all their girl problems.

"All my sisters," Baba said, "got married before they were fifteen. No, I'm lying; Kameela was seventeen. They got married against that whitewashed wall outside . . . like prisoners awaiting execution." Baba stopped and exhaled wearily. The wall was the one on the east end of the old house, the end facing the valley. I scanned the scratched-up floors, touched the worn door handles, and tried to imagine Baba as a child.

"I walked to school or rode the ass. I carried my books in a length of rope over my shoulder."

"Did you miss it here when you had to go to Egypt?"

"I was sad, but going to Egypt, going to university, gave me my freedom. Your aunts never received such an opportunity. I want more than anything in the world for you to have that opportunity."

I stared at the hills that surrounded us.

"Do you understand?" he asked me, his voice filled with urgency, and I nodded.

"I lost my home," Baba said, leading me outside, "and I gained an education . . . which later became my home. That can also happen for you." He paused, mining his mind for better words. "War is terrible. Terrible! But good things can come of it too."

He wanted to take a picture of me; he told me to lean and rest my back against the once-famous, now-dirty white wedding-wall. I stuck my chin out and smiled, my hands like soldiers at my sides. The flash made me see stars. Years later, I looked at this photograph closely and noticed a ladder at the left hand side of it, propped up against the yellowed wall. Baba had left me an escape route.

SEVEN

LIFE IS A TEST

• • •

THE ESCAPE ROUTE WAS DUG, ASPHALTED, AND PAVED IN MY twelfth year, the year before secondary school, also known as the Year of the Long, Hard Study. Mama woke me up every dawn for breakfast so I could have energy to study for my entrance exam, which was a month from when Ramadan ended. The results of the exam dictated your class rank for the next four years, which eventually shaped where you went to college.

"Your father was the #1 student in all of Jenin!" Baba said proudly one afternoon after supper. "I blew fear into the other boys' hearts. No one surpassed me. I rode the donkey down to school every morning and sat in the classroom—which was freezing in wintertime since some of the windows were broken—and I always had my hand up: I could answer any question. Without fail, my name appeared first on that list every year."

I wanted Baba to tell me more about this donkey, about growing up in Palestine on the small hill in the small house, spreading mats for beds on the floor of the one-room house. "I'd rather hear your stories than study any book," I said, and, unfortunately for me, he took this announcement literally.

"Then bring me a piece of paper!" he commanded. "And bring me a pen!" he said, so I did, and then he said, "Sit! Now write: Ever . . . wait." He stared off into the window, or at the branches in the fake forest we painted on the wall. "Evergreen," he said, "write it," so I did. Then he said, "Now write, A Memoir, Waheed Ammar," so I wrote, A Memoir, Waheed Ammar. Then he stared off again and anxiously bit the inside of his cheeks, his mouth twisted to the side and his lips pouting.

"There . . . NO! Don't write that. Wait! The hills in 1901 . . . No! Did you write that? Don't write it. Wait till I say full stop. Wait! Fuck, you're ruining my inspiration. Kids! You can't be an artist and have kids! Now sit, don't stand there leaning that paper against the couch, didn't you hear? I said a memoir. So sit."

I sat at the oak-finished table and waited like he said. I waited and waited; I waited until my feet went numb and my hands too. I waited until I was starving and craving water more than anything in the world. "Uh," I started to say. "Shutthefuckup!" he yelled, "Inspiration!"

Baba had it in his head that books should be dictated, a romantic notion that a good book had to be spoken out loud to a scribe who put it down on paper.

"Why can't Mama do it?" I whined.

"Mama? *Your* mama?" He sucked in his lips as though he'd swallowed ten pickled beets. "Why, does your mama know anything about Arabic? Does she even know how to write it? Her with those *oui ouis* and *comme-cis* and *kussys*?"

"*Kuss ummak*—your mama's cunt," Mama chimed in from her nightly post at the toilet, where she read sheet music.

"Shutthefuckup!" he screamed. "Sit down now," he pointed to me.

I began to come prepared. I'd have my *ʒa'tar* burgers, my guava juice, my sweet mint tea, and large slabs of *roumi* cheese all set up on the oak table in front of me. And while I'd wait for him to start his novel, I'd eat. I'd be done with all the food and be burping and ready to pee when he'd say, "Enough. That's all for tonight." I'd look down at the blank page with the heading, always the heading: Evergreen, A Memoir, Waheed Ammar.

Poor Baba. He used to be a good poet. Now he was a dad and a husband, and he couldn't write anymore. He had an idea in his head, but that, unfortunately, was all he had. Through the years he'd build on it, adding layers and characters, descriptions of places he'd seen, hundreds of twisting anecdotes and witty lines, and store it all in his head. But because he wanted it to come out of his head perfectly, fully formed, like Athena out of Zeus (like, on some days, he believed I had come out of him), he could never let it go. When I saw that Baba was afraid, I felt sorry for him.

"What's it about?" I ventured one night, in between a medjool date and a sip of tea.

"It's about your great family, on the Palestinian side."

"About Sido and Sitto?" I said, knowing that the mention of my grandfather still upset him.

"And the people before them. Yes, it's about how you come from warriors, and our connection to the land. How we fought all along, first by the side of Salahiddin, when he liberated Jerusalem from the Crusaders, against the Turks, then with the Turks, against the British, but never . . ." and his face came really close to mine, and he continued in a whisper, "never *with* the British. You know, they offered your grandfather a post to be a 'mayor' of the village, and he told them to eat the fucking post, eat it!" I swallowed a whole date. It felt stuck in my heart. "Then we fought before '48 and we lost. It ends there."

"The fighting?" I said.

"The book. The book, you donkey. Okay," he said, getting off the couch and stretching, "enough for tonight." And I looked down and saw the blank page with the title and his name.

I GOT A new mix tape days before the exam. Linda stole it from her brother, who went to school in my birthplace: Boston. I wished I could go to school in Boston someday and buy rap tapes. Linda felt so guilty about stealing the tape she crossed herself after each major transportation: when she got on the bus, off the bus, past the school's gates, up the stairs to class. She was convinced the Lord would strike her down, turn her into a miniature monkey with bangles up to her armpits, a million gold chains across her chest, and the ability to speak only in rhyme.

"He will not," I convinced her, listening to a tape on Rama's walkman. Rama was a new student from the Sudan; she was taller than everyone else and blacker than the asphalt in the street. The playground was crowded with kids from Junior and Senior school. I looked over in the seniors' direction and thought about the entrance exam, and a boy—a senior—waved at me.

"Shit, he thinks I was staring at him," I said. Rama looked up with a glitter in her eye.

"You said shit . . . from now on it's tihs, you have to say cuss words backwards or you'll be in deep tihs."

"Rama, the boy is waving, what the kcuf should I do?"

"Wave back!" she said, holding my arm up and waving it. My hand limply obliged.

"Nmad, I'm in love," I said, staring down the curly-headed cutie.

The next day, Ramadan would start: goodbye food and gum, welcome bad breath. I wouldn't be talking to him up close.

Mama woke me up just before the sun rose so I could do *suhoor* and study for the exams. I drank water until the first rays of sun shone through the kitchen window. Mama got back into bed with Baba, and I peered into their dark bedroom and watched them sleep, their fingers twitching wildly: Baba's right forefinger pressing circles into his palm, writing proposals and chapters of *Evergreen* in his sleep, Mama's hands playing a dream piano, her thumb, her forefingers, all her fingers, rising and falling on the bedsheet while she performed air Bach.

It was on mornings like these, when I stood in the doorframe of their bedroom and spied on their failed artistry, that I questioned the reasoning behind all this studying. Why would Mama and Baba want me to be a professor, anyway? Why didn't they want me to be an artist, like they once were? Maybe it was because their art had failed them; sometimes their love for each other had failed them. I understood that that was why they were always steering me away from dreams of an artistic profession, dreams of marriage: they wanted to save me from disappointment.

"Forget about marrying anyone," Baba liked to say in between soccer matches or during the commercial segment, as though this piece of advice concerned my excessive usage of ketchup or something similarly trivial.

"Husbands are useless!" Mama would shriek in the middle of any activity and point her index finger at me. "Do yourself a service and don't ever acquire one."

On the morning of the exam, I stood in the doorframe and watched my parents again. They shared their bed so peacefully; they got along so well when they were unconscious, when they were both dreaming. I dug my sweaty palms in the pockets of my ugly uniform skirt and walked to the gate; I kicked rocks with my shoe, bit the inside of my cheek, and waited for the bus to come.

The exam was in the assembly hall, where every year each class put on a play. The year before, I'd played silly Billy. I went up to the roof and memorized my lines while all the kids played in the courtyard and on the sand hills. Now, I sharpened my pencil and waited for the teacher to say begin.

"Begin," the exam proctor said, and my heart leapt like a flung rock against my getting-big chest.

I flipped through the exam booklet and balked. The questions were impossible and I didn't know how anyone answered them correctly. I'd never be in senior school; I'd wither away in the junior school and wave at boys in the seniors' courtyard till I turned fifty-six and died like my yia yia.

When the question time period ended, the essay section period began. The teacher told us to write about the longest day in the world.

I chose to write a short story about aliens coming to earth and stopping time. I befriended them because they unfroze me, and I showed them our planet. It took forever to explain to them why we had war, food, and religion—especially since I didn't even know. I showed them the Koran and we flew over the pyramids. "Oh, yeah, we built those," they said. I said, "Impossible!" And they said, "Oh, didn't you know?" Then we flew to libraries and cafés and I made them take me to bookstores and record stores in America so I could swipe naughty books and good tapes. When they'd had their fill of our world they restored time and disappeared: the longest day in the world took no time at all. As the exam monitor rang the bell, my chest filled with a strange satisfaction. Taking the test was the most fun I'd ever had . . . taking the test and writing a story.

After school, I waited for the bus with Tamer and Rama. Tamer had recently told Rama that he loved her, and she had given him some gum. Linda was mad because nobody loved her. I told her it was because she kept crossing herself.

Mama suddenly appeared in the Olds: she came careening down the street like she'd just robbed a bank.

"Is that . . ." my friends asked in unison.

"*Yes*," I said, covering my face with my hands.

And we stood there as the beast came nearer and nearer.

We stood in line on class assignment day and waited to see where we'd placed. It was a month after the test and we still felt as though a giant white beast were approaching us. Once in a while we heard someone getting in much lower than expected and letting out a sharp scream. Some girls fainted, scared to tell their parents they were in 1C. Students in eighth grade were separated into classes that grouped them with their equals, grade-wise, so that A students went to 1A, B students 1B, C students 1C, and so on. Then there was 1X, also known as The Nerd Class, but that was for super-geeks who scored exceptionally high on the multiple-choice and essay questions. This class was usually filled with Southeast Asian science nerds and Palestinian Christian math nerds.

I was one person away from knowing, and I was chewing my nails and jumping up and down. I accidentally jabbed my fingernail into my gums and tasted my blood. Oh God Oh God. Blood. Baba would kill me if I didn't make it into 1A.

"Oh my God!" I screamed, reading the letter after my name. "NO!"

"Oh no!" Tamer said as he read the letter, and he reached over and stroked my shoulder.

"Your dad's gonna massacre you!" Rama said before she even read the letter.

"He won't need to, I'm killing myself!" I stomped off to the principal's office. "I'm filing a complaint!"

"What's with you?" Linda shouted after me, and I could hear Tamer whispering, "She got into The Nerd Class!"

THAT FALL, DURING eighth grade at the New English School, I'd wake up, bang the off-button on my alarm clock, make Gamal brush his teeth and get his uniform on, and we'd farewell Mama, who was ready to get us the hell out of the house so she could practice piano and complete whatever composition she'd begun a year ago. We'd run down the hourglass and onto the bus, and when we'd get to school I'd walk him past all the stuffed peacocks and foxes, and withstand his daily barrage of questions regarding the nature of gypsum and death, and then drop him off at the elementary school. I'd run to join my class, which was waiting on queue, listening to our headmistress's speech.

The complaint never got filed. I walked to the principal's office, no, ran, and when I got to the door, it hit me: I was in 1X. And since I knew I hadn't scored exceptionally well on the multiple choice, I must have scored high on the essay. Which meant writing a good story got me into 1X. And, embarrassing as being in 1X was, I felt proud of myself.

"Late again, Ammar," my form teacher hissed, and shocked me out of my early morning daydream. He was tall and skinny and had a head of orange hair, and was convinced, like I once was, that I didn't deserve to be in this class.

"Sorry, no excuse," I said.

Just as I'd been rewarded for my writing by getting into 1X, I eventually got punished for it by getting detention. The first time, it was because I didn't do my French homework "properly." The assignment was to write a small essay on French history. I chose to write a short tale about how in 1798, when Napoleon's army invaded Egypt, a soldier entered a small village with his brigade and saw a woman washing her clothes by the river. After she wrung them dry, she piled them into a pot, which she then balanced on her head, and once she neared a small adobe hut, the soldier abandoned his brigade, raped her atop all the wet clothes that now fell out of her head, and caused her to conceive a blue-eyed child, who was most probably my friend Sandy's great-great-great-great-great-great-grandmother, because Sandy is Egyptian yet has blue eyes.

The French teacher spat "detention" at me the next morning and handed me a slip for my mother to sign. She would never return the essay, because, she said, she burned it in her sink and then flushed its remains down the toilet. I was to attend detention that very same afternoon, and when I got to the hall in the science wing where the school's delinquents gathered every Wednesday for their collective punishment, I was thankful for this brief stint of coolness far away from The Nerd Class. The students sitting at their desks and staring into space were mostly Arab boys, with the exception of a Dutch girl, Olga, who flirted shamelessly with everyone and was regularly in detention for being caught smoking cigarettes in the boys' bathroom.

The curly-haired boy I'd seen in the courtyard a few months earlier was in detention often. I found out that he was Egyptian, that he smoked with Olga, and that he constantly wrote, but that they were never notes.

"So, what are you writing all the time?" I asked one day in detention.

"Letters," he said, and yawned. I bored him; I knew I bored him.

"Oh," I said, "whom to?"

"People. People I don't know. Presidents. Actors. Dead singers."

"Like whom?"

"*Like whom?* Like none of your fucking business."

His name was Fakhr el-Din, which literally meant the Pride of Religion. He was Egyptian but he looked Chinese too. I asked him if he was part Chinese, and he answered swiftly, "None of your fucking business." Then the weary teacher, who

was annoyed at having to be in class after 3 P.M. because of us,
yelled, "Not another word!"

Fakhr passed me a letter. It said:

Dear bitch "whom" always bothers me,
I write letters to Jimi Hendrix and John Lennon, Ibn
Battuta and Ibn Khaldun. Do you even know who these
people are? And no, I'm not Chinese, I'm part Japanese,
because my grandfather was based as an ambassador to
Japan and cheated on his wife with a Japanese woman who
had my father, who was then raised by my grandmother
(the Egyptian one) as her own. It's supposed to be a big
secret, so try to spread it around. The pride of the religion
is really Japanese. You're cute but you're part Falasteezi
—Palestiniass, and so you're probably insane. I heard you
were born in America. Are you a liar like me? Because I'm
not really Japanese.

—Fakhr

After that, I tried to get detention at least every other week.
One afternoon after detention, Fakhr and I went around the
entire school, which was deserted for the weekend, and painted
lipstick and earrings onto all the portraits of the Emir. If the portraits were behind glass, we'd take them out of their frames, paint
on the lipstick and earrings, then slide the portraits back in.

"They'll dust for fingerprints," Fakhr said before we began.

"How do you know?"

"I read crime novels. We'll be thrown into a Kuwaiti prison,
which is really just a boat they'll send across the Gulf to Iran,

and when the Iranians see us approaching their shore, they'll empty their Kalashnikovs into us. Better wear these." He handed me dishwashing gloves.

"Okay," I said, and proceeded with the mission.

When we were done sabotaging royal portraits, we sat in the courtyard and he looked at my legs.

"You're hairy," he said.

"What's a Kalashnikov?" I said.

"You call yourself Palistiniass?"

"No, I call myself Palestinian."

"It's a Russian rifle."

"You're lying again."

"No, I'm not. And you're hairy."

"Do your parents fight?"

"They're both dead."

"No, they're not."

"Yes, they are."

"No, they're not."

"No, they're not."

"Mine do."

"Then get a Kalashnikov. And a razor."

"Fuck you."

"Okay."

"My mom's here."

"Bye."

By the end of eighth grade I'd accumulated twenty-three detentions, received all *A*s since I studied super hard and aced all my tests, written a small book about detention, which I self-published courtesy of Baba's stapler and Mama's pretty sheet paper, and kissed Fakhr three and a half times.

The fourth time, a janitor was still on the grounds and caught us, and we ran like hell, fearing our parents would try to pull us out of school, or worse, marry us to each other.

His lips were full and wet and he let me suck on them. I liked his scent; he smelled like sweat and he never tried to touch my breasts. We kissed in the hallway, in front of the menagerie of stuffed animals; we kissed beneath the stuffed vulture's glassy gaze.

On the last day of school, there were dozens of kids going off to a pizza place to eat a celebratory early dinner. I was ecstatic since I'd dropped down to 2A for ninth grade.

"What's it going to feel like now that you're once again one with the masses?" yelled Linda, and thrust a make-believe microphone under my chin.

"Well, Linda, it feels lovely. I bloody well missed the masses!" I said in a fake English accent. "To the masses!" I said, toasting an invisible drink.

I asked Mama if I could go to Pizza Italia. She lifted Gamal's lunchbox up and tucked it under her arm.

"You know your father," she said.

"Please?"

"He doesn't want you going out without supervision," she said.

I didn't say anything, just looked down at my uniform. I wanted to remind her of the time she and my aunt Sonya got drunk on beer when they were my age. I wouldn't do such a thing. Except for the three and a half kisses, I was a good girl.

"Go," she said, and tucked some money into my ugly skirt's pocket.

"I love you!" I said, and hugged her. I sprinted off to the parking lot, where seven of us crammed into Tamer's big brother's car.

I was sure Fakhr would be there. We acted like we didn't know each other when we were around other people. I asked him once if he thought we were embarrassed by each other, and he looked down and said, no, we're just Arabs, so we're scared. I thought you were Japanese, I teased him, and he wrestled me.

The pizza place was on Kuwait City's main avenue, which was only a block away from the Gulf. We all sat at a giant table, and Fakhr and I didn't ignore each other, which confused our friends.

When the pizzas were all eaten up and our bill was paid, we sat outside on the steps and watched the people walk by. There were veiled women, men in suits, women in tight jeans and makeup, men in long traditional robes, beggar boys who wanted some leftovers and we gave them some, white people with their white kids in strollers. The giant lampposts lit up and the sky darkened. Loud music blared from cars that passed by slowly, guys and girls showing off their new rides and the music they'd just bought from the mall. Little dots of light hung on strings from all the buildings up and down the avenue. I sat and admired this nightly festival that I rarely took part in. Fakhr sat next to me on the steps and we smiled at each other.

"Nidali," Linda said, tugging at my arm, "it's your dad!" She pulled me away from Fakhr because she knew how Baba felt about me talking to boys.

My heart beat fast, my arms went numb, and my feet felt like they were floating. It was as though someone had drained all the blood from my body, from my head, it felt so light and dizzy. I was like those lights strung up on the buildings, buildings that were probably commissioned by my dad's company; I was small and spent.

"Come on," my father said, and grabbed my hand.

"Hi, Baba," I said, attempting to sound fine. "See?" I wanted to say to my friends. "Everything's OK."

Once we were in the car, he said, "Wait till we get home."

And I did. I waited but while waiting, wished I could be singing. Baba didn't have any music on, and there was an anger brewing inside him that I couldn't reach, like a kettle that keeps shrieking but you're stuck somewhere and can't take it off the stove. Baba's anger was sitting atop a flame just like that kettle, and whistling all the time. I was not used to being in a car with Baba without listening to something, or him making me sing along to someone. I wanted to sing "You Are My Life" and pretend that I was Umm Kulthum, who began singing when she was little. I'd heard stories about how her baba didn't want her to stop but he was scared that his little girl would be taken advantage of or not be taken seriously because of her sex, so he put her in boys' clothes and pretended to others, and soon to himself, that she was a boy, and in this costume she was safe to be herself and to be happy. Soon, she was free and had enough money to move away from her family and into a villa in the Cairo suburbs and have dinner with her friends at all hours. I couldn't wait to have my own money. Baba had been pretending all my life that I was a boy, from the moment of my birth, even before. Tonight was possibly the first time he actually realized that I was on my way to becoming a woman.

He made a sharp turn onto the gulf road and soon we were home. I got out of my seat and slammed the door, then walked up the hourglass, and into the house, where Mama was sitting in a corner, her hand under her chin. I waved at her, then felt Baba's shoe hit the side of my bottom. The suddenness of the movement shocked me. I was on the ground and he was kicking me. Then he was telling me to get up.

"Get up! What are you waiting for?"

"What did I do?"

"You celebrated being demoted to 2A."

"No, you're angry because I was with boys!"

Slap. My cheek burned. I put my hands over my cheeks to protect them from his slaps. He grabbed my hands and held them both with his one big hand. With his free hand he slapped me again. I hated it when he held both my hands; it made me feel so powerless.

"Aren't you ashamed that you were demoted? You were exceptional and now you're nothing! You," he kicked my bottom, "are," another kick, "nothing!" he screeched into my ear, then pulled me up to my feet by my hair.

"No, I'm not! I'm still an *A* student, smart, and can do anything!" He didn't let me finish.

"Running around like a whore all day until midnight!" He slapped me again. "Get out of my sight. Go wash your face!"

I was weeping; my nose was stuffed; my face felt like a rock.

I wondered if Umm Kulthum's dad hit her. Everybody I knew had been hit by his or her dad. My eyes glanced at the clock. It was just before nine. Why did he always alter the time to suit his needs? Whenever Gamal and I were too noisy and woke him up at ten on weekends, he'd say, are you crazy waking me up at six in the fucking morning? And now, so I could be a true "whore," it was midnight. I thought about Fakhr for a moment, then shook him out of my head. I'd probably never talk to him again. I wished I was allowed to use the phone to call boys, but I wasn't, and they weren't allowed to call me. I put an Umm Kulthum tape in and brought the small stereo into bed with me. I listened to her mournful voice and pretended she was singing only to me, that she was in bed with me, her black sunglasses and beehive and white handkerchief and fat body, all with me.

I waited for Mama to come and comfort me but she never did. I remembered her face, her body cowering in the corner while Baba was kicking me. Why didn't she rise to her feet and protect me? Why didn't she love me enough? Why didn't she play piano in front of a bunch of people the way Umm Kulthum sang in front of a bunch of people? Instead of a pair of sunglasses, Mama had Gamal; instead of a white handkerchief, she had me. I didn't ever want to be like Mama; I wanted to be free and forever unmarried like Umm Kulthum was, and someday have my own money and my own home so I wouldn't have to answer to anyone. But until then I'd have to answer to him, and Mama would too. And he said I was staying home all summer and studying for next year. I looked forward to it like a prison sentence.

EIGHT

TANKS LIKE GREEN ELEPHANTS

· · ·

IN THE EARLY HOURS OF MY THIRTEENTH BIRTHDAY, I HEARD a loud airplane swoop and scream over our small complex. It sounded like a show-off dream, a cartwheeling nightmare, a pimped-out vulture. I lay very still in bed, afraid. The airplanes were louder than anything I'd ever heard. Or was it what the airplanes were dropping that was loud?

There's a moment when most children know their childhoods are over. That was mine.

The giant airplanes were dropping bombs. The other airplanes, the ones meant to protect us, were leaving and abandoning us in their wake. Then there was a rougher sound, closer to where I was, grinding against the street. I ventured out of bed the way I did whenever Mama and Baba fought, in hope that my presence would assuage their fighting or at least keep Mama safe from Baba's blows. It had rarely calmed anything then, so I didn't really expect it to now. This wasn't two people fighting: this was war, I was sure of it. My heart was a shell exploding against my chest. Like trick candles, this shell in my chest blew up and then lit back up again, blew up and lit back up again. I stepped gingerly over the cheap rug and to the window and my shaking hand gathered the curtains to one side. I saw tanks. I said, "Fuck." Again, I said "Fuck!" and I let the curtains go and jumped back into bed. So, where was the famous monthly emergency beeping system now, the loud country-wide siren with its ear-piercing "doy doy doys"? We'd had to listen to it on the first of the month every month for nothing; we'd even heard it the day before, on the first of August, at 11 A.M. Mama and I were in a small shop and she was buying me a bathing suit as an early birthday present. I guess I wouldn't be wearing it now.

I got out of bed again, this time to see what my parents knew. Mama was nagging Baba while he shooed her with a hairy hand, squinted his eyes, and listened to a small radio, which he hoped would not run out of batteries. I leaped at the telephone and checked for a dial tone. I found one. I dialed my second cous-ins' number as instructed. Auntie Naila answered with a weary "Allo," as though to say, "Here we go again." Baba grabbed the handle from me and spoke to her in a whisper, as though there were some way to protect me from the truth: that there was a war happening outside.

Mama was in the kitchen, pouring out tea in demitasses. She gave me a cup and walked out to the living room window where she surveyed the scene, scratched her hair and then her behind. She took a sip of her mint tea and a deep breath. She didn't want to speak to me. I tried to guess what she was think-ing, then decided she was listening to a song inside her head. When she glanced over at the piano, I realized she was resent-ful that she couldn't play this morning; in fact, her anger over this was possibly greater than her anger about the invad-ing army.

After half an hour of sitting on the sofa and waiting in vain for my parents to act parentally, I did what I always did when I was bored and sitting on the sofa and waiting in vain for my parents to act parentally: I got up and turned on the fat old TV set. Mama swung away from the window like an agitated cat, Baba tossed the small radio onto his bed and ran out to join us; neither of them had considered turning the TV on. The man on the screen spoke from under his neatly trimmed mustache and we listened: Kuwait, the country we were in, was now the nineteenth province of Iraq, the country directly above us. Kuwait had always historically belonged to Iraq and now Saddam was reclaiming it, and we should welcome his army and abandon any ideas of resisting it. The standing army (four hundred guys, less than the amount of security guards that work at any major university) had been defeated (surprise!) and Kuwait, the country we were in, was now the nineteenth province of Iraq, the country directly above us. Kuwait had always historically belonged to Iraq and now Saddam . . . the man went on for an hour, repeating the same sentences over and over again.

"You animal," Baba said, not to the broadcaster, but to his ruler. "You brother of a whore!" He threw his house slipper at the television, then his other house slipper at the window, then he spat to the side. "May you burn in hell; may God destroy your home!" Mama gave him a cup of tea. We sat in silence for half an hour.

And no one remembered my thirteenth birthday.

LIFE DID NOT continue as usual but there were still family visits. Auntie Naila came over with her husband and kids; my cousins and I sat in my bedroom and drew enormous maps, planned out our attack on the army and a way to restore the natural order of things. Gamal invented a time machine, and then, when my cousin Hatim yelled at him that they would just invade again, my brother invented a vanishing machine. My cousin Tamara chewed on her hair and began fantasizing about her future life, away from the country's Palestinian ghetto of Fahaheel.

"I heard Baba saying we would go to Amman. Amman has nightclubs and a good sewage system."

"What do you think will happen to us?" I said.

"You'll go to Egypt," she said quickly, as though this required no further thought.

"Baba said we would go to Palestine," I said.

"No, you won't. There's an intifada. The place is in very bad shape. Throw in the fact that you would have to live with the aunts and the cousins and the operation comes to an end." Tamara was using her formal voice, so I knew she must have been repeating what she heard the adults say. Because Tamara was older she was privy to much more information; also, she went to an Arabic single-sex school and so I always thought she was smarter and more authentically Arab than I was.

"You know where I wish we were going?" I said. "America." She didn't respond. "What do you think? Will we go to America?"

"I hope not," she said, and pushed my shoulder with hers. "You'd be too far away from everyone."

I stared out of the window at the square of sky, perfectly framed by the walls of the neighbors' apartments; the sky was a cloudless and icy blue, even though it was the middle of

August. Tamara stared up with me. A fighter plane suddenly crossed it, its jet stream separating the sky in half.

On an afternoon when no one came over, when Mama was napping on the sofa, Baba on the bed, and Gamal biting his toenails, I heard a crackle that sounded like thunder hitting the ground so close it shook the apartment. Mama woke up lazily and looked over at the television. Then the thunder returned, this time louder. Baba came to the living room with a weary look in his eyes, and the third strike of thunder, when it came, affirmed to him that he wasn't just dreaming the sound.

"*Yalla*," he said, and walked over to the forest in the living room. "Under the table." We all followed Mama, who was crawling over to the painted purple grass. We huddled under the brown dining table and the bombing raid continued. Mama looked through the window and pointed outside at the gray and orange cloud that was rising in the sky. Baba stared at it too, his architect eye registering the smoke and sending the information to his engineer's mind, then calculating the distance between that smoke and our complex, then that smoke and our apartment, then, looking at us, that smoke and our bodies. He sighed a deep, post-fight-with-Mama-type sigh and said, "*Ma'lesh*. It'll be fine. Fine." I stared at the orange-red and gray cloud that was multiplying outside and I imagined that there was a giant outside smoking his giant cigarettes, inviting other giants to smoke with him, to keep his lonely self company. Plumes of smoke rose like those giants' cigarettes' embers, and every once in a while, a gray cloud of smoke, which a giant had exhaled, mushroomed up.

"Will we die?" Gamal said.

"No," Baba said, "and if we get buried under this table,

even without food, we will survive. Do you want to know how?"

"How?" Mama asked, knowing by the tone of his voice that he was about to make fun of her. She was still on all fours, her butt in the air. Baba smacked it.

"We'll live off of the fat preserves in your mama's ass, that's how." He chuckled endlessly, hiccupping, his eyes teary.

Here we were, under the table. We were four people, and as time went on, we each leaned on a different table leg, as though we were under the earth, the table legs the push and pull of its four directions. I couldn't tell if we could all sense the possibility of our destruction, as human beings and as a family, but right then, in that tender moment, we all stretched our feet so that they touched in the center of the space beneath that table. And, just like that, the bombing stopped.

We spent the next few days waiting for something worse to happen and then, for something better. The day Mama went into the kitchen and discovered that there was no more cheese to make grilled cheese sandwiches with, she got dressed and announced she was going to the neighbors' to see if they could switch foodstuffs with us.

"Just go to the supermarket," Baba said.

"To the supermarket?" Mama said, laughing. "You go, my love. Good luck. You won't find anything there; people are probably fighting for food."

"Sit down and shut up, lady, you're not going to the neighbors' and begging. Why should people be fighting at the supermarket; are we in Beirut or something? Or, don't tell me, is it suddenly Algeria outside?"

"Go, then," Mama said.

Baba went, and as soon as she heard the car's '84 engine fade away, Mama pulled out the piano bench, sat on it, and played the piano like her fingers were out of breath, like there was a contest for fastest waltz, like her arms were a starved child and the piano was a giant brown teat. I danced with Gamal; we danced all around the apartment the way we did when we pretended we were in Egyptian musicals, two orphans dancing for money. We twirled and skipped and shimmied and jumped. I took out one of Mama's scarves, which she reserved for belly-dancing or prayer, and tied it around my hips. Gamal picked up Baba's calculator, with which Baba had been figuring out our sad financial situation, and pretended it was a mic.

We were normal again. We were people. We were the Ammars, dancing and singing and living. We had exited the bored-population-of-invaded-country realm, a seriously wack realm that exists for wack and helpless fools who didn't have as a priority the goal to survive whole, with *spirit* intact. I felt real, alive, and high.

Baba came back and saw us like that, celebrating in the living room. He yelled, "*What* are you *doing?*" We stopped in mid-song, like someone had suddenly decided we were playing freeze-dance.

"What's happening here?" Baba said, again.

" . . . "

"Don't you know there are people DYING outside?"

"They're dying?" Mama said, truly surprised.

"YES!" Baba said, equally surprised, and carried a small bag to the kitchen where we all followed him.

He took out one cube of sliced cheese, a container of yogurt, and some bread.

"Those sons of whores, fighting over food like crazy animals!" His brow was sweating tiny water bombs and he was short of breath, as though he'd just returned from a wrestling match in which he'd been an unwilling participant.

My stomach sank as the silence of the apartment enveloped me and the reality beyond the apartment invaded my mind. I thought of death and hunger, and I shivered.

FOUR WEEKS INTO the invasion, Gamal discovered a black cat licking itself in the bidet and screamed at the top of his lungs. We all ran to the bathroom, and Baba yelled, "All that for a cat, you son of a bitch, you scared me!" Mama was already beginning her histrionic attempts at capture. As for me, I was completely relieved that, for once, there was someone other than myself masturbating on the bidet.

Gamal and Mama shut the bathroom door and followed the cat from bidet to bathtub, from bathtub to sink. Baba and I stood in the hallway outside the bathroom and tried to figure out how the thing got inside the house at all, let alone the bathroom. We hadn't opened the front door since my cousins visited last, and that was almost three days ago. We hadn't been opening our windows for fear of noxious fumes.

Baba suddenly lifted his hand. I flinched and stepped back, thinking he was going to slap me.

"What's your problem?" he said, in response to my flinch. "Something in your eye?"

"No, I thought you were going to slap me."

"Slap you? I was just thinking of the cat and trying to understand how he wound up in the house."

"She," I corrected him, since I'd noticed when the girl cat was licking herself that her space was completely absent of balls.

"Girl cat, boy cat, whatever," he said, lifting his hand. Again I flinched. "What's wrong with you? Are you on drugs?" he said, and folded his arms across his chest.

"No," I said.

Mama yelled after the cat, "You bastard pimp, you think you can escape me?" and for once, she wasn't addressing my father.

Baba turned to me. "Have you been smoking hashish in the stairwell?"

"Baba, I thought you were going to hit me."

"Why would I do that?"

"Because you hit me a lot."

"No, I don't."

"Yes, you do."

"I don't hit you that often."

"Ha!"

"I've hit you five times in my life."

I couldn't believe Baba was this deeply in denial.

"Try five hundred."

"I hit you? That often?"

"All the time."

"You're probably suffering from war stress syndrome or something. Great! Is this why I left my homeland, is this why I married an Egyptian and forsook all Palestinian women, so my children could have war stress syndrome?" He was yelling. He opened the bathroom door and pointed at my brother. "Do you have war stress? Are you pissing in the bed?" he said.

"No," my brother said. "I haven't peed the bed since I was three."

Baba went to our bedroom and felt Gamal's mattress with the back of his palm.

"Goddamn!" he said. "The boy's pissing his bed."

I stayed in the hallway. I heard Mama scrape the couch's legs: the old V trap. Gamal slammed the bathroom door and stayed inside. Baba slapped his palms together and said, "*La hawla wala quwata illa bi'llah.*" He repeated it over and over again. "Traumatized. My children: Palestinian refugees after all. What's the use, what's the use, I ask you? *La hawla wala quwata illa bi'llah.*" "I am an Egyptian!" Mama screamed at us during this stage in the capture attempt. "My ancestors spoke to animals and in many of their self-portrayals were part animal. I can deal with this cat." I stayed in the hallway between the bedrooms, listening to my brother's sobs, my father's laments, my mother's screams. I put my arms up to my shoulders, making a small shield. And I flinched.

The black cat was finally ousted from the *dar*, and Mama said there was no coincidence about the animal's appearance; it was a sign.

"This too is a sign," Baba said, and gave her the Arab arm, his left hand loudly smacking the bottom of his right forearm.

"It's a black cat, Waheed," Mama insisted.

"I'm not leaving," Baba said. "I don't care if God drops the sky on us. I don't care if the black cat itself began speaking words from the Koran. We're staying. They'll leave soon, and everything will go back to normal."

"Why must you be so stubborn? The children were supposed to start school last week."

"Yeah, Baba, we were," I said. "I'm bored."

He threw a slipper at me, so I retreated to my room. This was Mama's war, anyway.

The phone rang. It was so rare for the phone to ring those days. There were some people, unlike us, who were checking their phone lines every few minutes. The army connected it as sporadically as it bombed or otherwise destroyed palaces, hotels, and office buildings. Usually, we found out that the phones were connected only when someone called, as they were doing now. Mama yelled my name.

"Who is it?"

"Come see for yourself. Do I look like your secretary?"

"Well, life hasn't *completely* changed," Baba said.

I got off my bed and went to the living room.

"*Thanks*," I said in a bitchy tone, and took the receiver away from Mama. "Yeah?" I said.

"Hey Nidali, it's Rama."

"Can you believe this?" I said. "It's crazy!"

"I know. Did you hear about Linda?"

"No," I said, "why?"

"She left through Saudi last week. Her parents freaked out, 'cause they're Kurds, you know."

"Don't be an asshole," I said, because I thought she'd called them turds.

"It's really dangerous. Did you know they gassed the Kurds in the north a few years ago? Like three years ago."

"They gassed the what?" I said.

"The Kurds. Linda was a Kurd. Didn't you ever see her talking to her parents?"

"Yeah, they talked all fucked up."

"It was Kurdish, you idiot. So they had to flee, you know."

"Damn, I hope they made it," I said. "I wish she'd called me."

"She didn't want to call anyone. Her neighbors found out and they're friends with my mama. That's how I know."

"Oh," I said. I was really worried about Linda. Did she know all along about the people who were gassed? How come she never talked about that with me? How naïve was I not to notice that she was Kurdish?

"What the hell is she gonna do in Saudi Arabia?" I said.

"Leave it and go somewhere else. A lot of people are doing that now, apparently," Rama said. She sounded so much older. I *was* an idiot. "Look, I have to go now, my parents need to make their calls."

"Okay," I said. "Hey Rama, call me as often as you can," I said, sounding way too desperate.

"I will," she said, and hung up. I ran to my room and thought about Linda but every time I pictured her she was dead, lying on a mountaintop, her mouth stretched open, and I cried for a long time.

A continuous car horn noise. It wouldn't stop. It came after another noise—a loud crash from the bottom of the hourglass, where the bus usually picked us up. Baba was running his tongue along his front teeth; we ran out of toothpaste last week. His beard was starting to show itself off; all his razors dulled three days ago. He was still in his pajamas, even though it was almost time for dusk prayers. He wasn't praying. Mama got up and played the piano because she knew the music would drown out that other sound, the one of the car horn, so Baba wouldn't refuse it, and she was right; Baba didn't stand in her way, but Schubert didn't overwhelm the continuous beeping. She kept playing anyway. Baba stood up and walked toward the front door. Mama didn't notice.

"Where are you going?" I said.

"Someone is seriously hurt. That's the sound of their head on a steering wheel."

"So?" I said. "Let the ambulance get it."

"There isn't an ambulance," he said.

"Okay," I said. And Baba left.

I waited a few minutes and then bolted to the sand hills that were just outside the courtyard. I climbed the middle one and sat on its peak and watched Baba's white *dishdasha* against the stranger's white sedan. I rocked to Mama's music. The long beep stopped, evaporated into the desert air, and Baba dragged the man out of the sedan and carried him to our car. I could see a circle of blood on the man's headdress. Our car seemed human to me then, its headlights orange and its eyes transparent.

Baba started the engine and it revved like a long-ignored mistress. The man must have been lying in the backseat; I could no longer see him. Baba drove off and my eyes followed him until he turned the corner and moved away from the ocean road and toward Cordoba Hospital. I sat atop the sand hill and thought of how, when my neighbors and I were small, we carried plastic yellow pails and buckets of this sand to the bottom of the complex in an attempt to transfer the hills to the bus stop. We thought if the three sand hills could be consolidated into one giant hill outside the rusted gate of the brown brick complex, the school bus would be unable to get through and we'd be free of school. I imagined what we must have looked like from a fighter airplane then: our brown hair and brown skin and yellow pails and brown sand, running through an hourglass.

Mama didn't even notice Baba was gone until he came back less than an hour later and shouted about why the entire family had to listen to Mama play that son and brother of whores, what's-his-name. I didn't ask what had become of the man who'd prompted the long horn sound, and Baba briskly told us he'd been to the hospital and back, that was all. Then he asked Mama to play "Moonlight," because he knew she hated it. He put his feet up on the faux marble table, and, halfway through the lunar cycle, he fell fast asleep.

THE PHONE'S RING shot through the quiet apartment. Everyone was napping, so I ran to pick it up.

"It's Rama."

"Hi," I said.

"The Iraqi army lives in our school," she screamed.

"What?"

"I know. They moved into the classrooms, ripped up textbooks and papers, set up army mattresses and shit. Isn't it wild?"

"They're in our classrooms torturing people," I said.

"Well, probably that too. Imagine them in our kindergarten classroom, torturing dudes in the kitchen center. My baba said they're setting up for winter."

"They're staying through winter?" I said. They were here to stay. "Hey," I said, "can you come over?"

"Hold on, let me check." She asked her mama, who began screaming. "No. There's a war on. Gotta go."

One afternoon, when nobody came over and Baba and Mama were sitting in the living room reading old newspapers and magazines, Baba stood up and stretched his legs.

"I'm hungry," he said.

"Good for you," Mama said.

I heard Baba go into the kitchen. Then, I heard him cry out, "Where is the *za'tar?*"

Mama yawned, and said, "There's no more left" through her yawn.

"I couldn't hear you. You were yawning. Nidali, what did your mother just say?"

"There's no *za'tar* left, Baba," I said, and quickly covered my ears with my hands. Gamal did the same.

Baba screamed.

Mama groaned and returned to the living room.

"No, no—what kind of life is this? We're leaving. We have to leave," Baba said.

I went to my room, locked the door, and blasted music.

We would leave in a few days with Auntie Naila and my cousins; we would drive in a caravan of cars through Iraq and into Jordan, where we would be welcome and safe. Mama and Baba didn't want to stay in Jordan because we had nowhere to stay there, and they didn't want to go to the house in Palestine because going from one war zone to another made no sense. So it was decided that we would go to Alexandria and stay at our beach apartment until the war ended.

I thought about how we'd all have to run away, and when I pictured us leaving home I saw us literally running.

We were barefoot, like on the West Bank bridge.

I saw us running barefoot, the skin of our feet collecting sand and rocks and cactus and seeds and grass until we had shoes, shoes made of everything we'd picked up as we ran. When we had the shoes, the shoes the earth gave us, we stopped running, and maybe then we settled down somewhere we'd never have to run away from again. The thought comforted me, even though it was more of a fantasy than a thought.

"Telephone, donkey!" Baba yelled.

I went to the living room and reached for the receiver. Baba moved it out of my reach.

"Don't tell her we're leaving," he said, and when I nodded, he relinquished the receiver.

"Yo," I said. I knew it was Rama.

"The soldiers gave kids on my street rides on their tanks today."

"Did you go?"

She was quiet. Then, "No."

"Yeah you did. Why are you lying?"

"Because I don't want you to think I'm a traitor."

"Traitor what?" I said. "This isn't like World War II or some shit. I'm jealous. I'd want a tank ride. But I think I'd try to run away in it, put metal to pedal or whatever they say. Race away."

"Tanks are very, very slow. They'd catch you on foot."

"Figures. I miss school."

"You would. Guess what? Our maid and the Pakistani butler

from next door ran away in the neighbor's BMW. Just took off
in the direction of Saudi."

"Good for them!"

"I cheered for them secretly. My mom's pissed. Can you
come over?"

"Hold on," I said. "Mama, Baba, can I go over to Rama's?"

"Have you gone crazy, are you smoking hashish?" Baba said.

"No," I said to Rama.

"Let her go," Mama said. "She's been home for weeks. Her
face is turning yellow. She'll be safe over there."

I smiled a big smile and fluttered my lashes.

"You do look pale," Baba said, "Go. One less person to take
when we leave."

Mama drove me to Jabriyya, where Rama lived in a small villa.
Just as we got onto the highway, there was a checkpoint. The
soldier peered his head into our car and asked Mama to pop the
trunk. He opened it and then shut it. He asked for her bag. She
handed the giant, fake white Coach to him like it was an embarrassing diaper. He unzipped it and looked inside. His hand
made a small hurricane motion as he swirled receipts, Mama's
eyeliners, mascaras, and shredded tissues. He gave up and
handed it back to her. He asked who I was. Mama said, My
daughter. She doesn't look like you, he said. More fair. Mama
nodded and waited for him to let us pass. He winked at me and
waved us through. Mama waited until we were on the highway
to yell, "Animal. Did you see how dirty his nails were? I'm
throwing away all my makeup." Mama transitioned into driving so swiftly, like it was any other day, without war. I thought

of how accustomed she was to soldiers and checkpoints because of her upbringing in the 1950s and '60s. I wanted to yell at her that I was not used to it. I wanted her to comfort me and tell me that my fear was unwarranted. But I just watched the road and drew my knees up to my chest.

Rama's maid didn't answer the door the way she did the last time I visited. Instead, it was Rama's mother—a tall black woman with a beautiful nose ring. Mama embraced her and they sat in the living room. Rama took me to her bedroom and shut the door.

We heard the first blasts. The army was shelling the palace. We sat in her room and listened to Indian music and read old fashion magazines. We drew mustaches on the models and sniffed the perfume inserts.

The army was bombing the last of the palace's buildings and the smoke sat on the horizon like a premonition. We stared at the vanished palace and opened the window to see if we could smell it. The air smelled like dirt, wet wind, and sand.

I drew in a deep breath, breathed in the dust of the palace, and said, "I just inhaled a throne, marble steps, a swimming pool." Rama inhaled dramatically, "A Persian rug circa 1780, a golden coffee pot, a diamond tub." She flung herself onto her bed and watched the ceiling. She pointed up; there was a long crack in it. The bombing and the house's shaking had created the crack; it was a long line that separated into two small lines at the mouth of the room's corner. It looked like the Nile.

"Do you miss Fakhr?" Rama said. I was surprised to hear his name; I'd tried my best to bury it.

"Yes. He was fun."

"Did you guys fool around?"

"We kissed."

Rama turned onto her side and propped her head up in her palm. She stared at me long and hard and I gave her a look. I couldn't tell exactly what she was up to. She reached over and pinched my boob.

"Ow! You pinched my boob!"

"I know."

So I pinched hers.

Soon we were tickling each other and she stuck her knee right in between my legs. A moan escaped from my mouth; it felt good, her knee there, and she moved it over me in a circle. I grabbed her thigh and guided the circle until I felt the way I felt whenever I sat over the bidet for too long. I turned away from Rama and jumped off the bed. I had no idea what had just happened and Rama seemed just as confused as I was. She turned on her music and we read magazines until Mama called to me from downstairs.

Mama rushed me out the door—she'd turned this into her own social call—saying it's almost dark, let's move it, and I gave Rama a quick goodbye hug. When we got in the car and I turned and saw Rama's dark hand shutting her heavy front door, I knew I'd never see her again. In a few days, my family would pile into our cars and leave Kuwait through Iraq.

I cried quietly on the way home, at my bewilderment and at all the injustice that had been decreed unto me, unto us. I felt as though I no longer understood the world. A soldier stopped us at the checkpoint; I looked at his green uniform,

at the rifle in his hand, at his stubble, and my stomach sank—
I knew that nothing would ever make sense to me, ever again.

The night before we left, I stayed up, refused to fall asleep as a
form of protest. At around three in the morning I heard the
voices of women on rooftops, chanting. A few minutes later I
heard gunshots. After that, I fell asleep and I dreamed: I was in
Saddam's palace on the Tigris. I was wearing a beautiful gown
and was being escorted to dinner by Saddam. He seated me next
to his son, who was reading an English-language book. Saddam
ate his meal and told me to make him laugh. I did my best, tried
some funny stories, and he laughed. Then, he led me to the back
gate, a gilded collection of fake gold and iron. We swam in the
Tigris, and just as I lay on my back and watched the green scen-
ery, I heard a loud sound and the river turned red. Terrified of
the bloody river, I looked at Saddam, but he reassured me and
pointed to a man with a lever at the bank of the river. The man
pulled the lever and the loud sound came back, but this time
the river turned purple. The man pulled the lever over and over
and the Tigris turned orange, white, green, and so on and so
on, and Saddam stayed alive and I stayed alive and I woke up
shaking because Mama was shaking me and telling me it was
time to leave home.

II

As one long prepared, and graced with courage,
as is right for you who were given this kind of city,
go firmly to the window
and listen with deep emotion, but not
with the whining, the pleas of a coward;
listen—your final delectation—to the voices,
to the exquisite music of that strange procession,
and say goodbye to her, to the Alexandria you
  are losing.

—C.P. CAVAFY,
"THE GOD ABANDONS ANTONY"

NINE

THE TRAVELERS

• • •

IN NORTHERN KUWAIT I KEPT WAITING FOR THE BORDER TO come. I didn't know that there wouldn't be a fence stretched for miles and miles, or a clearly marked thick black line in the sand the way it is on a map, extended like the Gulf's horizon. Someone once told me that a straight line on a map isn't straight in reality. The closer you get to the straight line the more expansive it is. And Kuwait kept going and going, even after the road signs had ended, after there was nothing but yellowness surrounding us. It was bigger than I had thought. We'd never come this far north. Nothing would mark our entry into Iraq; I never knew when it was that we were officially there. The geography stayed the same; it could have all been the same country—it had been before. It was a people's tribe that grouped them together: the Shiites, the Sunnis, and the Kurds, and in the past, the Zoroastrians, the Jews, and the Christians: all on different sides of mountains, valleys, and fields, all there.

Mama and Baba had found a way to get papers. Mama had an Egyptian passport and I had an American one, and Egypt and America were about to come to Iraq to whoop some ass, so Baba added us all onto his Jordanian pity-passport. This was the sort of passport Jordan gave to Palestinians who were born after the 1948 partition but before the 1967 war. He added Gamal and me as his dependents and Mama as his spouse. In this way we hoped the Iraqis at border crossings would be duped, that they wouldn't ask more questions, and that they'd let us through to the only country they didn't have serious problems with. There were American troops in Saudi Arabia so we didn't want to go through there, in case the troops were to question Baba with the pity-passport. Palestinians were unsafe anywhere but at least we could hope to get to Jordan without a fuss.

I don't know where we got the gas; I don't remember stopping at any gas stations, just rest stops. Maybe the adults filled the cars with gas while I stood over toilets, my toes poised precariously, the skin on my legs shrinking far from the cracked seats—at places that had toilets. The rest stops past Basra and to the west had only holes in the ground, and those were covered in someone else's rest stop experience. The boys—Gamal and Hatim—pissed at the side of the road, stood at the tip of a golden plain, and pissed a golden arc into it. I started my period in a village in the west called al-Rahhaliya—the Travelers—and didn't want to tell anyone because I could imagine, from the sparse agricultural surroundings and the smell of sheep and gasoline and burning garbage that had been following us, that there would be no walled "rest stops." The smell of the surrounding villages accompanied us the way Umm Kulthum's band accompanied her on the tape we were listening to. Her voice rose and undulated as she repeated herself over and over and the band tried to keep up with her, violins and *oud*s, an ordinary orchestra keeping up with a diva, and the smell in northwestern Iraq keeping up with the people in the van, the

Olds, and the firebird: back to back to back, to our roots, like a caravan.

Baba had a box of whiskey and a sheaf of silk ties. When we had to stop at a checkpoint or a civil soldier pulled us over, Baba tried to figure out if this soldier was a whiskey man or a silk-tie man. The whiskey man was not so religious, was fond of card games, and didn't mind getting wasted on good stuff now and then. The silk tie man was a little religious, or a little vain, or a closet fashionista trapped in a lifestyle of drab green. Baba, who had less than ten seconds to guess which one the soldier was, extended his arm out of the window with either a golden brown rectangle of liquid or a blue and green striped cravat.

I watched him do this from the van, watched his arm reaching out to a man with a rifle at his side. I worried about Baba every time he did it, worried that he would make the wrong choice and the soldier would empty the caravan and arrest us, one by one. Once in a while, this worrying was replaced by sadness, because I'd notice that the tie Baba extended to the soldier was one of Baba's favorites.

The soldiers always accepted the offering and waved us on, as if to say, "Thanks for the whiskey!" "Thanks for the tie!" and I wanted to roll down the window and say, "Thanks for this exodus!"

The van, the Oldsmobile, and the Firebird were at a synchronized speed level by the time we reached Basra. Mama was driving too slow, and since she was in the middle of the caravan sandwich, my aunt Naila in the Firebird flashed her lights so Mama could catch up with Baba and my uncle—who were in the van "without any children," Mama reminded us every few minutes. "Bastards." We were following the Euphrates. The adults had decided they didn't want to go straight west; they were scared of checkpoints, armies, vagabonds, highway robbers, the unfamiliar wilderness. They wanted to follow an old-school route, even "visit" a few historical cities along the way, or at least those cities' rest stops.

We saw goats, children, and in the west, three small sand twists rising up to the sky in whirling prayers. I had never seen a sand twist before; they looked like tiny tornadoes and I was mesmerized by how small they were. We did not see any ziggurats—those stepped, crude pyramids—even though I begged to go to Ur, Uruk, and Babylon. "Herodotus wrote that the ziggurat in Babylon had seven stages of color with a temple at the top," I said. Mama said those places weren't even on the map anymore, and the proud Egyptian in her said that even if they were she wasn't going out of her way to see wanna-be pyramids. Gamal wanted to see ziggurats. Mama told him to shut up because she knew he just liked the word "ziggurat." We saw the river for just a moment on the caravan's right en route from Basra to an-Nasriya, but we didn't see it after that. It hid from us like some of the women walking on the side of the road hid in big black wraps, virtuous. I envied them their hardness. They carried children, jugs of water, laundry, plastic bags, and rice on their heads and in their arms.

I watched a woman walk south and imagined I was she; I was walking and a small caravan passed me on the right. I was still walking, and thinking—about the rice, the son I might have lost in Iran, about my husband, or better yet, a man I loved who could never be my husband. Maybe I was not thinking, but humming a song; I hummed it and walked and looked at the road at whose side I'd walked every day for a thousand days, like a lover. A caravan passed me on the right and the firebird caught my eye: a bird on the hood of a car. Then it was gone, and I stopped thinking about it. I kept walking and humming my song. Then I was myself again, like in my head trick, and I imagined our caravan as a ray of light, and that woman as another ray, so that our two rays met when we crossed each other's paths. Our ray kept going up, to Samawa and an-Najaf, and hers went the opposite direction, to the river and home. She was just a spark along our paths, we, three quick sparks along hers.

Tamara and I started tapping against some pots we had in the car and singing. She wanted to sing "Where to? To Ramallah," even though we were going to Jordan, and Mama was daydreaming and following the silver van. The taps on the pots were light at first, and they gradually grew to poundings. Mama said if we were intent on making a racket we could sing something Egyptian. We drummed on the pots and sang the folk tune, *Al-Toba*—Mercy. We sang our favorite verse: "The songs have wilted in the green heart, love, have wilted in the green heart/ and it hasn't, since your absence, love, been able to drink from another ocean, love, to drink from another ocean, love."

My right hand was red from banging the pots. I rolled down the window and stuck my hand out. I pushed the air and I let the air push my hand back and forth. My hand still hurt. I remembered the times Baba hit me, over and over again. He'd push me and I'd try to push him. The slaps. Afterwards he would look down at his hands and I'd run to my room and cry into my bed. And then he'd yell out so I could hear, "My hands are red, as though they're on fire. She hurt my hands, the brat."

The irony and unfairness of his complaint was always the final and most painful blow.

We heard honks coming from Aunt Naila behind us.

Mama pulled over but Baba's van kept going. She got out of the car and I stretched my arm and honked the horn so he could hear us. He couldn't. Mama jumped in place and waved at him, but he drove on. I opened my door and ran out to the Firebird; Aunt Naila had already propped the hood open and was checking out the engine.

"What happened to it?" I said.

"Waheed, you animal, come back!" Mama screamed at the silver dot on the horizon.

"It's a real . . ." Aunt Naila paused, looked up at the sky, and reached into her purse, ". . . piece of shit." She took out a cigarette and dangled it, unlit, from her lips.

Hatim ran out of the Firebird with a box of his Atari games and a suitcase of clothes and stuffed them into our van, where Gamal was sleeping blissfully.

"Waheed's gone and left us in the middle of Iraq, at Karbala, to be massacred like Husayn. We're screwed!" Mama slapped her cheeks.

"He'll come back. Do you have oil in your car?" Aunt Naila said. She lit her cigarette and threw the match on the ground. I saw it in slow motion: the skinny, wooden, lit cylinder flying back up, as though guided by an invisible windy hand, and settling onto the engine.

The Firebird was on fire, and luckily, nothing else was.

"*Kuss ummik*—Your mother's cunt!" Aunt Naila yelled at the flame.

Mama panicked and threw sand onto the fire but it was stubborn. She gave up and sat on the dune at the side of the road and crossed her arms. Baba's van was back on the horizon, facing us this time. Hatim ignored Aunt Naila's staunchly worded orders to "stay away from the burning car" and reached in for the last bag. My aunt puffed hungrily at her cigarette and rubbed her temples. Baba parked the van by the dune and he and my uncle got out to inspect the car.

Aunt Naila's hatred for the Firebird was almost more famous (in Kuwait's Palestinian ghetto of Fahaheel) than Arafat. In an attempt to destroy the car and get my stingy uncle to let her buy a new one, she had purposefully ignored each of the engine's warning signs and hadn't changed the oil since '87 (a personal intifada, if you will). Neighbors would hear her curse God for granting a car a bigger will than He granted her. The students at Al-Nur School, where she was headmistress, would hear her engine from a kilometer away and would accordingly scramble into morning assembly. Because I knew all this, her husband's insistence on roping the still-flaming Firebird onto the van's bumper and towing it all the way to Amman sounded like a joke. We all laughed. Aunt Naila crushed out her cigarette under her black strappy heels and looked at him, her right eyebrow raised, and tapped her foot against the dirt road.

From the velvety back seat of our van, I faced the rear window and watched the Firebird decrease in size, its orange flame disappearing like one of Aunt Naila's squashed cigarettes.

Aunt Naila sat in the front with Mama, and Hatim and Gamal were in the van with the men. They drove in front of us the way they stood in front of us at prayer.

We drove west as night fell and fell. It was a black cloak that draped us, protected our modesty, or disguised our bad intentions. But maybe it was the night whose intentions were bad. The stars appeared slowly, one by one, as though a long forgotten Zoroastrian God had risen from His heavenly couch to turn some lights on, room by room, in His astral house. Through the window I saw only darkness. There were no fields, no people, and no buildings. Our headlights broke up the night and Mama wondered aloud if Baba knew where he was going. His van slowed to a stop and Mama's foot rested on the brakes. She got out of the car to see what was going on, and when she came back she said, "I guess we should get some sleep."

We shut our eyes and stretched our bodies as far as the cars would let us. I imagined a host of terrible things happening to us: a vicious attack by soldiers; villagers robbing or raping us; snakes crawling up the exhaust pipes, coming in through the air vents, and releasing their poisonous venom into our unsuspecting skin; or worse, our night passing peacefully and uneventfully, and then, as we drove away, the mine we'd been parked on all night going off. I didn't open my eyes, and I wondered if everyone else was thinking thoughts instead of dreaming them. And with my eyes shut, my fingers searched out the door's plastic lock and pushed the knob down.

When I woke up we were moving again. I wrote a letter and tore it up into a thousand pieces, or more accurately, sixty, and though I am not normally a fan of littering, I threw it out the window. I imagined the bored secret service men finding all the pieces over the course of a month, taping them together, and delivering the letter to its intended recipient:

Dear Mr. Saddam Hussein,

I am in my parents' falling-apart car, and we are crossing
your beautiful country, fleeing from your ugly army. My
father has thus far distributed four bottles of Johnny
Walker and three silk ties to checkpoint personnel; my
mother has pinched my leg approximately 13 times in the
past forty kilometers alone, and my cousin, who is now
riding in my uncle's van after my aunt's Firebird caught on
fire and was abandoned in Karbala, has been giving me the
arm roughly every 45 seconds. And I, you may wonder,
what am I doing while these boring goings-on surround
me? I am bleeding in my panties and too embarrassed to
make the caravan pull over, and I am writing you this
letter to humbly inform you that, although I admire your
sense of fashion, green is so last season. Also, when you
decided to invade the country where I grew up (and when
you decided this, sir, were you on some seriously strong
hashish?) did you, at any point, stop and consider the
teenage population? Did you stop and consider how many
of them were dying, just dying for summer to be over and
school to restart, for classes to resume and crushes to pick
up where they left off in June? For your information, I was
anxiously awaiting to see a certain Fakhr el-Din, a very
handsome, sarcastic, 9th year student. I had kissed him a
couple of times by the dry-freeze animals in the school
entrance, and I've since been making out with my left
hand, but it's not the same. He was supposed to be my
boyfriend this year, but that's scrapped now, thanks to you.
I hate your fucking guts. I wish you nothing less than

violent anus-expansion via rocket ships launched from close
proximity, and I hope that you too will be expelled from
your home and forever cut off from your crush and sen-
tenced by almighty Allah to eternity in the final circle of
hell where you will forever make out with your left hand,
the skin of which will burn off and re-grow for all of
eternity.

Yours sincerely,

N.A.

I spent the rest of the trip writing and sleeping. In the spirit
of Fakhr, I wrote more letters: to Fakhr, to Sitto, to my dead
cursed Yia Yia, to the Iraqi girl who just passed our caravan,
and to Umm Kulthum.

The caravan pulled over a few hours later in the village of
al-Rahhaliya (the Travelers) west of Shithatha, at a small café
by the side of the road. A *small* café: three stools, a table made
of a smooth rock, its owner, a one-hundred-and-four-year-old
woman, sitting on the ground, smoking an argila. She told me
to go behind the shack and use the outhouse. Surprisingly, it
was the cleanest thing I'd seen the entire trip. A beautiful brown
and green pot filled with clean water sat in a corner. I washed
myself between my legs and shivered. The water felt cool and
soothing. There were four strips of paper hanging on a nail in
the wooden door. I ignored them and kept washing. I started
to wonder if it would be all right to shower there. Of course it
wouldn't be; I was going crazy. Well, why not? Everyone was
sitting around drinking tea and coffee by then. I could hear
demitasses clinking against trays, the voices of everyone inter-

mingling; I could smell my uncle's cigarette. They were wind-
ing down. I could shower there, couldn't I? There was enough
water, and I was sure there was more. I remembered something
in geography class about the Kuwaitis traveling to Iraq for
water. Iraqis had water. I started taking my clothes off. No, they
didn't: what about the ten-year war? And, more importantly,
what if someone could see me? But there was no one around,
no buildings, nothing. I was at the back of the house.

I was at the back of the house in a small roofless room, naked.
I poured small amounts of water onto my shoulders, my stomach, my legs and feet. It was colder outside now. I watched the
skin around my nipples tighten. The small hairs around them
gave a standing ovation: Bravo, hard nipples! The hair on my
arms did the same. Now I was imagining there was a boy who
lived there, that old lady's great-great grandson, and he needed
to use the bathroom, bad, so he busted in and found me. And
then he reached out to me, caressed my hard nipples, and . . .
my mother was at the door now, banging it down.

"What is it, girl? Did you fall into that hole in the ground?"

"No, Mama, one second." I dried off with an extra shirt and
put my clothes back on. Thank God I hadn't really wet my hair.
She would've killed me. I opened the door and walked out.

"Finally," she said.

"I have my period," I whispered.

"Is your *hair* wet?" Mama yelled.

"Just greasy," I yelled back, and kept walking, quickly, to
the front of the house.

The old woman had my father on her left side and my uncle
on the other. She was looking at my father's palm. My uncle
was clicking his prayer beads and listening to everything the

woman was saying. I could barely understand her strong accent. Aunt Naila sat on the stool and crossed her legs. She drank out of a silver filigreed demitasse. Gamal and Hatim were fifty yards down the road, chasing some sheep. Aunt Naila signaled to the spare demitasse on the smooth rock. I picked it up and took a sip. My nostrils expanded to breathe in all the scents: tea, sage, mint, sugar, something else. The cool water on my skin and that hot herby tea inside me gave me proof that I existed. I sat on the ground by the old woman. I could understand her accent now. Her voice was the only sound; even the beads' clicking had muted. She looked at us kindly, her eyes surrounded and encircled by lines, lines within lines, like dry rivers, each one constantly branching off into the next.

The old woman told us she was born in 1886. "I was here for everyone," she said. "They all come and go." We watched the horizon with her, hung onto her every word. "The Turks, the English, the kings, the presidents, and Saddam too; he'll go too. And the Americans, I say let them come! Soon, they'll be gone too. Even me, me. I will go." She reached for her cane. "Welcome to al-Rahhaliya," she said as she got up slowly and left.

TEN

IN TRANSIT

• • •

WHEN I SAID GOOD-BYE TO HATIM AND TAMARA AND AUNT
Naila, I knew I wouldn't see them again for a while and the
knowledge stained my insides. On the plane to Egypt, I watched
the tourists that surrounded us and thought how nice it would
be to travel just for the sake of traveling, how nice it must be to
leave one country for another willingly . . . for fun! I wondered
how many planes I'd been on. I thought of my ancestors going
from country to country, and a little silent film played in my
head, all sped up with crazy music playing loudly as a soundtrack: A Turkish woman gets in a carriage and goes to Palestine. She marries an Arab and they have little Turko-Arab babies
and their babies have babies and one of those babies grows
up and begets my father. A Greek woman with a black shawl
and massive boobs gets on a ship in Crete, goes to Alexandria, Egypt, gives birth to a girl who falls in love with an Egyptian and they beget my mother. My father gets on a ship from
Jordan to Egypt and finds my mother and they marry. They
get on a plane and go to America and beget me. We all get on
a plane and go to Kuwait. My child someday will tell this entire story and tack on in the end that I got in a car and fled

Kuwait and then boarded a plane to Egypt. I didn't know where my story would end or how many planes, carriages, cars, or ships my offspring and the offspring they beget would go on, only that I hoped in the future travel would be more comfortable, because right then I was sad and dizzy and my goddamned head hurt.

LOOKING BACK, BEING in Alexandria that winter was like being in the company of a man in a suit who is usually a fabulous drag queen. Everyone else thinks he looks average in the suit, or more likely, they don't even notice him. They walk on past him—past his dirty necktie hidden behind the suit jacket, the faint remainder of mascara on his left eyelid, his overly sure swagger—and their voices rise above his. Only I know what he's usually like: festive, grouchy, colorful, dramatic, the possessor of the closest possible shave.

Geddo picked us up from the airport the way he usually did, except this time we were there to stay. And Baba was with us. And he didn't have a job. And Mama was quiet. And I was hungry. And a Cairo-Alexandria drive was unnecessary thanks to the newly anointed Al-Nuzha airport in Alexandria.

Gamal and I sat in the back of Geddo's Fiat with Mama while Baba and Geddo talked politics up front. "The war is starting soon," Geddo said. "They're preparing us for it on the news every few minutes." Baba nodded wearily. I stared out the window at my day-job-drag-queen of a city. I felt guilty to admit it to myself but I knew why this city was my favorite of all places: it used to be just mine and Mama's and six million others' during summers. Now it was real, permanent, and its flaws peeked out at me every time Geddo turned a corner.

The people still lined the streets and pawned their wares or bought other people's wares and shouted and spat and cursed and laughed and smoked and teased the women who passed by holding Cleopatra cigarettes in their manicured fingers fresh from salons where you could see them getting perms and sweeping multi-colored multi-textured hair out onto the sidewalk where they grilled their corn and hung about the *corniche*'s railing instead of finding a job or leaving a job and rendez-vousing in alleys and on balconies where they watched their imported soaps and their Egyptian soaps and dangled down their baskets which carried shopping lists (going down) and groceries—mallow leaves, chicken bouillons, tomatoes, onions, garlic, flour, salt, eggs—(going up) and looked down at the street where they saw traffic upon traffic upon traffic that cradled us in it, the new refugees, continuing a tradition of refugees by coming to Alexandria. My grandma came here with her family from Crete when things were bad there. My baba came here from Jordan because he couldn't go back home. And now here I was, back where we all eventually went.

We left downtown and passed Chatby, and I wished we could stop here and stay at Geddo's but Baba was too proud to live at Geddo's and would rather us all live in the small beach apartment, so the car kept weaving past Chatby, and past San Stefano, and past Myami and Sidi Bishr and Mandara and Montazah Park and soon we were in Ma'moora, and we were the only ones there since it was a summer town. I didn't see a single soul. The streets were empty as though the small neighborhood had been through a war too. We parked in front of the apartment where 'Abdo, our doorman, greeted us, and his face looked exactly the same. His wife kissed both my cheeks and thanked God for our safety. Their children weren't there because they got married and I'd probably never see them again.

'Abdo brought our luggage upstairs to the apartment, four times as much luggage as usual, and he didn't look at me the way he used to; the two bumps underneath my shirt would keep him from dangling me over the balcony and threatening to let me go because I'd already gone. My room was the same, my bed was wooden and cold, the sheets smelled like time. I lay in it and faced the cracked wallpaper, my old graffiti, the caked boogers I thought I could hide by the bed's frame.

Mama opened the balcony doors, even though it was cold, and stretched her legs so she could walk over to the souk and buy some food. Baba was already unpacking luggage and making Gamal help him. He called to me but I didn't budge. I knew I could catch a beating right now; his temper was abominable under such circumstances (thrice refugee-d). He called for me again. I heard the cheap wicker chair croak on the balcony, followed by Mama's voice, "Waheed, leave her." I turned away from them all, turned away from my sadness and tried to shut my feelings out, and fell into a light, dream-riddled sleep.

When I woke up it was still nighttime. I sat out on the balcony and tilted my head over the rails so I could see the Mediterranean. The ocean's water was still, like a rug. This was our home now; our old home was gone, and no matter how far I tilted my head, I'd never be able to see it. I went back to my bed and once I'd wrapped the sheets around my head, I cried; I cried a mini-Mediterranean of tears.

. . .

"You're lucky," they said. That year was *I'dadiyya*, and I wouldn't have to repeat the year; I could just begin school and take the final exam in May.

"How come?" I said, twirling one of Baba's ties that had been in the box from the trip out of Kuwait, the only surviving bribe.

"Because," Mama said, "in Egypt, the ninth year students don't get graded for anything during the year, just for what they get on their exams."

I was ignoring her and imagining the silkworms that made the tie, envying them their cocoons. I didn't want to be around anyone for a while.

"The final exams determine their grades for the year, see?"

"Yes," I said, "but that doesn't make sense."

"Stop fucking with my cravat," Baba said. "It was from London. Harrod's!"

"Don't argue," Mama told me. "What makes sense, anyway? Does it make sense that we live in a summer beach town in our summer apartment, or that our neighbors invaded us; that America actually cares and is going to war for it; that my ass is as big as it is now when it was twenty-four inches in diameter when I married that bastard?" She points at Baba. "No. Nothing makes sense. So, we need to get you a uniform, *wi bas*, that's all."

"I'm not going to school this year," I said calmly, and tied the cravat in a Parisian knot around my neck. "If all I have to do is take an exam in May then why should I enroll at school and meet new people and new teachers who will doubtlessly hate me?"

"Because you'll fail your exam if you don't."

"I'll probably do better at that exam if I have all my days free for study. It could be beautiful; I'll read eight hours a day and I'll write, instead of sitting in a classroom and listening to one person, an idiot, talk all day long."

"I'm telling you, you're not hanging around this apartment for five months, your face constantly in mine, that's why!" Baba said.

"You're selfish," I said.

Mama came running out of the kitchen because she heard it, his big palms against my cold cheeks. I didn't care how many times he slapped my face, I wasn't going to school for five months. I was planning out my hunger strike, my days as a professional studier rather than a bored student. I was fantasizing about reviewing for physics by the ocean, history by the cannons in Montazah Park, mathematics by the eastern quay, English and poetry while I held vigil outside Cavafy's old apartment—if I could find it. I wanted to study for this exam and ace it, slay it like a paper dragon, but I wanted to do it on my own terms.

Mama surprised me then when she pried Baba off me. Mama had always stayed out of it; she'd almost never intervened on my behalf before, so why was she doing so now? Maybe it was the fact that the apartment was in her name, or that she was in her own country, or that she had had enough bullshit for the month. Invigorated by her boldness, I began a rant.

"You can hit and hit and hit me but I'm not going to an Egyptian ENGLISH school in stupid DOWNTOWN which will probably take me an hour and a HALF to get to on a BUS full of sweaty MEN who'll try to grope me every goddamn

MORNING for the next five MONTHS when I can just take a final exam in MAY."

"You're going to school and that's final," he said. "No discussion."

I blew my snotty nose, all my glorious green boogers, into his fancy Harrod's whateveritscalled handkerchief cravat. It took Mama another five minutes to pry him off me.

"I'M NOT GOING TO SCHOOL!" I managed to say through the struggle.

The El-Nasr Girls' School downtown was marble floors, arched doorways, mosaic pillars, a garden, and teachers who were so underpaid they wore their stockings for months after the first run showed up, as it invariably did, right on time, unlike the lousy students. The school had been a fancy boarding college back in the thirties and forties, before the revolution and the nationalizations and the overall undercutting of decadence. Now it was an "affordable" girls' school where some subjects were taught in English, especially English literature. The other students were hard-haired and chatty, strong-willed and naïve, skinny and fat, short and tall, light skinned and dark skinned, and almost no one was half-Palestinian here except me. And everyone knew it.

"Hey Nidali, where's your *keffieh*?"

"*Ya* Nidali, why'd Arafat support Saddam?"

"Why's your leader so stupid?"

"Doesn't he know that the Palestinians who lived in Kuwait will suffer now because of his support? That anyone who supports Saddam is about to be fucked?"

I didn't tell them, "No shit, my family just lost its home and its life savings because of that, and millions of people on the West Bank and in Gaza will lose income families like mine used to send them from Kuwait." I didn't tell them that my heart was broken. I didn't tell them how I always felt like I'd left something behind at home until I realized that what I'd left behind *was* home. I kept my mouth shut and raised my hand to talk only in class. The classroom had light blue walls and gigantic windows without screens. The blackboards took up most of the wall opposite the desks. The desks were narrow and wooden and at least thirty years old. I was secretly in love with our classroom because it was so old and historic and the windows were peeled open.

There were a few boys in my class because their mothers taught there and they got free tuition. One of them was a freckled redhead. Even though there were a lot of English people in Kuwait, I'd never seen so many freckles in one place, on a single nose. I stared at them, tried to count them. They were like a constellation.

"What are you looking at?" he said.

"Nothing," I said.

"Liar. You were staring at me," he said.

I ignored him, and I decided to call him Red from then on.

"Nidali Ammar," my teacher said. "Stand up and list the leaders of Egypt starting with Muhammad Ali, please."

Everyone waited.

"Muhammad Ali was a boxer who converted to Islam in the sixties and when my parents were in Boston where I was born they saw him on the street and my mother took a picture of us together," I said, as though being quiet all this time had taken its toll, "and my father explained to Muhammad Ali Clay what my name meant and the great one said, so she's already a fighter."

The room exploded with laughter. The window by me creaked open and little drops of rain dripped on my half-broken wooden desk that was covered in carvings of the names of every hot boy who'd lived in Alexandria since the fifties.

"Silence!" the teacher said to the class. Her face was lean and long like the run in her stocking.

"Sorry," I said.

"Answer the question," she said.

"She doesn't know," Red said, and the whole class laughed again.

"Of course she doesn't," the teacher said. Someone threw a spitball.

The class was laughing at me and pointing at my sad, sad half-and-half self and the teacher hark-hark-harked in slow motion, her laugh guttural and phlegmy and her wart getting bigger and bigger as my heart sank and sank.

The blue walls turned bright purple and a huge silver disco ball descended from the ceiling.

"Muhammad Ali!" I screamed. "Wali Ibrahim, Wali Abbas, Wali Sa'id . . ." and a bright green and yellow spotlight shone on me and no one else. "Khedive Ismail, Khedive Tawfiq, Khedive Abbas Hilmi, Sultan Husayn Kamil . . ." the teacher's faint mustache suddenly grew into handlebars and curled up at the edges. "Fuad, King Farouk, Gamal Abdel Nasser, Anwar Sadat, Hosni Mubarak, the end!" As a form of protest against their housing conditions the freckles on Red's nose evaporated and distributed themselves on the faces of all the students.

Silence descended on the class.

A moment later the chatting resumed and the teacher sat down and read. A paper plane made its way across the room: a note from Jiji, a dark-haired girl in the front row. It said, "You're a tough girl, Nidali, by God."

I took a bus from school to Mandara, and another bus from Mandara to Ma'moora. The buses were packed with people and people smells and it took two hours to get back to the apartment. Every night Mama made us dinner, even if it wasn't great. We only ate meat once a week, if that, and sometimes it was just heated bread or *fateera* with a little honey. Baba put on his reading glasses and read his Tawfiq al-Hakeem or Yusuf Idrees or Naguib Mahfouz or poetry deep into the night, his lamp the only one on in the entire house. He let me go sit on the street corner by the mosque after *athan al-maghreb*—the dusk prayers, since no one molests girls outside mosques, and I read by its green light: assignments in history or religion or the only English book we read that year, *A Tale of Two Cities*, and wondered who the hell would stand in for me if I had to die. No one talked about Kuwait or our apartment or if we'd ever go home again. This was home.

One night Mama gave me dinner and I ate most of it by the mosque, and there were leftover pieces of *baladi* bread. Birds wanted to eat it so I let them. Then I remembered my summer friends. I walked over there and I screamed their names and the street seemed so much narrower, smaller than it used to be; my voice echoed less. And when they didn't answer since they were away at their regular home in Cairo or wherever it was that they lived, I threw crumbs onto their balconies, arched my arm and threw them there for birds to go visit, for birds to eat.

I looked up from the street at our dimmed balcony and saw my family moving around inside, barefoot. I wondered about all the sand and rocks and cactus and seeds and grass we'd picked up so far running away—if we had the shoes that the earth gave us, and if we could stop running and settle down.

I WORE MY uniform in the toe-pinching dark cold every morning: a gray skirt we borrowed from Mama's friend's obese eight-year-old daughter, black tights that were yet to run, my old black shoes that were a size too small, a gray blazer, a gray tie, and a pink button-down shirt that all used to be Mama's. We went to Chatby one afternoon, made Geddo lunch, and fished the uniform ingredients out of her old closet, pausing every few seconds so she could explain to me what recital this skirt or that blouse was for and how she wore this pair of bell-bottoms and that tank top to date Baba. The clothes had been sewn by my yia yia; I could tell by the way Mama had painstakingly conserved them, had folded them like delicate origami. The requisite piano pounding was performed, as was the requisite opening of shutters and the walking up and down on the wrap-around balcony.

I watched the photos again, and again wondered things. But mostly, I wondered how I could convince Baba and Mama to let me move in with Geddo, into this museum. I watched him intently that afternoon, amazed. Remnants lined the walls, lived on, just as he did. Pieces of Yia Yia were stashed in closets, cupboards, and drawers. Her cross still hung on her side of the bedroom. Some of the couches were covered in white sheets. The books on the shelves were in Russian and Greek; they had been hers, notebooks with thick films of dust on the topmost layer of once-white pages. I wanted to ransack the place, wanted to understand Mama's past, to understand Mama.

Jiji was the redhead's girlfriend. He had at least eight girlfriends that were accounted for. Jiji said he probably had more in other schools. She'd never been kissed.

"Have you?" she said one day during recess, while we were hanging out on the diving board over the "pool," which was covered in a stratum of green-black film and buzzing with the rich soundtrack of frog symphonies and bug sonatas.

"Yeah," I said, "in Kuwait, I had a sort-of boyfriend. We kissed after school a lot."

"Was it disgusting?"

"At first, yeah, because their tongue is in there and you wonder, why does it feel so slimy? And you try not to laugh. I don't think you should kiss Red, though," I said.

"I want to," she said.

A frog stuck its head out of the swamp and croaked at us.

I wanted to tell Jiji that I'd give her her first kiss. I hadn't thought of it before but just then, when I saw that slimy frog, I thought, *I* should give her her first kiss. I'll go to hell, I thought. I liked boys, I assured myself, because I did. I wanted to kiss them. But I wanted to be the first one Jiji kissed instead of some slimy toad of a guy.

The school library was gorgeous: walls gilded in gold, mirrors, lamps that hung down like movie stars' breasts, their bulbs shiny bright nipples. The bookshelves were old wood, the books inlaid with gold, their pages thinner and softer than petals, and the whole place smelled like an abandoned oyster fisherman's ship. I liked to go in there during free periods and pretend I was studying for the exams, but really I was reading poetry, Shakespeare, and novellas, and avoiding Jiji. I wished Mama and Baba had saved the money they'd spent on this stupid school so I would have never met Jiji and never felt guilty.

At home, Mama and Baba didn't fight because there was no money to fight over, because there was no piano, because Baba had no job to complain about. Instead, they picked fights with Gamal and me. Gamal caught a beating almost every week at first, then twice a week, then soon enough every day. His school was in Mandara, and it was tougher than mine, and Gamal had never really been interested in school, and at this school, you didn't have a choice. They assigned him mathematics three times harder than what he was used to, history lessons he stayed up till midnight every night to memorize. I kept away from the scene, let Baba yell at me, and didn't talk back. I thought, I'm already going to hell for having lesbian thoughts and I might as well bide my time here on earth.

My time was sectioned between the tiny kitchen counter on which I did my homework, the sink in which I cleaned the dishes, and the bidet over which I had shuddering orgasms. I felt like I was constantly being observed, because I was. Baba and Mama had never had to watch us, really see what was going on with us. So they noticed that Gamal was not a school person and had attention problems, and that I was really into school and had to use the bidet a lot.

When they weren't on duty observing us, or beating Gamal, and when Mama was not busy crying into a towel in the bedroom and cursing her lot in life, they were watching the news. There was a briefing on the Gulf War, which had just started, and the goddamn segment had *theme music*. Military drums beat like at an ancient tribunal, and every few hours President Mubarak came on and said something even dumber than whatever he'd said last time. Nations from all over the world were invading Iraq—Egyptians and Americans and it seemed everyone in between. The cities we traveled through in the south of Iraq were all being obliterated just as I was studying geometry theorems. The woman I pretended to be at the side of the road was buried there now.

Baba was laughing at the television. "Everyone, you have to see this," he yelled. We huddled around the blue flickering screen, the only source of light in the small room.

A reporter asked Mubarak: "What about the threats Saddam has made about hitting Egypt with a Scud missile as punishment for its cooperation with the West?"

"Let him hit us!" Mubarak said.

"Let him hit us?" the reporter asked in horror.

"Yes, let him . . . it'll miss!"

Baba was hiccupping with laughter. Mama looked into our faces as though she were on her way to jail.

"We should have stayed in Kuwait," she said, biting her nails. "We would have been safer."

"Safer what, crazy woman," Baba said. "Didn't you see the fires burning, the madness?" Then, "I've never seen such a sophisticated method of defense. 'Let him hit us, it'll miss!' It'll *miss!*" Baba was doubled up on the couch.

On the day before winter break began, Jiji found me at the library and asked if I wanted to come to her house since her mama was making stuffed peppers and steaks. I hadn't had a decent piece of meat since before the Iraqi invasion. I told her I had to call my family and ask, but when I did, Baba said absolutely not.

"We're not beggars. You have to come home and study."

"Baba, it's the last day of school for a *month*. Please?"

"No."

"I'm going."

"If you don't get on the bus and come straight home, *ya* Nidali, you'll be sorry."

"I already am. Sorry," I said, and hung up. I wanted steak.

Jiji's apartment was a penthouse on top of a tall building in downtown Alex. Her terrace faced the sundial square and the University of Alexandria. She sat on a chaise longue holding a cup of tea and wearing a wool hat, and I stood against the terrace railing.

Jiji's mother called us in to eat, and her father, whom Jiji called Poppy, sat at the head of the table and didn't say a word. He ate three times the amount of meat as her mother, and her little brothers squirmed and chewed the meat and spat it out and rechewed it and kicked each other under the table. I tried not to look like someone who'd just given up a hunger strike, but my mouth watered and I could feel the drool coating every bite I took. Jiji's mama asked if I missed my old house. I hadn't much thought about it because whenever I felt the memory approach my mind, I drew the gates and turned my back on it for fear of the pain it would cause. So I answered, "Yes," because that was the polite answer. Jiji shifted uncomfortably in her chair and announced that my mama was a great pianist and that, since they had a piano and no one played it, Mama should come and give them lessons. Where the hell did that come from? Mama would love the idea, so I hated it.

"Mama is really busy with my little brother. He's retarded," I said, tapping my head. I loved to lie.

Jiji squinted and made a face, and her mama reached for my hand and her face sagged with false empathy.

In Jiji's room we listened to Amr Diab's new album and she asked me the same thing her mama asked me: Do I miss my old house, do I miss Kuwait?

I sighed.

"I mean," she kept going, ignorant of how much talk of home pained me, "If I had to say goodbye to everyone, to my house, my room, the place I'd grown up, I'd be so . . . *sad*."

I changed the subject because thinking of how much I missed home was excruciating. I told her she could practice kissing on me if she really wanted to impress Red. She jumped off her chair and stood with her arms at her sides, confused.

"You mean like lizzies?" Lizzy was a word someone started for lesbian.

"No," I said, "like a pillow, but with real lips. And you won't be in trouble 'cause I'm your friend. If you wanted to, I wouldn't care."

She looked down at her fingernails, turned her hand over, stared at her palm, and then turned her hand over again.

"*Tayeb*," she said. She locked her door and I stood up to face her.

"*Tayeb*, open your lips slightly and lean in on me," I said. She leaned in too hard and her teeth hit my teeth.

"Ouch!" she said.

"Never mind, I'll lean in," I said.

I put my hands on her compact shoulders and kept my eyes open. Hers were closed. Good, I thought. It felt like a mini-pilgrimage, my traveling the space between our heads, like running down the street when my legs were shorter, when I had another home to go to after the summer. I longed for that time again, for home. I imagined the apartment in Kuwait, its doors locked, the hourglass complex deserted, the sand hills like somnolent gravestones, the shells and the secret notes and the toys from kids' meals and the memorabilia of our youth that we buried inside them—all relics now that we were gone. I imagined the hills lifting up and the sand shifting and floating up to the sky as though it were a sieve transferring them from our ownership to its own; unkempt grass gathering like dirty hair at the would-be woman's waist swaying and then catching fire; flowers in the pots outside the apartment doors and on the terraces cracking and emptying themselves of jasmine roots and dry sage leaves; the white-washed walls blocking the Gulf's spilled oil from slicking against the ivy that spread over it like a disease; and inside the apartment, our made beds staying made; cups lining the cupboards and the tea tinned and dry; cockroaches creeping in and out of the piano where Baba had saved some of our bread (in case we ever got robbed) which he never remembered to throw away; old cassettes silent like men at Friday sermon; birds struggling out of the Gulf, managing to flap their wings only three dozen times before the oil hardens on them and they stop, like time, and spiral down into our *manuar*, where they die by the bicycle, whose gears have gone orange like a lazy flame.

Our lips touched and I parted hers until I found her tongue. I was licking a gelato on the beach at summer; Fakhr's tongue hadn't felt this smooth or slippery or cold. She laughed, then moved her tongue around in rapid circles. I slowed it down and then brought it to a halt and sucked on it. She made a whimpering sound. I opened my eyes and saw that hers were open too. I reached up and closed them with my thumbs, then caressed the side of her face, stuck my fingers in her thick knotty hair. I kissed her lips, quick pecks that she returned, and I tugged at her bottom lip with both of mine. I felt dampness in my panties, as though I'd left them out on the humid balcony overnight, and a hard pain between my legs, which I tried to ignore. We kissed until my lips felt electrocuted, until someone knocked on the door and asked if we wanted dessert.

I replayed that kiss over and over in my mind, tried to figure out what it meant that I liked both girls and boys. It was bad enough to like boys! It was bad, bad, bad, and I was bad, and Baba told me so as his hands slapped and his feet kicked and his house slipper struck my skin over and over again. But he thought I was bad because I hadn't come home straight after school. If only he knew! I was cowering on the floor, or running toward my room, or he held my hands with one of his big hands and slapped my cheek with his other one. Yes, I deserved to be punished, I thought to myself. Punish me. And then it didn't hurt because the memory of the kiss, of the way it transplanted me back home, made the pain loosen and drift away from me, like a plucked eyebrow hair, or a clump of dirt worried free of the earth and away from the buffalo's hunger.

"Why did you disobey him?" Mama said, patting my head as I put a cool towel over my eyes, which had swelled from crying.

"I wanted to have dinner with my friend. Is that a crime? I never visit anyone. We never leave this place! Baba makes me feel like a criminal!"

"Shhh! Are you crazy? He'll come in here and finish you off if you talk like that."

"I hate him," I said.

"No you don't. We're all going through a tough time."

Gamal, in his awkward way, came in and gave me a glass of lemonade. I kissed his warm cheek and wanted to hug him.

"Your father misses home," Mama said. "He misses his life, his mother, even his sisters. Also, he's uncertain about our future, ya binti. He doesn't know what he's going to do and what the war will result in and if he'll be allowed to go back and get our stuff or our money, much less his job back."

"Wait," I said, "do you expect me to feel sorry for anyone other than myself right now? It's going to be pretty hard to do that while my bruises heal. Try again in a few days."

Gamal began to sob on the mattress, facing the wall. I wondered if I'd miss him when I grew old like Baba, or if he'd hit his daughter when he grew old because he'll miss me. If he really loved me, he'd never hit his daughter. If he really grew up, he'd never love anybody. Mama took my towel and turned off the light. She warned us not to talk, shut the door, and watched the news about the war.

Gamal and I compared our bruises like bomb sites on two different maps. "This is where Baba's foot landed; this is where his palm exploded; here is the site of the house slipper mine; please note the series of detonations along this arm's terrain, the craters in this butt's field; see how this cheek encampment was burned down to the ground." We giggled. Gamal said, "Sometimes I dream that Mama will turn into a super mom or a witch, and her hair will become snakes, and her boobies will turn into missiles, and she'll save us."

"Keep dreaming," I said, and I tickled him until he said mercy and we passed out, our bodies folded-up maps under the thin sky of our worn blue blanket.

That first week of winter vacation I avoided Baba's hands and eyes, ate with my head bent over my plate, and never asked him to pass the olive oil, which was always at his side. Mama stared off into space all morning, slept on the sofa in the front room all afternoon, and watched the news all night. The military song grew on me, and I began locking our bedroom door and dancing to it whenever it came on—every hour. Kuwait would be liberated soon; our chance to go home might be coming any time. But I knew in my heart of hearts we would never return.

Things I miss:
My old stereo.
The living room wall.
My bed.
Mama's piano.
Za'tar burgers.
Fakhr el-Din.
The sirens on the first day of every month.
The water towers.
The gulf.

Linda. Rama. Tamer.
The frozen animals at school.
School.

ONE OF GEDDO'S old army buddies called: Geddo had gone through an insulin withdrawal and fallen while crossing the street. His friend picked him up and took him back to his apartment in Chatby, where Geddo ate a chunk of *basboosa* dessert and revived well. The friend was calling because he knew Geddo never would have told us; his friend thought we should keep an eye on him. I volunteered my services immediately.

"No," Baba said. "Mama can go out there in the afternoons and check on him."

"No, I can't," Mama said, looking at me. "I have responsibilities here, and I have Gamal to look after, and you to cook for, and myself to watch. She doesn't have school and it'll be good for you both if she went and stayed with him."

Baba didn't say anything for a minute. "One month," he finally said, and gave me a hard look. "And Geddo's going to keep an eye on you, so there'll be no whoring around the streets until midnight."

That's right, Baba, I wanted to say, I'm dying to be a whore.

Mama and I took a pot of stuffed grape leaves and a small bag of clothes and books to Chatby. Geddo was in the living room, watching the window and pretending to read the paper. His record player was on, something by Chopin. Mama took the needle off the vinyl and kissed Geddo's cheek. "Would you like to hear it live?" she asked, knowing he'd never refuse. She went into the next room and played Nocturne no. 1 in B-flat Minor, which was flat but not too minor on the long-out-of-tune piano. I didn't go out onto the balcony that time. It was too cold outside; it had been drizzling. I hung my coat in the closet by the piano room and began emptying my clothes on Mama's old bed. There were Beatles posters on the wall, a worn photo of Mama at a recital, Baba's first poetry flyer, and a plastic rose tacked in a corner. I wondered if Baba had given it to her.

After Mama left, Geddo and I listened to records and I set the table for a late lunch. "Did I have to get sick for you to come stay with me, you monkey?" Geddo said.

"You know Baba, he would've never let me. I wanted to live here. It's a short walk to school."

"Yes, I know your baba," Geddo sighed, as though he wanted to say more but was holding back.

After dinner he made me do ablutions with him and pray in the drawing room. The prayer time was announced on the television and from the neighborhood's minaret, but I usually took it as a signal that it was time to get up and make a cheese sandwich or a cup of tea. While I prayed, my mind wandered around the rooms and wondered about the future. I wanted more than anything to know what was going to happen to us, to me.

ELEVEN

THIS IS WAR

• • •

THE ALLIES WERE BOMBING IRAQ EVERY DAY. EVERY DAY, THE
Egyptian president said something stupid. One day, he said if
Saddam was willing to call it all off, he'd make a statue of him
and put him on his shoulders and run him all around the main
square. On his *shoulders*! Geddo went to the Sporting Club
every morning, played cards and backgammon and talked with
his old army friends, and then headed to the mosque for evening prayers.

I went out, the ten-pound note Geddo had given me in my
pocket. I waited five minutes for the old wooden elevator, and
when it arrived, hesitated to take it. I'd been taking the steps
up and down the building because I was afraid of the ancient
lift. In the end I got in, closed the iron gates behind me, and
then the wooden doors; I felt like I was shutting myself into a
cupboard. I swung down the lock and pressed the 1 button. The
elevator smelled like the inside of an old Russian doll, her wood
intestines mildewed but sweet. The walls of the elevator shaft
slowly reeled upward. I held my breath in between floors, and
after the fourth, turned around to face the mirror in its gilded
frame. I imagined that Geddo must have taken this elevator

the day Yia Yia died, and Yia Yia must have taken it hundreds
of times before that. Once at the bottom floor I stepped over
the black-and-white-checkered marble tiles, then made it a
game, challenging myself to step over only the black ones.
The *bawab* greeted me on my way out of the building.

The streets of Chatby in general, and the ones connecting
the Awqaf buildings in particular, were heavy in air stream
traffic. The cold wind whipped through the streets like a phantom in a hurry. Mama used to scare me when I was little and
tell me it *was* a phantom of all the old Greeks who wanted their
city back, and all the old Egyptians who wanted it with them,
underneath the water. I wrapped my scarf around my cheeks
and pushed against the current of air until I was on the *corniche*,
where I had to fight against a human stream. Dirty papers flew
off the ground and wrapped themselves around my ankles. I
kept walking and they flew away. The ocean was wild, its waves
like the blunt punches of an angry boxer. A black flag was at
high mast. I turned left and walked toward the center of town.
There were people everywhere selling fruits in wooden fruit stalls
and carts, hanging out in front of shops. I wished we could live
here forever. I walked into a paper shop and fingered the notebooks and the envelopes. I left, and darted in and out of shops
like a frenzied mother-of-a-bride dancing to the minute waltz.
Into Bata Shoes, out; into the coffee shop Mama and Baba once
told me they loved to go to, gulped down a hot chocolate, out;
into a jewelry shop, tried on some hoops, pretended to bargain
for them, told the man he was a thief and a bastard, and out.

On my way home, I stopped by Trianon and bought an
umm ali. The waiter gave it to me in a little transparent box; its
coconut puff-pastry skin and pistachio topping greeted me. I

looked around at the fancy gilded walls of the restaurant. I
wanted to pretend I was rich and sit in one of the seats and order
a veal scallop pané, but I didn't. I just took the box and left,
thinking of how the original Umm Ali threw together all the
ingredients in her pantry that day the ravenous Ottoman sultan stopped in her town.

At a florist's in St. Mark I thought of my grandmother. This
was where Mama had always dropped me off to pick up flowers for her grave. I decided to visit it. I bought a single white
rose and I already knew I wouldn't be able to take it home, that
it would die soon. I walked five blocks to the Greek Cooperative Cemetery. Once there, I told the guard I didn't have any
money to tip him, that I was just here to visit my relatives and
leave. He let me in begrudgingly while his dogs barked at me.
I was still afraid of them so I ran all the way down, past and on
top of the bodies. Then, set loose in the cemetery, I realized
that I had no idea which one was hers. I didn't read Greek. I
knew that her grave was a plain Jane compared to the others.
Most of the graves there had elaborate head stones, enormous
Greek crucifixes, and Greek stories about heroic deaths in
wars. These were the men's graves. Then there were babies'
graves, with naked cherub statues to their right. Yia Yia's
grave was short, small, and had a simple cross. That sounded
awful: a simple cross. I wondered if, back when they used to
crucify people, the crucified people ever thought their crosses
were simple; if they ever thought, "My cross is simple compared to that guy's over there." I thought they must have
crucified bigger assholes on more elaborate crosses than small-
time crooks. Maybe it was the other way around? They felt
pity for the small-time crooks and gave them more fancy

crosses. I doubted people who crucified people had any pity, though.

I found Yia Yia's grave because I saw Geddo. He stood over the rectangular plot, talked to it. I was afraid I had intruded on him and turned around and ran again, the dogs chasing me out of the gates and the guard calling me a crazy whore. I ran out of the cemetery lot and further on, wondering when I'd die. I ran out of Chatby altogether, away from the crazy spirits fighting in the wind. I clutched at the white flower against my out-of-breath chest and ran parallel to the tram now, up and down small hills and trestles and old tramlines. I saw a boy on a bicycle heading for me, so I ran to the left, but he also chose to turn left, and crashed into me.

"Bastard!" I yelled at him. "Where the fuck were you going? Do I look like a street to you? Is there a line of paint going up and down my body? Son of a whore!"

"*Mish mumkin!*" he said, straightening up and pulling his bike off my body. "Nidali?"

I knew right then that no one would ever believe me. I didn't even believe it. Was this considered a coincidence? Fate? A really weird bicycle accident involving two people who'd known each other hundreds of miles away and who'd been each other's first kiss—could it be?

"Fakhr el-Din?" I raised my hand and he helped me up. Then I looked down at myself: what was I *wearing*?

"What are you doing here?"

"I live here," I said.

"Me too!" he said.

"Where . . . how did you come here? Through Iraq, through Saudi?"

"Through Saudi," he said. "We brought our car and everything."

"Are you staying at your apartment in Sidi Gaber?"

"Yeah," he said. "Damn you. You fucked up my brand new bicycle."

I looked at the blue bike's wide handlebars, its gorgeous white-walled tires.

"We're staying in crappy Ma'moora," I said. He and I automatically began walking over to the *corniche*, his bike at his side. The alley was narrow and its walls were covered in calligraphy and graffiti.

"In a summer apartment?" he said.

"Yeah. I thought I was never gonna see you again," I said.

"Me too," he said, and looked up and down the alley searchingly. "I'm gonna kiss you," he said, and grabbed my arm so hard it would bruise later that night. He snatched a kiss and looked away like nothing happened, as though he were a pickpocket on the bus.

Kissing in public is illegal in Egypt. The foreigners—American archaeologists and English teachers—all kissed on street corners and in alleys and on the beach, and people would stop their cars to watch as though the blonde people were television stars showing themselves in public. If Fakhr and I got caught, someone would beat us and possibly send us to the police station.

"Don't *ever* do that again," I said, and looked down at my now-crushed rose.

"So if we're both in the same city, does that mean—" we were crossing the street now, a near-fatal act for any Alexandrian, "—that I can still be your boyfriend?"

"Yes," I yelled over the din of cars and car stereos and horns and people.

Fakhr and I sat against a railing and talked about everything except Kuwait. He told me about his classes at the *Academia*, a private school in Sidi Bishr, and I talked about EGS and Jiji. I didn't tell him about the kiss, just about Red. Fakhr wanted to beat him up. We bought *kushari* from a peddler and when we were done we each had orange tomato sauce stains on our shirts. The cold set in and I knew I had to go home before Geddo started to worry. Fakhr bowed, called me *Ameera Falastiẓiyya*, a Palestiniass princess, and said goodnight.

"We have to make plans about where and when we can see each other," I said.

"How about the bicycle renter a few feet away from where you bumped into me?"

"This isn't your bike?" I said.

"Of course not," he said.

Geddo was lying sideways on the couch and snoring when I got home, and I took the opportunity to sit in bed and daydream about Fakhr. My heart raced when I thought about kissing him. He smelled faintly of sweat when I saw him. I loved that scent; it made me want to wrap my entire body around him. My face got warm at this thought and I took a deep breath.

Geddo fell as soon as he got up from his nap, and I already had the *umm ali* ready to help revive him. I spooned the sweet cream into the corner of his mouth, and he got up and told me to set the table so we could eat *ẓay elnas*, like people do.

"I saw you at the cemetery today," he said, scooping fava bean dip onto his bread.

"I didn't see you," I said.

He stared at me.

"*Tayeb*, I saw you too."

"Garifalia was my sweetheart," he said. "I miss her every day that goes by. Don't worry about me."

"I'm not worried," I said. "Although, you should go to a doctor and get some insulin."

"I will, God willing. Did you know you have another month of vacation now because of the war? I heard the teachers at the Sporting Club talking about it."

"Really?" I said. "That's so great! I want to stay here with you, Geddo."

"No one's forcing you to leave!" he said, and smiled.

"War is good for school kids," I said.

"But it's bad for soldiers and nurses," he said, still smiling.

Geddo and Yia Yia met during the Second World War in a Greek orphanage that had been converted into a hospital. He was evaluating injuries and she was too, except he was with those who caused injuries and she was with those who healed them; he was a soldier and she was a nurse. In the beginning there were a dozen tuberculosis patients in the basement, and Geddo didn't know Yia Yia's name. Then they began talking and seeing each other outside the hospital. They talked about everything. He told her stories about the shelling, she told him stories about the doctors and nurses, and they talked about their families. Soon the war ended: the tuberculosis patients died, the orphanage shed its hospital gown, and Geddo and Yia Yia got married in a civil ceremony at the government building in Ramle station. She wore a plain dress and held flowers. Her Greek Orthodox family shunned her. There were no photos.

I'd always wanted Geddo to tell me more about Yia Yia, but instead he talked about the war and the revolution. We were going through the fifth album he'd dug up from one of the storage closets and my eyelids were drooping.

"And here's the Fox. He was such a bastard! And here's the Bear. Another son of a bitch! And this is Amr . . . he was a huge coward. You never know what people are like until the bombs start falling. So we're all in the field, lights out. And the bombs start dropping this way and that—normal—I mean, it's war. And Amr is screaming like a child, jumping around, hiding under sandbags, running left and right, crazy! I was calm, you know me, they can tell me now, the Iraqis are sending a nuclear bomb, I'll say okay. Just like that.

"And this is when the peace-keeping delegation went to Spain. Franco brought us to Spain, the bastard. We were doing our best not to kill him. And we went to Russia, look, here's the Kremlin," a line of men in uniform, standing in the rain. "We bought those Russian dolls from there, the rotted ones in the living room.

"And here I am on our family land in the South. That man standing with me helped us make an accurate map of it. The English had made one in 1898, but we started over. Do you know that a large-scale map creates a better relationship between people and their land? I know they didn't teach you that in the English school in Kuwait because they knew that power is the knowledge and command of land, and they wanted that knowledge and power for themselves! So here I am standing on the land, and you should learn that when it comes to maps, accuracy is always a question of where you stand.

"And this is the delegation I went to America with: we were in Washington, and this was in the sixties, the middle of the civil rights movement there—you know about that? What do they teach you in those schools, those colonial schools?—in the heat of the movement, and the *wafd* is eating dinner at the restaurant in DC and the maitre d' tells us, 'Colors sit over there.' Just like that, 'No colors here.'" Geddo did a funny American impression. "We tell him, 'We are Egyptians. We are eating our chicken.' He kept saying 'colors over there.' We refused to get up. Here is a picture of us all outside the restaurant."

They still had their napkins in their shirts.

FAKHR AND I met daily at the bicycle renter—who was certainly a hashish addict and convinced me that all bike renters were hash fiends—and we rode the Prussian blue bike across town, stealing the paper from stationery stores, reading it in cafés where we never paid for our chocolate milk, drawing our own backgammon board on a piece of cardboard and playing with shiny coins, always losing track of which coin was supposed to be white and which black. Once, we pretended we were orphan brother and sister and begged women in *ʒan'et el-sittaat*, the women's jewelry and fabric quarter, for money, which we then used to get into the Rialto to see a supremely crappy film that redeemed itself by allowing us to suck face for an hour and twenty minutes until the usher approached us with a stick and beat us both, sending us out of the theater, yelling after us that we were banned from it forever. I rode behind Fakhr on the blue bike and he pedaled it extra long when it rained so we could be dirty and wet and uncaught. I loved when we went down a hill by the tram tracks, how my wet clothes clung to my chest and rippled off my back. I loved Fakhr's hair by my nose like black bunches of grapes. I saw the faces pass by me and the ocean playing peek-a-boo on my left, and I heard beautiful harmonies inside my head. I inhaled his scent and the aroma of the humidity all around me, and the mixture of the smells and the bike's speed made me feel high. We kissed in elevators and abandoned beach cabins until our lips turned blue and the dusk call to prayer reminded me that it was time to head home. I traced his eyebrows and his big nose to my memory in case I never saw him again.

The last night at Geddo's I found an Arabic translation of Cavafy in a closet by the scarves and the shawls. I read him as Geddo prayed: the God abandoned Anthony over and over again. Geddo had given up on my company for prayer weeks before. The news was on every hour and the military music played. Kuwait had been liberated. Baba wanted me back in Ma'moora. School started in two days. In my head I made lists of things I loved and things I hated: I hated Saddam and uniforms and the possibility of being called a lesbian by my only girlfriend. I loved Fakhr and Cavafy and Geddo . . . and the Alexandria rain, which, I was convinced, was probably also male.

I RETURNED TO school eagerly; I'd missed the everyday gossip, the library, Jiji's funny stories about Red, and now I had my own story to tell: Fakhr. I sensed a small ridge form in Jiji's brow when I told her about him and was about to attribute it to jealousy when she said: "You mean you have a boyfriend like me? Now we can sneak around and use each other as excuses. You know, double date." I didn't want to double date, was sure Fakhr would kill Red if he ever saw him.

During recess, a girl from second form approached me and said she was Fakhr's neighbor. "And he wants me to give you this," she said. "What is it what is it what is it?" Jiji said, jumping in place. It was a triangular piece of paper, sealed with tape. I undid it and unfolded the triangle until it revealed words. A letter. It was cheesy and sweet, and, I found out later, mostly lifted from LL Cool J's opus, "I Need Love." I began sending triangles back too, sometimes in Arabic, until he sent back an octagon (show-off) and, in Arabic *ruq'a*, poked fun at my Arabic script.

In April, a month before exams, the school announced that we would have three weeks off to study.

The night before the start of my long study period, our usually mute gray telephone rang long rings and paused briefly in between—a long distance call. Baba ran to pick it up and listened silently to the words that were being spoken on the other end. When he hung up, he went to the bedroom and locked the door, staying inside for at least twenty minutes. We stood at the door, waiting for him to re-emerge. When he did, it was clear he'd been weeping. He told us what over 300,000 Palestinians would tell their families that year: We were not returning to Kuwait. We were not wanted there; no Palestinian person or family with a Palestinian member was. Saddam had made so many promises to the Palestinians, had talked about opening

Jerusalem's gates so often, that Arafat had supported him. Because of this, the Kuwaitis decided to collectively punish all Palestinians. My father's work permit had been revoked indefinitely. He had to come up with Another Plan.

Baba told Gamal and me, "I can relate to what you're going through. After I came here, to this very city in 1967, I never got a chance to say goodbye to any of my friends or belongings. But I survived. And well! I ended up having a great time here. What a lucky family, a lucky people we are to have Egypt!" He was relating to us. And pretending not to be sad. For our sake. Which endeared him to me for the first time in months. I leaned forward and hugged him, hard.

I worried about Baba. I watched him over the next few days sulk in a bathrobe, his beard growing, his brow furrowing. He said very little. At night, he didn't read his books, just sat on the couch and stared at the wall, told us all to leave him alone. I heard him going to bed when I got up in the morning. While he slept, out of my view, I worried about us. We couldn't live in a summer apartment forever, could we? Where would our food come from? How would we live?

One afternoon, I sat at the dining table and drew a map of Palestine from memory. Baba walked by, coffee cup in hand, and said, "You still remember that?" I nodded and looked at the map nervously, hesitant about whether I'd drawn it right. I pointed at the western border and asked, "Is that right?" "Who knows," he said, waving his hand dismissively. He walked onto the balcony and sank into a chair. The steam from his cup rose and made a phantom out of his bearded face. I approached him timidly. I wanted to know more.

"What do you mean, Baba, when you say 'who knows'?"

"Oh, *habibti*. That map is from a certain year. The maps that came earlier looked different. And the ones that come after, even more different."

"What do you mean?"

"I mean . . . there's no telling. There's no telling where home starts and where it ends."

I sat with him on the cold balcony for a while. When I got up to go back inside, I noticed that Baba's eyes were filled with tears.

I took the map I drew to my room, flipped my pencil and brought the eraser's tip to the page. I erased the western border, the northern border. I erased the southern and eastern border. I surveyed what remained: a blank page, save for the Galilee. I stared at the whiteness of the paper's edges for a long, long time. The whiteness of the page blended with the whiteness of my sheets. "You are here," I thought as I looked at the page and all around me. And oddly, I felt free.

I spent fifteen days in the kitchen studying chemistry, mathematics, Arabic, and English, from eight in the morning until eight at night. It was as if the bad news fueled me, infused me with the desire to work harder.

In order to dodge my sadness, I began writing a musical while studying for history and helping Mama stuff vegetables. It was based on what I'd been reading about the opening of the Suez Canal. I was writing song lines for everyone invited to that opening: the Khedive Isma'il, Napoleon III's wife, the empress Eugénie, Prussia's crown prince, the emperor of Austria, Gautier and Zola, Fromentin and Ibsen. I'd read *A Doll's*

House so I made sure Ibsen sang about it endlessly, and I made the empress into a little coquette who slept around during all the ceremonies, which were held by Muslim and Christian clerics. I also attempted to make parallels to the Suez Canal crisis of 1956, so the writers exclaimed drunkenly that it was a shame the Suez was drawing attention to itself, forcing England to come in and rape Egypt's resources and its people, as it was doing the world over.

I wished I could stage the play, wished I could be allowed to hold auditions (although I already knew that Red would make a great Prussian crown prince and Fakhr a fabulous Isma'il). I wanted the tickets to be modeled on the invitations to Verdi's *Rigoletto*, which had opened at the Aida opera house to coincide with the Suez opening; this last idea convinced me of my genius. I stuffed peppers and zucchinis, and thanks to some imagination and lack of sleep, the pepper became Gautier, the zucchini, Fromentin.

I worked on the play day and night, stopping only to help Mama make omelets or to walk to the market to buy new cheese and bread. On one of those shopping visits, I ran to the *centrale* station's payphones, which were right across the street from the market, and called Fakhr about not going back to Kuwait. He said he was sorry, and I told him I was sad. He asked if I'd ever go back to Kuwait again and I said no. I told him to cheer me up. He was building an RC car from scratch and told me he couldn't wait to race it. I said I hated him because he was a boy and building a car and sure that whatever the fuck he wanted to happen would happen while I was trapped in the kitchen writing a play that starred vegetables. "Sorry, *habibti*," he said, confused, and I hung up on him.

I walked down to the paved boardwalk by the beach, carrying my sack of vegetables: my future stars. I looked up at the horizon expecting a straight line and instead found a wraparound horizon like a semi-circle. I thought of the semi-circles beneath my eyes, how they swelled out like every other woman's in my family. I thought about all the main events of my family history and discovered that they were all wars. I imagined my family history without war. My grandmother would not have lost her father in the first war in Palestine and would not have been sold to the family through whom she met my father's father. My yia yia would not have met my geddo had it not been for World War II and that dress-up orphanage. I wondered how many wars waited in my future, and if my children—if I had any—would be products of them. I got angry and picked up rocks and pebbles, threw them into the sea. I threw harder and harder and yelled out things that didn't make sense. A couple of boys were sitting and fishing on boulders on the edge of the sea; they turned to watch me and laughed. The sun was in its Alexandria show-off setting state, streaking eggplant purple, mango orange, and watermelon red. I was hungry. I put the last rock in my pocket and ran home.

The morning of my exams Mama overslept, I overslept, and Baba stayed up so late—or so early—thinking of Another Plan that he ended up passing out just when we were all supposed to wake up. I jumped out of bed, cursed and swore, and wore my skirt inside out. I didn't even bother with my tie. Gamal snored peacefully; his exams weren't for another three days. Baba ran downstairs and started the car, which we'd borrowed from Geddo for exam week. I put my knotty hair in a bun, stuffed pencils into my shirt pocket, and raced down the stairs three at a time. Mama appeared a few seconds later in her nighties, carrying a copper coffee pot and three demitasses in her hands. Trailing her was Gamal, who was also in pajamas but wanted to come along anyway.

By the time we left Mandara—the Montazah Park farewelling me to the right, followed by the glittering sea and the small dark heads that bobbed along its surface—the traffic was so congested I was sure I would not graduate, that I'd be doomed to a lifetime in ninth year. Mama poured out the coffee and distributed it among us and Baba gulped his down in a millisecond. None of us spoke. I drank my coffee in silence and wished Mama could read the cup when I was done. I wished she could see a play in it, or a new home, or some sign that I'd make it to the damn exam, or that we'd make it as a family.

The car was still and the silence deepened. I began to worry, as I was sure Mama was worrying, and Baba, and Gamal, that we'd be like this, still and arrested, stuck in one place, the place of no-place, forever.

And then, like a beacon or a war alarm, a siren was behind us and we could hear it louder than our own thoughts. Its screams rose higher and higher until Baba saw what it was in his rearview and sat up straight, like he finally had A Plan. "*Aiwa*," Mama said, "Yes," as though to encourage his unspoken thought. The bearer of the siren approached the left side of our car at full speed, and as soon as it passed us, Baba gunned the engine and raced behind it, raced like our lives depended on it, and we watched the picture of the snake climbing up the pole painted in red on its backside, the Hippocratic seal of this

old Greek city. We followed the ambulance all the way downtown, tailed it leaving only a few hand-lengths between us, the
whole time clutching onto our seats for dear life, my family
and I, not only following disaster, but chasing it, thankful for
it, depending on it to get us where we need to get on time.
And it did.

TWELVE

THE PRIDE OF RELIGION

· · ·

FAKHR WAS JEALOUS OF MY PLAY AND MY THREE-WEEK STUDY
break, and after that weird phone call he had given me up for
dead. I decided to rent a bicycle and pedal to Montazah to meet
him for a truce. Besides, I missed kissing—not him, per se, but
the act itself, like one who goes hungry not for a certain food
in particular but for food in general.

We couldn't find a single empty spot: the once-deserted park
was overcrowded with summer transfers from Cairo, mothers
and their winter babies, married couples, *higab*-wearing women
and their wayward boyfriends. I wanted to find a hidden place.
Fakhr was one step ahead of me; he found a deserted corner and
it took us half an hour to reach it. I sucked on his lips; they tasted
like the salty coats of watermelon seeds, and he took his shirt off.

"I want to take *my* shirt off," I whined.

"Okay," he said, truly shocked.

I slipped it over my head and stood there in front of him, in
the corner, my bare bosom blocked from view by huge boulders that the ocean supervisor had installed in the sixties to
soften the crashes of waves. (That's what Mama once told me.
I wonder if she, too, stood behind the boulders topless.)

"Your nipples are pink," Fakhr said, balking at them. "I always pictured them brown."

"You pictured my nipples," I said.

He kissed me again but didn't touch my breasts. I rubbed them against his bare brown chest but he didn't get the hint.

I waited a few weeks, then, halfway through summer, when he still hadn't touched them, I grabbed his right hand and placed his palm over my left nipple. This seemed to open a floodgate. Now we were kissing and he was touching my nipples and slipping his hands into my shorts, his fingers blunt stones against my walls. I eased his hand out and told him I was used to water, and when he looked confused, I told him about the bidet.

"I'm competing with a *bidet*?" he said.

"No, just with water. Water is gentle and falls very consistently. That's what you have to be. Consistent and gentle."

We sat and watched the sea and talked. After sundown, I pedaled the rented bicycle (which was two days late and which Fakhr was trying to convince me to keep/steal) home, terrified I'd be punished for being late, but no one noticed me. I ran straight to the bathroom and sat over the bidet until my thighs went numb.

I taught Fakhr to move his fingers rapidly over the spot that made me shudder in the bathroom. He watched my face and made me nervous. Then, I enjoyed his audience. His two fingers spun, like two swimming legs, gently over the ridge of my sex until I came, for the first time, in front of someone else. It felt like a miniature person was playing a drum from inside me.

MAMA PULLED THE television out to the balcony, its black wheels squeaking against the white tiles. Her feet were bare and the red nail polish had worn off, so that her toenails had little shy red lines in their corners. Gamal sat by the railing and kicked his feet against the balcony's cracked wall, and Baba sank into the mildewed cushions of the straw chair. I sat on the white tiles by Mama's red-lined toes and we watched whatever was on. Baba was still busy thinking of A New Plan; his job applications had yielded no results, and he seemed like a furry grouse, nesting and complaining from various spots in the apartment at all hours of the day. A car sped through the street below, Egyptian pop blaring from its windows. "Animals!" Baba spat in its direction. Mama turned the volume of the television up to blot out his seething voice. An astronaut filled the screen, his face concealed, his body padded and safe and upside down. I envied him his free-floating, untethered existence. A purple planet shone in the corner of the screen, waiting.

Over the course of the next few weeks Baba groused, read, and thought, and the more he thought, the more he saw the inevitable, only choice: he would look for a job in America.

Baba had a dream that reassured him that this choice was the right one. In the dream, our family asked him to find us a home. He replied, "How can I when I've never had one?" We shrugged and asked him again. He looked up into the sky and saw a giant planet approaching us. It was a purple planet. He realized that we have to move that far away in order to start over again. He woke up and promptly, excitedly, related the story to us.

The idea of moving to America intrigued me, though I also had reservations. I always used to think about what it would be like if we'd stayed in America after I was born, but the idea that we could return to it always seemed too much of a dream, one that could never come true. It *was* kind of like moving to a purple planet, and often, when I rode my bike to the beach or sat in the sand and watched the water, I'd wonder if one could really do such a thing.

When I thought of living in America, I pictured straw yellow hair, surfboards, snow; I saw girls and boys holding hands and breaking up and kissing in public; I heard rock music and rap music and pop music and throngs of people swaying and singing; I tasted ketchup and mustard and mayonnaise; smelled streets and new cars and sometimes horses and barns, dollar bills and bacon. I tried to imagine a school; it would look like my new school: arches, a courtyard, old desks, and my old school: concrete, gray, sandy playground, but I would add one thing to my vision, and this was my own ideal symbol for America: Privacy, as embodied in Lockers. Lockers, rows and rows of silver, gleaming, tall, rectangular lockers; lockers with locks on them, lockers labeled and numbered, lockers with young people leaning against them or slamming them or stuffing them with whatever they wanted to stuff them with. I tried to imagine myself leaning against a locker but all I saw was my puffy brown hair, the unfortunately cut bangs stretching like a sun visor over my bushy eyebrows, and my lanky arms hanging out of a black sweatshirt Mama had ordered from a catalog. It had a picture of a shiny, short-haired puppy in its center, so that it made me look like a ten-year-old, not the almost-fourteen-year-old I was. Even in my fantasy I looked like a geek, and I was terrified of never fitting in, of that new place that was my birthplace, that place I belong to only on paper, in the confines of my small blue passport.

. . .

Baba was our only ticket to America, which was ironic considering he was usually a ticket out of places, not into them. He executed his Plan with enormous energy and grace, took the bus to coffee shops downtown daily, and worked on his C.V. the way he would have worked on a novel in another life, a life in which he hadn't met Mama by the tram tracks. He poured himself into his cover letter, making sure someone somewhere would want to employ him just from reading it.

On his way home every afternoon, he stopped at the *centrales* and bought three-minute phone calls to America. He called old colleagues in Boston who flatly denied knowing him and others who remembered him fondly. He did research, bought all sorts of newspapers, called companies and contractors, architects and engineers. It was clear that they would not be able to find him a job at the level of his old job in Kuwait but he believed they would find him one, nonetheless.

He went to copy shops after the coffee shops and faxed his spanking new C.V., along with blueprints and all the news stories Middle Eastern architectural journals ran on him and his designs in the past ten years. This preparation reinvigorated him, it seemed; he moved with light feet around the apartment, swept Mama up sometimes and planted wet kisses on her dark cheeks. Mama was optimistic in front of him but on the phone I heard her telling Sonya she was doubtful he'd find a job in Boston. And she was right.

He found one in Texas.

. . .

The night after we got the call, Baba, Gamal, and I were all sitting on the sofa watching old footage of Gamal Abdel Nasser's resignation. Mama and Geddo were sitting on the balcony drinking coffee and talking about Baba's new job offer. We didn't talk about it with him because Gamal and I were afraid of Texas, afraid of the cowboys that would lasso him away from us, possibly forever. Where would we fit in with his Plan?

"He was a great man," Baba said about Nasser.

We all watched the street scene: women slapping their faces, men crying and shouting.

"Arabs are so emotional," I said.

"This is not about emotions," Baba said.

"So what's it about?"

"People who love their leader."

"Isn't love an emotion?"

"Yes, but it's racist to say that Arabs on the whole are emotional."

"I think it's a good quality. Look at the English. Stone faced and boring. I'm saying it's good to be emotional."

"We're not emotional," he said again.

"Then why's that man slapping himself and screaming?"

"Because these people knew what the alternative was. These people knew that if Abdel Nasser walked out, some other idiot would walk in. They didn't like the alternative, it worried them."

The next morning, my grades came out, my own good news: I got an incredibly high 92 percent average. I jumped up and down and pretended to fling myself from the balcony. 'Abdo laughed from his post at the bottom of the apartment building and sent me air kisses. I felt like a superstar and an audience member at the same time. I was proud. That would show them, all those girls who teased me last year. Then I knew why Baba liked success: it's vindicating.

There were celebrations for the country's top-scoring students on television, and we watched them all day. Then they showed old footage of pop star Abdel Halim's funeral. We watched women throwing themselves off balconies and men crying and screaming and more women, this time stabbing themselves.

"And what about these people?" I said to Baba. "Are they afraid of the alternative? Are they worried because they know that they'll have to listen to Hassan El Asmar and Magdy Talaat with their boring *mawal* songs?"

Baba exhaled and went red, then banged his fist against the table and shouted, "ARABS ARE NOT EMOTIONAL!"

"OK" I said and giggled. I was satisfied with his answer.

Baba bought his ticket to Texas. He made the announcement seventy-two hours before he was scheduled to leave. Mama was in a state of shock: she couldn't believe it was easier to leave for America than to find a job close by, a decent place to live, and a piano. To celebrate his leaving us, Baba took us all out to Zephyrion restaurant in Abu-Qir that night, a seafood place on the east side, by the ocean. On the way there we made fun of the name "Abu-Ear." I called it Father-*widn*, and we all decided that's what we'd call it from then on.

We ordered sea urchins whose spines moved rapidly when we squeezed lime juice over them. I ate a grilled fish and choked on its bones. Gamal ate pita bread and tahini sauce: he hated fish. And Mama ate two dozen oysters back to back like they were watermelon seeds. Baba winked at her and said, "Are you planning to give me a memorable farewell then?" and Gamal and I almost burped up all our food.

When all the food was put away, along with the sun and the bright sky, and when all the stars peeked out; when the swimmers in the ocean got rowdier and the mosquitoes swept down at us with an almost martial vengeance; when Baba took Mama's arm and kissed her cheek, whispered in her ear, then looked over at Gamal and me as though wishing we would disappear— I believed that this was a farewell dinner with our dear Baba, our last supper. I thought (or wished, or dreamed, or feared) we'd never see Baba again.

So when we all went to drop him off at al-Nuzha airport and Baba got out of the car and waved at us, saying, "See you soon, monkeys," I didn't understand why my stomach folded into itself or why my hands balled up into fists. His back disappeared into the crowd and I imagined him being questioned at the airport for hours (why else had we arrived there five hours before his flight departed?), the Americans stealing him away from us forever. What if he never sent for us? What if he got himself into trouble and ended up dead in a ditch after a duel? What if I never saw Baba again?

I was the only one crying in the car.

THE COOL THING about Baba being gone was I could do whatever I wanted. One night I lied and told Mama I was sleeping over at Jiji's and I indulged myself and took a taxi, orange and rickety, its leather and driver scented with fumes, out to Montazah. I had fears, fantasies, of the driver swerving into the wood in the pitch dark and raping me beneath the sky. He didn't, and I forgot to tip him. I walked to the fence by the private beach and skipped it, then tiptoed around onto the sand. It was closing time and no one was in the water.

I slipped off my shirt and shorts, balled them up into my high tops, and left them in the sand. The grains were cold and soft, like semolina, and I got into the water slowly. It swallowed me in its darkness and I floated in to honor it, closed my eyes and listened to its familiar sound. Under the water, a few miles out, lay ancient ruins, and I pretended to swim down to them, to those sunken subkingdoms and cities of Heracleion and Canopus where I touched the statues' eyes, watched their dead-awake faces. I saw pink granite gods, and a sphinx of Cleopatra's baba, Ptolemy XII. I saw silverware; I saw pots and pans, bottles and plates, weapons from Napoleon's sunken 1798 fleet, and a green statue that held something huge in its hand. I couldn't tell what it was until I swam closer; it was a pen. I opened my eyes again. I was just a few yards from the shore, and I saw Fakhr sitting in the sand, his shirtless torso facing the street, waiting for me. I waved, then decided to wade out and get him; he saw me before I was out all the way and came after me.

I swam away from him and he swam faster toward me. I didn't say hello, he didn't either, and I stopped stroking the waves when I could no longer reach. I turned around and watched him watch me until he stood in front of me; he could still reach the sandy floor bottom, and I wrapped my legs around his waist. He cupped me in his hands and I kissed his salty mouth, salty with sweat and salt water, and he grew against my bathing suit bottom. I rubbed myself against him then and the waves gently rose and fell, and he bit and licked my neck as I found out again how used to water I was and the wetness inside me rivaled the wetness that surrounded me.

I SAT IN the balcony, completely bewildered, after she told me the news. "I can't move to America," I said. Mama looked at me, waiting for a reason. "I have nothing to wear. And my hair is stupid!" I didn't want to tell her the truth: that I didn't want to move again, to work at feeling at home again, to lose that home again, then have to start all over again.

Mama wheeled the television onto the balcony and we watched a Greta Garbo movie on Channel 2. We drank tea and Mama babbled about all the things we'd have to do for the move while I daydreamed, sleep-deprived, about what it would be like in America.

My friends and I had always thought of America as the coolest kid in the world, one who would never acknowledge our existence. When *License to Drive*, the Haim/Feldman *tour de force* finally arrived on SECAM in Kuwait, we'd watched one scene over and over again, the one where the cute girl (the one Corey Haim's character was in love with) verbally bitch-slapped her possessive boyfriend, saying, "This isn't . . . Kuwait!" We were thrilled to hear the name of the place where we lived—a place we believed to be a tiny spot of spit on the map of the world—uttered by a gorgeous actress in an American movie. We'd never stopped to notice, though, that it was being uttered negatively, in criticism of our place of residence. Still, the fact that we were noticed! That we existed! We relished it. America actually cared that we existed, and this somehow made us feel like we were worth existing.

So now that America itself had proved that it cared about Kuwait's existence, or at least about controlling Saddam and oil prices, now that it had gone to war for it, America was not as unattainable as it once used to appear. It was like a cool kid coming over to your nerdy table in middle school and kicking a bully's ass for you. Never mind that he kicked the bully's ass because you have a huge wealth of information you share with the cool kid during tests. The whole school sees the cool kid fighting for you and now *you're* cool. You're important. You exist.

When I thought about it this way, I realized that moving there was actually doable.

Mama spent her days packing and unpacking and packing again. What she couldn't fit she gave away to 'Abdo and his wife. She chewed a lot of gum and tapped her foot against the floor constantly, filled with anxiety and restlessness. She leapt to her feet whenever someone knocked on the door or called on the phone. She invited Sonya and Geddo over for tea every day so she could get her fill of them. She gave Gamal random English exams to make sure he was up to par. She asked Baba a hundred questions when he called, about our new house and our new town.

Fakhr and I spent our afternoons hiding in stairwells and abandoned beach cabins to kiss every day. He held my hand two days before I left and said, "What do you want to be when you grow up?" "Why?" I said. "Because I won't know you then, and I want to be able to imagine you in the future, as you go about at work." "I don't know. What do *you* wanna be?" I said. "I asked you first!" "I can't tell," I said. "Tell me!" he said, suddenly straightening up, as if his new posture made him worthier of my telling him. "No," I said, "it's embarrassing!" and I tickled him and kissed him before he could ask again.

He bought me a necklace of jasmines on the way to the bike renter and gave the garland peddler a whole pound. The peddler laughed and prayed for Fakhr, saying he hoped all Fakhr's dreams would come true. I did too. We rented bicycles and rode them on the asphalt-paved boardwalk, dodging women and children and old men, racing each other to the buildings at the end of the walk. I took my hands off the handlebars and the wind whipped my knotty hair and my jasmine necklace so that everything around me smelled sweet.

Before we returned the bikes, he brought out a permanent marker and wrote my name on his bike's handlebars. "Give me that," I said, and wrote his name on my bicycle's frame. "There," I said. "Now we'll always be two bicycles in a city we both love."

That night, Fakhr called me, his voice filled with urgency. He asked me again what I wanted to be when I grew up and insisted I tell him. I resisted, but he said he wouldn't be able to imagine me in the future if I didn't tell him.

I'd never really said it out loud to anyone because I didn't want to be teased, but I said, "A writer," my cheeks getting hot and red. He repeated it and exhaled. "I like that," he said, "it suits you. Will you send me some of the stuff you write?" "Sure, if I write anything," I said. "Well, then," he said. "Later." "Yeah, later," I lied, because there wouldn't be a later.

Geddo came over the night before our dawn flight to say goodbye and brought me a farewell present: Cavafy's poems in English. I thanked him with a long hug. Sonya showed up too, later that night, and she and Geddo and Mama sat and chatted on the balcony till dawn. I was proud of Geddo for still partying hard. Sleep-deprived, I began to hallucinate and banged a moth against a wall with my notebook, mistaking it for a cockroach.

When I pulled the notebook away from the wall, I saw the moth's golden guts—such beautiful guts. Then I looked at the wall and saw all the blood on it from mosquitoes we'd killed since 1980, and the blood, I noticed, looked like commas. So I sat on the couch with the tea Sonya made me and watched the wall while Mama and Geddo and all of Alexandria talked on its balcony, filling in the words between the blood's punctuation marks on the blank page of the white wall. Convinced it was time to go to bed, I kissed Sonya and Geddo good night, took my new book to my room, opened it to *God Abandons Anthony*. I read the lines, *As one long prepared, and graced with courage / as is right for you who were given this kind of city . . .* I read and read until I fell asleep.

III

When I started this narrative, I knew that sooner or later I would have to have a go at Texas, and I dreaded it. . . . Once you are in Texas it seems to take forever to get out, and some people never make it.

—JOHN STEINBECK,
Travels with Charley in Search of America

THIRTEEN

FINDING THE CENTER

· · ·

BEFORE WE ALL CAME TO *AMREEKA*, MAMA AND BABA USED TO love telling their own '70s Coming To America Story. We'd sit on the floor in pajamas and sip tea and they'd take turns narrating in English.

"So, we had an apartment near ze Charle River, and ze first morning in America, your Baba took me out to breakfast," Mama said, in her French-Egyptian accent.

"Yes, and we sat at a big table and the waitress came and asked us, would we like to drink tea or coffee?" Baba said.

"I told her neizer, *chocolat* milk please, because I sought Americans loved it and also because I love it."

"And I said, tea and coffee. And the waitress said, sir? Would you like tea or coffee? And I said tea and coffee, and she said, no, tea *or* coffee, and I said, both: tea and coffee, and she said, you cannot have tea and coffee, you can have *either* tea . . . or coffee, and I said, I would like tea and coffee, miss, and she said, well, it's either tea or coffee, and I said, in my country we have tea with breakfast and coffee after breakfast, so I want tea . . . and coffee!"

"Can you believe it?" Mama said proudly and pursed her lips.

"So she snapped her gum, turned around, and brought them both to me, a cup of tea and a mug of coffee, and then asked me what country am I from."

"And zen your baba says, 'Neptune.'"

"I think that waitress had a heart attack that day."

GRETA GARBO ONCE said that she never said, "I vant to be alone." She only said, "I vant to be left alone," and that "there is all the difference." So when the airplane hovered over the spiky buildings and I saw the statue standing at the tip of the capitol in the distance before it shyly disappeared, and an expanse of water underneath us again, then tarmac, then America, I expected all the difference. I expected Garbo-glamour and haughtiness, but everyone was very friendly and they were all average looking. Nowhere were the blonde bimbettes or the brunette foxes I'd seen on vintage soaps. The men at the airport didn't yell to their wives, "This isn't the last you'll see of me!" then disappear into season-long comas. They helped them with their luggage and bitched and moaned like the rest of us. The passports officer greeted me with a "Welcome back," even though I didn't have any recollection of my brief stint as a newborn resident of America. He then went over Mama and Gamal's passports very briefly, asking them a few easy questions, none of which included "Do you currently possess a weapon of mass destruction?" or "Are you a collaborator with the enemy?" and we were promptly sent off without a full cavity examination. "And they say Israelis learn their tricks from Americans,"

Mama scoffed. The airport was a lot more posh than I was used to: the ceilings were high glass, the floors shiny, and the carts had wheels. The trucks and cars outside gleamed, and we glimpsed Baba in one. His beard had grown out so that it seemed like he'd been in the airport too—for the past six weeks, getting questioned. But he hadn't, and he looked happy. I surprised myself (and I'm sure I surprised even him) when I ran to embrace him.

I looked out of the car's window, mesmerized by the highway. Cars stayed in their lanes. They stopped at the traffic lights: here, these red and yellow and green circles were not mere suggestions or street decorations. The roads were clean. The graffiti on the inside of tunnels was pretty, like a well-tended flower. The air didn't smell of trash. A woman was crossing the street and no one appeared to offer her his luscious love bone. In the distance I saw lights from the city; they hovered over us like the personal illuminations of a hundred tiny angels.

We arrived at our new home, a long, narrow house that was a little off the ground. You had to take three big steps to stand on its front porch. It was on a short dirt road (I called it a desert road) three miles away from downtown, lined here and there, and here again, with cans of Lone Star. This must be the soda they drink here, I thought. The short trees surrounded us and some roads were cut out of rock, like in Palestine. A small river peeked out to greet us in the city, and here, by the house, a little creek ran like a secret faucet. The yard was covered in small flowers that consisted of round bunches of tiny orange and pink petals which, in turn, were also flowers, and smelled like sage. These were called lantanas. Bluebonnets would come later in the year, but the possibilities of them hovered a little in the air, as did unambitious fireflies that shone their green lights sporadically.

There were two AC wall units in the house and Mama immediately turned these on and sat by them as though holding vigil. The property was wide and pretty, and every few yards a birdbath or a twisted tree or a bird feeder or a tiki lamp shot out of the ground like a silent offering. By the house was a cement porch, and to the west of this, a small pond some hippie once dug out and poured cement and water and koi fish into. Beyond this, two poles stood ten feet apart, and between them hung a rope, I assumed for drying our clothes. The washing machine was outside the house under a wooden awning, and the rest of the patio was covered partly with thatched wood and partly with corrugated metal.

Mama claimed to hate it. Baba repeated to himself, as much as he did to her, that it was temporary. Gamal was already playing with a soccer ball he'd found in the yard, pretending that the poles were goal posts. I sat in a swinging chair and watched the koi fish, wondering how long this had been home to them. For the first time in months I was not missing anything. I repeated a line from the cinematic masterpiece *Desperately Seeking Susan*: "A girl could get used to a place like this."

But then I went inside. The rooms were tiny. Gamal and I had rooms on one side of the house and Baba and Mama had a room on the other side with their own bathroom. In between were the living room and the kitchen, which actually blended into each other. The bathroom Gamal and I shared had a tilted toilet (which we eventually got so used to that we almost always fell off the level toilets at school). There was no bidet. This came as a shock. "How did Americans wipe their asses?" Gamal asked. He asked people at school, at the grocery store, and definitely when he tagged along at PTA meetings.

I wanted to know how they masturbated. Eventually, I discovered that one could lie on her back in the tub and extend her feet up the wall so that the faucet would be perpendicular to her tummy, and let the water gather into her crotch for mind-blowing orgasms. The only downside to this was if one's mama put a load of laundry in the washing machine, one's orgasm was instantly and irreversibly ruined by the sensation that one's crotch was engulfed by roaring flames. Also, one could develop power issues orgasming in the tub: in a bidet, the girl is on top, but in America, where one has to do it in the bath, one is on the bottom, and so is always dominated. Oh well, one decides later; it's a small price to pay.

Exploration began shortly after our arrival and before we got over our jet lag. It took approximately three days of expeditions to the bus stop to figure out the bus schedule. It confused Mama that the buses here arrived on time. Buses in Egypt went by a very strict beans schedule: their arrival depended solely on the driver's acquisition of, or search for, a bean sandwich. Here, the bus driver followed a time schedule because he actually made money worth following the schedule for.

On the bus, Mama had to tell people every 12.7 minutes that she didn't *habla español*. But then people wanted to know what she did habla, and where exactly she was from, this hot-looking chica with a bangin' booty and two half-gringo-looking kids. She would smile big and say she was from Egypt, and they would be confused and ask, *Qué?* So she'd say "The Nile? North Africa? Gamal Abdel Nasser?" but they'd shake their heads, and she'd revert to stereotypes, say, "*Momias?*" But then they'd think she was from a place in Mexico that had mummies, so she'd finally say, "Cleopatra?" and they'd laugh, slap their thighs, and say, "*Mira*, she says she's from Egypt!"

We got off at the stop on campus and Mama told me this was probably where I'd go to college in a couple of years. I looked around at the university with a different attitude now, like a man sizing up his intended. Baba told stories about men in Palestinian villages, ugly, toothless, super-fat bald men who'd stand in village houses and stare girls up and down as if the girls weren't good enough for them, the girls with the black black hair like granite or asphalt, like a paved road cascading down the mountainous terrain of pale boobies. I looked at the campus now and wondered if I was like those undeserving men and hated myself for being judgmental. *Your grandmother didn't know how to read*, I shouted inside my head, and *you're lucky you get to go to college at all.*

At night I would wake up and search the room around me for a clue about where I was: in Kuwait, in Alexandria, or in Texas. It would take minutes. I had dreams about great fires and swooping airplanes, that the earth in Texas would open up and swallow me. When I woke up and heard birds chirruping I wondered if this was the calm before the storm and I worried. I would have to remind myself that America was the one that attacks people and that I was safe here, because it was too strong and no one would dare invade it. That would set my mind at ease until I began to feel guilty about being in a place that never gets attacked but attacks others.

When our white neighbors came to visit I told their daughters, who were ten and eleven, that I was half-Egyptian, half-

Palestinian. "We are half-German, half-Irish," they said, not batting an eye. It turned out everyone here was half one thing, half another. I thought this would make me feel at home but instead I was sad that I was no longer special.

Mama and Baba tried to make us speak nothing but Arabic in the house; instead, they spoke to us in Arabic and we answered in English. Pretty soon they spoke to us in a mixture of the two, and outside the house, they had to speak in English, their accents keeping them company when no one else would.

The first day of high school approached like a bowling ball, and we hoped it would miss us. At sunset, I sprawled out in the grass by the house and watched the blackbirds settle on high cables and imagined them chatting about us. The sky was like a flag, all red stripes topped with a solid blue. The horizon wrapped around me as a distant truck moved steadily west. The wall unit hummed in the background and Mama and Baba were in the house, and if they were fighting, the air drowned it out. I wished I didn't have to go to school, that we could buy goats and cows and sheep and I could stay out here with them—anything to avoid meeting new people and walking around lost in a new school. It wasn't as though I was unaccustomed to starting anew but I was unsure of myself, of my appearance, of my accent, of my intelligence. I was unsure if I could really, fluidly transition again, and I was scared. At least when I went to school in Egypt there was a uniform and I couldn't wear the wrong thing. And I could speak the language with the right accent, albeit an imperfect one. But here all that was gone, and I felt as though I was expected to know what to expect. And that seemed really unfair.

There was a ballpark by the house and every few minutes someone yelled and people cheered and a batter swung and I could hear the sound of the wooden bat against the white ball. I picked a blade of grass and stuck it in my mouth, but I could only chew it over twice before I spat it out, the insecticide leaving a weird taste in my mouth. Pretty soon the seat of my jeans was covered in fire-ants and afterwards I itched my ass for hours.

AT SCHOOL WE started the day with homeroom; everyone stood up and recited something, all together. I thought it was a prayer so I didn't stand, and the teacher motioned to me afterwards.

"I noticed," he said sternly, "you declined to stand during the pledge of allegiance. Did you fill out a conscientious objector form at the office?"

"A who?" I asked, shaking. I thought I'd already managed to get into trouble, and it was only 7:49 A.M. "I'm sorry, I didn't want to pray."

"It's not a prayer. No. It's a patriotic thing."

The next few weeks I slowly got used to the pledge and then, one day, recited it, even though I didn't want to. It's not because I wasn't patriotic—I was just really, really confused.

There was a lot that confused me. Why were there so many commercials on TV? In Kuwait and Egypt there was a commercial segment and you could opt not to watch it. What exactly was daylight saving time? And did it mean I had to stay at school an extra hour? What was a tag sale? Why would anyone want to buy a tag? What was homecoming? Was it something political, because everyone was asking me to vote for a

Queen? What was Memorial Day? Veterans Day? Why were there so many special days? Where was the call to prayer? I didn't hear it anywhere. I had a friend who once lived by the airport, and when she moved she couldn't stand the absence of airplane sounds. That's what was happening to me then, but instead of airplane sounds, I was missing a hundred different things from "home," and the sad part was, I was starting to forget what they were and where home really was.

People sat in a student center in between periods and for lunch, and this student center was like a map of the world: the white kids with money, the ones who showed up in their Beamers and their Pathfinders, sat in the top left; the white people with no money, the ones who drove Metros, sat in the top right; and the thesbians, who were also white, sat in the middle (around where France would be). Then the black people sat in the bottom center; the Latino kids sat in the bottom left; and the nerds sat on the bottom right. I discovered that no one was interested in where I was from because people in this high school didn't ask, "Where are you from?" They asked, "Where do you sit?"

I sat in the bathroom with my backpack and the meal Mama made the night before in a small Tupperware container balanced precariously on my lap. On the school's map of the world the bathroom stall was at the South Pole.

My favorite class was English Honors—the only honors class I was in. We read *The Scarlet Letter*, *The Red Badge of Courage*, *The Inferno*, and *The Decameron* and, being the nerd that I am, I skipped ahead and read the parts that were too naughty for school. I loved the story about the married woman who was talking to her husband while she sat in a barrel, her lover inside the barrel fucking her and the husband oblivious to it all.

The first time I read this story was during class, and I wished there was a bidet in the South Pole because I would've run out there as quick as I could and jerked off; my clit seemed to swell to the size of a plum.

Ms. Balducci, the English teacher, told me *The Decameron* was actually inspired by old Arabic tales. "Really?" I wanted to know. "Yes," she said, and asked me to write a story for the next assignment and model it after *The Decameron*, which was great because I wanted to write a story about an Egyptian woman fucking some dude in a barrel while her husband was outside of it.

At home in my bed I'd masturbate, but I didn't think of Fakhr el-Din; I thought of Omar Medina, this kid who sat next to me in my fifth period pre-calculus class. Medina was tall and brown and wore baggy pants that were constantly threatening to fall off and expose his boxers completely. He always said hi to me and never asked to copy my homework, which this other kid Donald always did. His hair was thick and black and his eyes were green by Arab standards, but I guess in America they'd be called hazel.

In order to stop being a pariah and start eating lunch with the rest of the world I would have to be the funny person I had been in Egypt and Kuwait. American teenagers couldn't be so different from any other kind of teenager, and from what I could tell, they were nowhere near as mean or as tragically cool as the people I'd grown up watching on *Dallas*. I had to join the world.

When I was little, during one of his breathless lectures on Palestine, Baba had explained to me that the reason his homeland was in constant turmoil was that it stood in the center of the world, and when an incredulous look shone on my face—even at eight years old, I was fully aware that that was *not* why this tiny place was in turmoil—he'd grab my arm and thrust me in the direction of the atlas and tell me to look up Palestine and see how it was in the center of the world. On the map, sure, it was in the center, but wasn't the world round? I'd worry sometimes about Baba, who built buildings and was a grown man. Didn't he know that any point could be the world's center?

This memory raced through my head while I stood at the top of a staircase overlooking the student center, trying to figure out where Palestine would be. I saw a brown table abandoned by students and headed for it, desperately hoping no one would sit at it before I did. I pulled out a chair and sat down, took out *The Decameron* and started reading. A strange smell wafted toward me from the cafeteria and I struggled to ignore it. I also struggled to ignore the couple that was practically humping two tables down from me. I looked around for teachers, expecting one to come out of the shadows with a giant stick and beat these two for dishonorable behavior. You're not in Kuwait or in Egypt anymore, Nidali, I told myself and laughed.

"Yo, what you laughin' at?" A tiny girl with long brown curls and a baseball jersey attempted to tower over me.

"This thing I just remembered."

"Oh yeah?"

"Yeah . . . from when I was back home."

"Where's home at?" she said, now completely interested.

"Far away. You wouldn't understand."

"Try me."

"Egypt. And Kuwait," I said.

"Dang, you from there? Yo, Camilla. Camilla!" Now she was yelling at another girl, who was pale and sitting at another table.

"What?"

"This girl's from Egypt. Camilla," she turned and looked at me, "is from Croatia. Y'all should talk."

"It's really not the same place," Camilla and I said at the same time to the tiny girl, who later on revealed that her name was Dimi.

"Shit, never mind. What's your name?" she said.

"Nidali," I said.

"A-ight, Dolly, come sit with us." I was already moving. "Nobody sits at that table; it's cursed."

"Why?"

"'Cause these kids used to sit there, right, four of them, and then like eight years ago, they were all in a car and it crashed," here she banged her small hand against the table, "into a fucking tree, right, and they all died. So nobody sits there, 'cause they ghosts still hangin' out, and that's where they chill."

"That's so sad," I said, glancing at the table again, half-expecting to see white sheets.

"I tell you what's sad, those motherfuckin rags you're wearing."

"Dimi, stop. You're cold," Camilla said.

"Well, do you know a good shop to buy exciting ensembles, you know, not too expensive?" I said.

The girls exhaled loudly.

"Yeah, we'll take you to a store. To buy cool clothes," Camilla finally said.

I don't know what we babbled about later, but every few minutes they corrected my English. "This one talks like she's on public radio," they said, which at first I thought meant I talked a lot, because in Egypt when you wanted to make fun of someone who talked a lot you said, "she's a radio!" but here they meant I spoke like a white girl on NPR, all boring and with nary a crazy emotion. I remembered how in Egypt I listened to Voice of America and tried to speak like the girl on the radio. And how in Egyptian my language was full of songs and lilts and catchy turns of phrase. I wished, then and for many months later, that I could translate the way I was, my old way of being, speaking, and gesturing, to English: to translate myself.

When the last period was through and the bell beeped a shrill ring, I was accosted by Camilla and Dimi, who were ready to take me shopping.

"But I have to speak to my mother. She's waiting to pick me up outside."

"You don't take the bus?" they said.

"Mama likes to pick me up," I said.

"OK, you think your moms would give us a ride to the store?"

"Uh . . . I believe she would."

Mama was surprisingly amused when I peered into the car's open window and introduced her to these girls.

"Yes, yes, sure, we will go to the shop," she said.

At the mall, Mama waited for me at the piano, which was by the escalators in a wide, empty space. It was surrounded by long carpeted steps that resembled stadium seating. She was trying to figure out whether or not she was allowed to play.

Dimi and Camilla spoke a mile a minute about boys and their broken-down cars. They ushered me into a men's shop and held a pair of jeans against my waist.

"These are perfect. They're affordable and they sit right below the waist," Camilla said.

"Yeah, try them on."

I did, and although their pant legs were thirty inches in diameter, each, agreed to buy them.

"Now we gotta go to the Salvation Army," Dimi said.

"The army?" I was horrified. "Why?"

"Not the army you crazy ho, the Salvation Army," said Camilla. She took out a cigarette.

"They got used clothes for cheap," said Dimi, lighting Camilla's cigarette.

"You smoke?" I asked Camilla, terrified that Mama would catch her and punish me for her blackened lungs.

"You want one?" Dimi said, taking out a pack of Newports.

"No!" I said, then yelled, "My mom will be enraged if she sees, or even smells, you smoking. Please extinguish it, please!" I was hopping from foot to foot, like a six-year-old who wants to pee. Camilla stared at me blankly.

"Didn't you hear what she said?" Dimi snatched the butt out of Camilla's mouth and put it out in the mall's sand-filled ashtray. I wondered where all the sand had come from, if it was imported like the sand hills by my old apartment. An image of the old apartment flashed across my mind but I put it out, like Camilla's cigarette.

"No, what did she say?" Camilla said, obviously irritated. "It sounded like Shakespeare or some shit."

"She said her mami don't like her hanging around smokers."

When we got near the mall's center, I heard it: an interpretation of "Across the Universe"; a little bit of John, a little bit of Ringo, a little bit of my insane mama and her Egyptian beats. Mama had gotten her hands on the piano and it was impossible to leave. The mall manager, a weary-looking man in uniform, with a gigantic bald spot and a haggard face, stood next to her, his arms and eyes crossed. Every once in a while I saw him mouthing something to her, and when I got closer, I discovered it was "What a bitch," and "I told you I'm not hiring anybody." Camilla and Dimi sat on the carpeted steps that resembled stadium benches. When she was done, they clapped. Mama looked at the man and said, "Who said anything about hiring? I only want to come in once in a while, maybe once a day, and play. For free." Mama smiled; it was her theory that Americans accept anything and do anything if it's free. "Believe me," she said when we first moved, "if you give them flat soda for free, they drink it, you tell them they can see a very bad movie with fat-ass Sinatra free, they watch it, you try to sell them a bag of chips and say fifty percent more free, they buy it. Never mind it is fifty percent more chips compared to the old bag, which the greedy company had decided to put six ounces of chips in. People buy it."

It wasn't going to work this time; I could tell from the look on this guy's face. Mama was wrong. I wanted to gloat. But then he rolled his eyes and said, "Fine."

"Congratulations, Mrs. Ammar," the girls said, and Mama told them she is Mrs. El-Guindi.

"Your parents divorced?" they asked me, but I shook my head.

"In my country, a woman doesn't change her family name,"

Mama said. "But her children keep their father's name. It is more feminist than you thought, yes?"

In the car, when I told Mama, who was still bouncing, that we wanted to go to the Salvation Army, a cloud of gloom snuck right into the Olds and threatened to empty itself over our heads. We argued in Arabic for fifteen minutes about how we weren't "beggars yet in this country," and "we should wear the same outfit every day if we can't afford new clothes"; that's what she'd been doing. Day in and day out, a comical dress that looked like it was made from leftover curtains. I told her this. She said, "Style is personal: it varies from person to person." "Or from window to window," I said, and she nearly slapped me in front of my new rock star friends.

In school the next day, when Camilla wanted to know why Mama wouldn't take us to the Salvation Army, I told her it was because she thought I could catch other people's diseases if I wore their old clothes. "She thinks anyone who'd leave their clothes behind has a disease."

MAMA MANAGED TO find a Lebanese woman who lived three blocks away and had two sons: one son went to Rice (he was the failure) and the other to Stanford. Mama made her Turkish coffee and read her fortune almost every night. They talked about opening a business together, a little restaurant on the main drag. Other neighbors came over almost nightly with a bottle of something: Texas red, cheap cabernet, whiskey, Shiner, or Lone Star. (I soon discovered this was not a soda, but that some people could drink it like water.) Baba never came to the door and he never made any friends. He said he wasn't interested in friends. Again, his mantra: "We're here to be educated and make money, not friends." Mama was here for friends, for life. She accepted the bottles, opened them on the spot (except for the Lone Star, six-packs of which were accumulating under the sink), and invited these sweet people to sit with her by the koi fish pond, eventually introducing them to her hookah (which she'd brought all the way from Alexandria), packing it with apple tobacco and, to their amusement, lighting it with a brick of coal. She strung up little lights and planted lilies in pots, which she lowered into the pond with a newfound gentleness. She even bought sidewalk chalk and encouraged us to draw designs on the concrete patio to make it look more inviting. She weeded the yard as best she could, and when fleas hitched rides into the house and bit us mercilessly, leaving a thick red banner at the bottom of our legs, she borrowed a neighbor's mower and spread flea killer granules with an odd ferocity. Like the lilies in the pond, Mama bloomed, while Baba drooped like a weed.

One afternoon, I watched her draw with a dwindled piece of blue chalk (I'd used it for "sky effect" on a botched corner of the patio) an old-school lotus, outer petals first, filling in more petals last "like the ones back home, the ones on the walls of Aswan. Remember?" I nodded my head. I wanted to ask her if she missed home, but, as though she'd read my mind, she said, "I'm glad we're here. I've wanted to leave Egypt and Kuwait ever since I was young, to see if there was life elsewhere. And there is." She finished her drawing and winked at me.

In the morning, a real lily, a lotus, floated in the pond. Baba tried to explain it away: "The old hibbie must have planted those long ago" (he still had trouble with his Ps and Bs and with his wife's tendency for superstitious thought), but the lily floated triumphantly adjacent to Mama's chalk drawing.

I found her doodling a piano by the front steps with the same chalk later that morning, and when I asked what she was doing, she said, "Look, Nidali, I'm going to tell you something about Baba's mother that he doesn't even know. It is a woman-to-woman story, and so she told it to me.

"When she was young, you know, she worked for those people her mama left her with, and one day, she broke the water bucket for the well. She didn't have the means to replace it, and she was very young and loved to daydream, so . . . she drew a bucket with a flaky, rained-on rock, as if this drawing would be some kind of replacement. But the next day, a new bucket was there."

I didn't want to believe her but I did.

"So she saw this as a good opportunity and she drew a man by her window, so a man could come to her, but instead, a woman did, her mother . . . so Sitto added to the picture of the man a penis, a big penis, in order for God, or whoever was granting these wishes, to know it was a man she wanted.

"Your Sido came by that very night. And here's why your Baba doesn't know this story: Sido had a giant penis. Do you understand this?"

"I don't want to hear about Sido's penis!" I said, nauseated.

"Stupid girl," Mama said.

"No, I'm glad you told me, Mama."

And her picture was finished.

When all the plants had been potted and every last flea massacred, Mama found an ancient used piano at a yard sale and somehow got the poor old man to cut the price in half (it was already lowered to two hundred dollars, and she bought it for ninety). It was a Bush & Gerts, the heaviest motherfucker you could find (naturally), and took twelve grown men, a handcart, and a truck (all solicited at the yard sale by Mama, who had to pretend she was Mexican for at least three of the men to agree to help her) to move, and when the monstrosity was dismounted and carried over the steps (on which there was a chalk picture of a piano) and set up in the tiny living room, Mama cracked open forty-eight Lone Stars (hard-working-man's water) as a thank you.

I sat and watched her, jealous of how easily she seemed to root herself here. Me, I felt splintered, like the end of a snapped-off tree branch. I had even taken to talking to myself, keeping me company, narrating my own movements. In this way, *me* became *her*, *I* became *Nidali*, *you*, *she*.

FOURTEEN

YOU ARE A FOURTEEN-YEAR-OLD
ARAB CHICK WHO JUST
MOVED TO TEXAS

• • •

THAT FALL YOU MOVE WITH YOUR FAMILY TO AMERICA, YOU are diagnosed with TB, and the old white doctor points at the five-inch red rectangle on your forearm and announces, "That should be three inches smaller." He puts you on a battery of medications, which worsens your acne, makes you gain thirty pounds, and gives you an overall sense of impending death. As usual, your mama is jealous of you and wants to be the one dying instead; for the first few weeks there, it is her first time without a piano, and your first time without friends to comfort you. TV is full of commercials and your family goes to McDonald's too often. The first few times you're excited to be eating hamburgers and then a few months later you realize that it's a nasty fast-food restaurant. When you go to the movies, you have to explain to your parents why the jokes are funny. Long after the credits begin to roll, the three of you still sit in the dark, you translating the movie's murder mystery into Arabic. There's nothing sadder than a fourteen-year-old explaining a movie to her middle-aged parents. In America, you think, not understanding a movie is the same as being illiterate. It could break your heart if you really think about it, so you should never think about it, you should just go to school, eat your lunch on the floor outside the library, then go into the library and spend the rest of the period reading the dictionary.

Every day, Dimi wants to have lunch with you. Soon, so will Camilla and Aisha, who is black and Muslim and wants to hang out with you during Ramadan so y'all can give each other support. When these girls call the radio to request songs, they send you mad shoutouts. You don't know what a shoutout is, but you like that your name is on the radio, even if they mispronounce it. They are sixteen and drive beat-up cars and want you to hang out at the park with them when it's dark. You tell them your Baba doesn't allow it. "She said her papi don't play that," they'll translate to each other.

There are things that make it bearable: that bicycle your father bought you when you weren't looking, its handlebars shiny, nothing like the tattered, rusty bicycles you had to rent from the hashish fiend at the souk back in Ma'moora; Oreos; MTV; but mostly, the letters you get from Fakhr el-Din, your boyfriend who is still back in Alexandria renting bicycles from the hashish fiend at the souk in Ma'moora; letters that always begin, "I miss your face your eyes and your smile what is America like is it cold there and do you like the blond boys better than me and my big nose?"

You write back that it's a total letdown, that there aren't any cute blond boys, and he's the best. You're lying; there are blond twins that are straight out of a movie, and they're gorgeous, and one day you drop your box of charity chocolates so one of them can help you pick them up. "Hey, I read about you in the newspaper," he says, and you blush. "Did you used to live in a tent and stuff?" You lose your breath, then say, "No actually, a glass pyramid." "No kidding? Right on . . ." and he walks away. What a fucking waste, you think to yourself.

You finally have a locker, something you've been dreaming of since you saw that 7UP commercial when you were nine. But lockers can't make a girl happy forever. One weekend afternoon, when your father comes into your bedroom with a letter from Fakhr in his hand, you brace yourself. There is a huge harangue. Girls should not be addressed this way, he tells you. And this boy says he misses kissing you. Did you actually kiss this boy? "No!" you say, a memory appearing in your head like a movie of yourself rolling around topless with Fakhr in an abandoned beach cabin. "Absolutely not!" you shout. The letter is torn up and discarded and you are officially cut off from the Pride of Religion.

When Dimi and Camilla and Aisha insist that you go to a rap concert with them at Stubb's, you are met with complete resistance.

"Enough, man," Mama tells your baba. "Let the child go, she's suffocating here."

"You, you be quiet, the girl's not going to rap concerts and getting drunk and pregnant. No, no, and no. Full stop." And to seal it, he farts three times.

"I want to have friends!" you scream and run to your room.

"We are not here to make a friend, we are here to study and get the best out of America!" This is your baba's mantra the entire time you are living under his roof. This is why he is in America, but not you. You want a "life," a concept you've just learned of.

You all go to the McDonald's drive-thru, and upon inspecting his cheeseburgers and finding them with pickles, your baba backs the car up and yells into the intercom,

"I said no *bickles*, you *pitch*!"

You hate the idea of having no friends here and not being allowed to write to your best friend, who isn't here. So, one morning, after listening to Nirvana half a dozen times, you pack a bag, kiss your brother's forehead, and sneak out of the house, balancing the bag on your bike's handlebars. You wear the bowler hat you and your mama'd bought from a street vendor by campus when you first moved here. Your bike flies downhill, and in your jeans' back pocket is your father's stolen credit card and around your neck every single gold pendant you've ever owned hanging from a sturdy gold chain.

Selling the gold and getting some cash to live on is the first logical step, you think, starving out of your mind. So you go into a small shop and give your chain to an older man with little hair. He weighs it and tells you sixty bucks. Sixty bucks? you yell. Man, I know I should've gone lower, he says. No fucking way, that's all my gold, that's all I've got in the world! Only sixty bucks? You think of your mama walking around with all that gold hanging from her ears and wrists; does she know how little it's worth here in America? You snatch the necklace back and clip it around your neck, and as you turn away, the man tells you if you come home with him he'll buy you a new dress and you can have a place to stay for free.

The solution is to be a taco vendor you decide as the day nears to a close and businessmen in their suits are flooding the avenue. You go to the place off Congress to apply for a cart and the man asks you how old you are. Seventeen, you lie, and he asks if you've got proof. No, you say, and that's the end of that.

But I'm a taco vendor, you say, I need to sell tacos, it's part of a bigger plan to unite all people, especially Palestinians and Israelis. Oh really, he wants to know and smiles. He's almost as old as your father and he wants to know if you want to go home with him because he can take real good care of you and you wouldn't have to worry about a thing. You turn around and sprint to a pizza place, your mini-suitcase banging against the asphalt, its wheels worn.

Quickly realizing you are prey, you walk to the nearest motel, a shit hole, and check in under a fake name, Madonna Nirvana. The man looks jaded and wearily gives you a key. In your room, you decide that you're fucked and call your parents.

"Goddamn you, we thought you'd been kidnapped!" your Baba yells.

"It's her, thank God!" your mama says.

"Where are you? We're coming to get you now!" he says.

"Not so fast, buster," you say, can't believe you just called your dad buster.

"What?"

"I have conditions."

"There's no condition, you give us direction, we come get you right now, little girl."

"Bye," you say and hang up. You call back five minutes later.

"OK, OK, what is your condition?"

"Curfew extension."

"Nine P.M. is the final offer," he says.

"And resumed contact with Fakhr el-Din?"

"No, no, and no!"

You hang up again. This time you wait about an hour, strolling down to a shop on the drag and using the stolen credit card to buy a dog collar.

"OK!" he yells when he picks up the phone. "Letters allowed between you and Fakhr el-Din, but there is absolutely, positively no dating allowed!"

"Fine," you say. "I'm in the motel on San Jacinto." In less than one year, you will regret not having negotiated more on the dating bit.

When they arrive you are waiting on the street corner, sleepy and hungry. Your mother gets out of the car to hug you, and you see her face is pale like your Sitto's white cheese. You hug her hard and cry; you wish you hadn't hurt her. She thought she'd lost you, she says, and you tell her she shouldn't have worried, that you're tough. She laughs and tells you to get in the car, and sits in the back with you.

That night, you hold her hand and look out of the window at the city's lights fading away, and see for the first time how you were braver than your mother. As though she'd read your mind, she gently curses you, slips out a "*Yikhrib baytik*," and then whispers in your ear, "I've kept all the letters for you anyway. You never asked for them!" So you'd never seen that she was an ally. How could you have missed that? It was really your fault.

Your baba puts in a tape of Abdel Halim singing *sawah* but in the middle of it, Marky Mark and the Funky Bunch comes on, and your father says he heard it on the radio and had to tape it because he thought it gave him a good feeling. The night folds over, your head settling on your mama's shoulder, as you fall asleep and dream of a new life, an existential restart button, and a slice of pepperoni-less pizza.

FIFTEEN

MAKE IT YOURSELF
• • •

MY SOPHOMORE YEAR PASSED BY UNREMARKABLY. AND THAT was precisely the problem.

"She's bored," Mama said one day in the kitchen while I sat in the hammock, my butt almost touching the ground. I was reading *A Passage to India*, which I checked out of the library along with another dozen books. She didn't know I could hear her.

"So am I," Baba said. "Life . . . it is boring. But she is doing her own damage control." Baba liked to whip out construction-type lingo once in a while now because it was really the only new English he was learning. "She challenges herself."

"But shouldn't she be in a challenging setting? I went to pick her up from the library yesterday and she practically cried. I've never met a teenager who wants to stay longer in a library."

That was true. I had a 9 P.M. curfew, and the library shut at 10. I wanted to be able to stay until closing time.

"What, you'd rather she stayed in a bar or a club or a den for crack? The library is fine." Baba stretched loudly from the kitchen table. "Make me some tea."

"I think tenth grade is not advanced enough. I think she should be in eleventh."

"No, Ruza, she is in tenth, she must create her own challenges, she must make it herself. You'll see, she'll do it. She's already doing it. Tea."

"Make it yourself," Mama said, and the next week she went in to talk to my principal and schedule a meeting with him and the school's superintendent. By the end of the meeting I had skipped tenth grade altogether and was going into eleventh. Mama explained that in Egypt I had already taken most of the subjects I was now studying and that I was ready to move up. Later, she told me that the superintendent had said, "But Ms. Ammar, your child is not emotionally ready to be in eleventh grade."

"I think *you're* not emotionally ready for her to be in eleventh grade," Mama had said, and that was that.

Struggles for the next few weeks revolved around curfew extension. I wanted to stay at the library till 10 P.M. on weekdays and go to a poetry slam on Saturdays. It started at nine and took place at an all-ages bar.

I brought both cases to Baba's attention. He asked me to write him an essay explaining why these activities are important to me.

"You will thank me for this one day, ya Nad-dooli," he said, as I huffed off to my room. "You will write the greatest dissertation of all human times. People will make *bilgrimage* to see your manuscript, like they do for the guttenburger or whatever it's called . . . that bible. You will become a world-renown scholar!"

"Renowned!"

"Yes!"

"No, renowned, not renown."

"See? Already on your way."

I wished Baba would enroll in a PhD program and get off my ass. Why couldn't *he* write the amazing dissertation? I wanted to write songs and poems and stories about women fucking in barrels.

I pictured him as a seventeen-year-old, in the *pension*, his hands dirty from work and poetry. I hated how he created this folklore around himself so that I could never hate him, because the folklore constantly reminded me of how history fucked him and how he just couldn't do a PhD. He couldn't afford to.

I doodled at my desk for a little while, wrote "library" in one corner and "poetry slam" in the other. I watched a dog sniff cactuses out in the neighbor's yard. I scratched my crotch. I wrote:

Dear Mama, Baba, Gamal:
  By the time you read this, I will be dead.
  I am sorry to have left you like this. I'm sorry about the mess. I'm sure Mama, you'll have to clean it up, all the pieces of my brain and such, and I'm sorry for that. Yeah.
  See, the thing is, I really wanted to stay at the library till 10. I like the peaceful brown cubicles and the gray carpet. I like the smell of all the books.
  I also really wanted to go to the poetry slam. They don't serve alcohol to minors there, it's against the law, and it's

*just a place where people recite poetry, like Baba used to. I
just wanted to hear it.*

*But I wasn't allowed to do either, and that is why I'm
dead now.*

Oh, good-bye, world! Good-bye!

I signed the bottom, got up, and went to the living room. I
handed it to Baba and said, "Here's your essay."

He read it, looked up at the ugly wooden paneling for a second, and said, "I did not know there was alcohol at the slam
of poetry place. You are forbidden to go there. But . . . 10 P.M.
for the library approved. Now," he said, handing me the paper,
"tear this up and throw it away before your mother finds it
and faints."

"Why don't *you* rip it up and throw it away," I screamed,
"the way you rip up your crappy poems?" I ran to my room to
get my library card.

SIXTEEN

THE SHIT NO ONE BOTHERED
TO TELL US

• • •

I.

OUR SECOND YEAR IN AMERICA, APPROACHING OUR THIRD, and Baba still comes back from work on a bus. He hates the city. He likes the bus. It is efficient and cool and clean. The bus races through neighborhoods and picks up people in uniform. Baba smells his hands when the bus stops at our neighborhood. He burrows them in his coat. The weather is odd and Texan; it is hot, it is cold, and Baba loves it because it is like him and can't decide which one it wants to be or even if it wants to stay or leave.

Baba wants to build his own house. He has visited fourteen banks and their loan agents all flip through his paperwork and remind him of the soldiers at the Allenby bridge. They read it quickly and send him off. He has to build his credit before he can build a house, they say. He applies for more credit cards. He buys Mama an Olds and pays for it in cash. The Olds reminds him of the one he had to leave in Amman. He couldn't drive it to Egypt, even though Egypt is for sure within driving distance from Amman.

He takes the bus to work. He works sixteen hours a day. He pays for dinners with his credit cards. He goes to the banks again. They remind him of the suspicious security agents at airports. He takes the bus home. He sees the uniforms on the bus. He comes home and screams at his daughter, who is turning into a slut, he's sure of it. He washes his hands; they are dirty from the bus. He goes to the bank. He leaves it without a house. He takes the bus to work.

2.

WHEN ON A rainy evening, we go out to check the mail—we made checking the mail a regular family outing in the second month since it's free—and find a large letter proclaiming us the winners of $10,000,000, we scream and jump up and down and bless America over and over again. Gamal does a cartwheel and I stand on my head. Baba shushes us and makes us get in the house "before people start begging us for a cut." We stand around the kitchen and plot out how we're going to spend it.

Baba wants to buy a house in every European city and furnish it with fine prostitutes. Mama wants to pay a hit man to kill Baba. Gamal wants an airplane and parachutes. And I want money to pay legal fees to emancipate myself from this family and live in a penthouse in New York. We stay up all night, giddy and giggly, and talk and plot until our mouths are dry deserts, drier than the fenceless and defenseless north of Kuwait. Then Mama breaks it to us slowly, what Ed McMahon says in the letter's fine print.

3.

MAMA MAKES MAD dough teaching piano classes. People all over
town want cheap classes from the "Mexican" lady. She says not
Spanish, Egyptian. They say, "Oh," and they say it the way
adults say Oh when a kid tells them he's Superbat. "Oh." The
rich kids pay a lot and the poor kids pay almost nothing. Mama
likes to talk to their mamas and pretty soon everyone in the
neighborhood is coming over, even the Jehovah's Witnesses.
They come to the house every Sunday with *Awake!* and a kid
who wants to play piano. Mama takes the magazine and uses it
when she fries her potatoes. The excess oil runs over prophe-
cies and Mama waits. She makes so much money she opens her
own account and gets a credit card. She teaches one kid the
Fantaisie-Impromptu and tells the mama about how this com-
poser brought her husband and her together. The mama nods
and asks, "Back in Mexico?" Mama goes to the bank and waits
for a loan officer. She applies for a mortgage. The woman asks
to see her taxes. Mama hasn't filed any. Mama uses the money
from the next 133 lessons to pay for her back taxes so she won't
go to jail.

4.

WHEN A BOY asks you on a date and you say yes, and he says
you should come over to his house, and you say you'll have to
sneak out because you're not allowed to go on dates, he'll say,
"Just say you have an after-school activity, we can date during
the day. I understand." Don't go. If you fall for this, if you go
on your after-school activity to his house, he will stuff his hands
down your pants and when you try to explain that you don't

do that, he'll say, "OK, but I've got blue balls now and if I don't get off I'll die." Don't believe him. If you do, he will force his dick in your mouth, so don't just sit there and let your nose run and your eyes tear and your throat gag when he does, bite him, bite him and run. Fucking haul ass out of that house. When he tells everyone at school you're a whore and everyone believes him, ignore them. They are nothing. When your father says you're a whore, ignore him. He can't even get you guys a house.

5.

MADONNA IS AN uncool music choice. Gamal knows this so he steals Baba's credit card and goes to the record store to buy some hip-hop: Bizmarkie, Pete Rock and CL Smooth, NWA, Beastie Boys, KRS-One, A Tribe Called Quest, Erik B. & Rakim. He goes home and jams out. He remembers the stories about Arabia, how disputes over property, family allegiances, gold, and women were all solved by two warring poets who stood on top of a big, sturdy boulder. The poets rhymed until one was defeated, solving the case. Gamal knows he's not black, but he comes from the home of the original rap battle.

6.

WHEN ONE IS used to two seasons, this is a miracle: in the fall, the trees turn brown the way they do in art. It really happens. Then the leaves fall down and encircle the trees like children and grandchildren, like we encircled Sido and Sitto in Jenin. The rain grinds the leaves into the grass and afterwards they get dry again. When I step on them they make a crunch sound

better than any other sound in the world. I seek out the crunchi-
est leaves and step on them with my boot. I rake leaves and
put them in a corner. The wind comes and picks them back
up again. I get yelled at and told to control the leaves. I rake
them into the street and hope they'll fall into the drainpipe and
wash away. I come home from school and see them, dull brown
in front of the house, like a pool of dried blood. I take grocery
bags and fill them with leaves. The bags burst or tear. I think
and think and think, and finally I get a garbage bag and stuff
them all in.

7.

BABA TAKES A bus home from work and at one stop sees a house
split in half: a cross-section of a house. He stares at it and
realizes it's a half-put-together mobile home—a double-wide,
which means it's twice as big as his. He watches people outside
work on it while the owners sit in the kitchen and drink tea.
He thinks it's tea. The wife is in a robe as though the house were
already put together. The husband is hanging a painting. Baba
wonders if they're shooting a scene for a movie. He doesn't see
any cameras. He imagines that he's got X-ray vision. He wonders if he should buy a double wide. And some cattle. And a
gun. And a cowboy hat. And his dignity back.

8.

MAMA DOESN'T LIKE the idea of a mobile anything. She wants
a place with a foundation and the only wheels she wants should
be on her car and her son's skateboard. And when did he be-

come such a little punk skater? She fries potatoes and eggplant and zucchini and puts them in a colander. The colander is plastic and it melts. She throws it away and takes out a back issue of *Awake!* She doesn't want the mobile home. She never again wants to hitch her home onto a car and drive away and flee. Mama wants to stay in one place. She arranges the potatoes in the glass baking dish. She layers lamb meat and tomato sauce on top. She arranges the eggplant. She pours more red sauce. Zucchini. Lamb. She sautés flour in oil, adds milk and cheese, boils the béchamel sauce and ladles it on top of the layers. The music is blasting from down the long hall. The kitchen is directly next to the girl's room on the left and the boy's room on the right. Mama hears Gamal rapping about something "is over, the bridge is over" and Nidali singing about "with the lights out something is less dangerous." She opens the oven door and slides dinner onto the middle rack. Mama imagines that she is in a movie and that a cross-section of her house is being filmed, with her daughter on the left side of the screen singing, her son on the right rapping, and her in the middle. Like a moving train. And in the scene she wipes her brow and says out loud the thing she is thinking: "I can't tell which one of those kids has a bigger identity crisis."

9.

THE FIGHTS ARE different. Baba and Mama no longer choke each other or argue. Sometimes Baba will throw a plate and that will be that. Sometimes I'll see him eating a sandwich he obviously made—untoasted white bread, cheese, pitted olives—and wearing a creased shirt and a stained jacket. Sometimes I'll start walking to school and notice that the car is tilted sideways and when I peek inside I see Mama sleeping in her nightgown and I open the door and try to sound nonchalant while uttering a sentence like "Hi Mama, do you have keys to get back inside the house?" At their worst, Baba stands at the doorstep with all his clothes packed into brown rectangles and Mama comes outside, tries to negotiate, gets rebuffed and goes back inside. Baba glances at his watch now and again and cusses the long-awaited pimp of a cabdriver, then folds his arms against his chest. During these Camp David–esque scenes, I play Jimmy Carter to Mama and Baba's Begin and Sadat (respectively). Baba is Sadat standing outside his Camp David bunker like an unsatisfied lover, spawning a truce. I am Carter—succeed in bringing them back together for an agreement—and like Carter, I have an ulterior motive: to be rewarded by going down in history as a phenomenal dealmaker.

10.

IF AND WHEN you receive an anonymous letter saying your daughter sucks dicks, don't automatically believe it and beat the shit out of her. She doesn't. She was, technically, raped. She won't tell you this because you're strict. And when you beat her up, for the nine thousandth time, she will dare you to kill her. She doesn't want to live the life you've come all the way to America to give her. She doesn't want to live it. Reminding her how many hours you work so she can eat Oreos will not work. Attempts to gain recognition from a teenager rarely work, especially when said teenager is in a headlock. Neighbors in America don't call the cops when they see their Arab neighbor chasing his daughter around the house with a knife. But don't be surprised when your daughter runs out of the house after you're done beating her up and calls the cops. The cops will take pictures of her bruises and the marks your hands and fingers left behind in all the red places. She will take you to court. Parents in America can't get away with Everything. She will drop charges against you. She will assume you've learned your lesson. Daughters in America can teach their parents lessons. Cops in America don't like Arabs and they definitely don't like Arabs who hit their teenage daughters and chase them around the house with knives. But they'll eventually drop the charges.

11.

IT'S HARD TO buy a house when you have a criminal record.

12.

ONE WEEKEND MORNING they all wake up—for a reason they can't figure out—exceptionally early. They scratch their heads and look at their clocks one more time. 5:20 A.M. Is it really 5:20? Mama and Nidali make breakfast and they all eat together, quite civilized. Baba brings the chimenea up to the porch and puts logs in it and he and Gamal try to light them for half an hour. Finally Baba pours Drakkar cologne on them and they light up beautifully, warm up the front of the house. They drink hot chocolate and watch a football game, even though they all hate football. When night falls and their tummies rumble again, Waheed suggests that they go out for dinner, so they all put

their coats on and get in the Olds, and Mama puts on some Billie
Holiday. "What should I care how much it may storm," she
sings. "I've got my love to keep me warm." The first place they
go to is closed. So is the second; so is the third. Come to think
of it, everywhere is closed, even Whataburger, and there's
no one else on the street. Theirs is the only car on the main
avenue. Baffled, they go home and Mama cooks a turkey she
found on sale last night for twenty-nine cents a pound. They
eat it and watch more football and fall asleep on the couch and
on the floor and wake up the next day to Gamal's friend calling
to find out what he did for Thanksgiving.

13.

MAMA FIGURES IT out: they *are* living in a mobile home. A
neighbor one day notes that "this is such a nice trailer, in such
good shape." Mama doesn't know how she'll take her revenge
on Baba. She wants to end this, to divorce his ass, even if sym-
bolically, like the many times he's orally divorced her. She
remembers something she read once about pre-Islamic women.
She calls her piano tuner, who owns a truck, and while he hitches
the trailer onto his truck she tapes the cupboards, drawers, and
bookshelves shut and takes all the mirrors off their hinges. Then
she takes his keys and does it herself: turns the trailer around
so that instead of facing west, it now faces east. And when Baba
comes home, he—a poet who reveres pre-Islamic poetry—will
remember how Jahilia's women turned their tents around when
they wanted to divorce their husbands. And he'll stand on
the front "borch," now the back porch, and laugh a big, huge,
Texas-sized laugh.

14.

AT THE SUPERMARKET, which is where Mama and I get along best, they are selling holiday items seventy percent off. Mama leafs through them apathetically while I discreetly place a Marilyn ornament, featuring a pose from *Gentlemen Prefer Blondes*, into my left pocket, and a Wonder Woman ornament, featuring a fighting-evil-while-revealing-cleavage pose, into my right. Mama sighs and almost gives up on the discount items until something catches her eye: round, light brown, and dotted with reds and greens. Mama leaps for it, breathing lustily, "Oh, ze cake with ze frooooooooooooot." The entire grocery store— its every customer, employee, bagger, butcher, stocker—is staring at us. Mama piles the fruitcakes into the cart and people are looking as though she's loading up on hand grenades.

15.

MAMA BUYS A real Christmas tree for Christmas from a miniature forest in a parking lot. The man helps haul it to the Olds and straps it to the roof like the rug we strapped to the roof of our old car when we fled the war. Mama drives through rain badly and loses the tree halfway down the road. She flags down a truck driver who helps her put it back up on the roof, tying it tight, tying it on for dear life.

Mama arrives with it intact except it's missing some of its branches where it was tied down so tight. Gamal and I help her get it into the house and prop it up in a corner. It won't stay, keeps wavering and falling like a furry bum who's had too much bourbon. Later, we go to the store for ornaments and find a box that says "tree holder." We collectively mutter, "O-O-OH."

Baba comes home on the bus. He washes his hands and then sniffs around. He starts to sneeze. He sneezes one sneeze after another. He goes to the living room and sees the tree in the corner and blinks twice.

"Is that a fucking tree in my house?" he says.

"Yes," Mama says.

"Why? We are not Christians or pagans. We are not going to start celebrating Christmas now after years of not celebrating it. And I am allergic to it." Baba squints. "Am I imagining this or does it have a waist?"

"It has a waist," Gamal says.

"The man tied it too tight to the car," Mama says.

Baba sneezes.

"Get it out," he says.

"No," we all say, the way we'd said oh in the store. "NO-O-OH."

"Damn you, I said get it out," Baba says.

"This is a democratic nation," Mama says. "Three against one."

Baba screams for two hours till his throat goes hoarse and his nose gets red and he passes out from sheer exhaustion. He cannot change the fact that our household is changing. The next morning he wakes up. He showers. He gets on the bus.

SEVENTEEN

BIG PIMPIN'

• • •

PEOPLE WERE APPLYING TO COLLEGE. I STILL DIDN'T HAVE permission to apply anywhere but locally. Ideally (for Baba) I'd get into Texas and that would be that, a bus ride away. I filled out the application in glitter pen, picked my nose, extracted a giant booger, smeared it across the place where it said NAME OF APPLICANT, and left the sheet of paper on the dinner table. Baba tore it up and filled out a fresh application himself. I spied on him from my end of the long hallway, his knotted brow knotting further, his eyes glistening with excitement, his hands filling out the form carefully, like a cheerleader applying for new pom-poms. He looked sweet. I closed the door and turned on the radio, and a new song by Jay-Z came on. I opened the door again to spy some more. He looked so thrilled, I decided that he was pretending it was his own college application. He almost signed the bottom but stopped himself. A visible disappointment clouded his face. I felt sorry for him; he must have dreamed once of getting a doctorate from an American university. He got up from the table and I closed the door quickly, took out my chem homework, and pretended to work on it.

"Hi," he said, "you need to . . ." He stopped. "What is that music?" he said.

I rolled my eyes. "Jay-Z. You know, hip-hop?"

"Turn it up!" he said, urgently.

"OK, OK," I said surprised, and turned the volume knob clockwise.

"Sons of the whore!" he said.

"What's wrong?" I said.

"It's Abdel Halim's song."

"It's Jay-Z's song."

"Zay-G? He is thief," Baba said. "Don't you understand? Listen," he said, and sang the percussion in the sample. "*Khosara ya gara,*"—a pity, neighbor girl.

"Wow!" I said. "Jay-Z sampled Ab-Halim! Do we have it? The original?"

"We have every tape of every song the man ever recorded. But were you interested before Mr. Zay-G stole song?"

"I love Umm Kulthum and Fairuz!"

"Girl singers, and you are a girl: you should love them. But to extend yourself and love an Arab man's voice? That's dedication!"

"Why should I? Abdel Halim himself didn't like Arab girls," I said.

"What you mean?" he said, squinting at me.

"I mean he was gay. A cute, sweet-voiced homosexual."

"Abdel Halim was not a gay," Baba said.

"He wasn't *a* gay, but he was gay," I said.

"Then why didn't he want his neighbor girl to move?"

"Well, he goes on and on about his eyes tearing up. Because she lent him her mascara, I bet. I don't know."

"You are a stupid girl," he said. "Can't you hear the longing in the song?"

"It's just that jigga man pimp," said Jay-Z.

"No," I said.

"I will find the original," he said, and gave me the application. "Sign while I search for it."

He returned and slid the tape into the stereo just as I put down the pen. The song started and Baba whistled. Abdel Halim said that his eyes were shedding tears upon his neighbor girl with bitterness. "Then, I'm sure it was the mascara. Mascara makes me teary-eyed too."

"You are funny," Baba said and nudged my shoulder. I made a face at him. "Really. I mean it. You should go to *Saturday Night Live* and sit in their hallways until they hire you."

"It's in New York," I said, anxiously awaiting his reaction. How would he feel if I went that far away? Not for an *SNL* audition, but for, say, college?

"Not now," he said. "After you get your BA and your MA and your PhD . . ."

"And my GDSFER and my KIGJNVDRT. What the hell are you talking about?" I was feeling crazy; I wanted to test him.

"Why not?" he said. "Get a KIGJNVDRT. You can be whatever you want. You're a brilliant, beautiful woman."

Goddamn. He could be so charming sometimes.

I waited a few seconds and then asked, my heart leaping up, "Baba, what if I went to New York or somewhere like that for college?"

"What?" he said. "Why would you want to go all the way there for college when there is college close to your family?"

"Baba, even you got to go away for college!"

"Yes, but there was a war."

"No, you used to dream of going to college in Egypt. Even in America. I can tell."

He shook his head vigorously. "I did want to go away to college. But with you, it is different! You're . . . different from me."

"Because I'm a girl?" I shouted, and my shoulders shook.

"No! You are luckier than I was: you have a good college down the street! You can stay with your family, you are not forced to leave them."

"But I want to!" I said, and instantly regretted it.

"Why would you want to?" he said, his eyes glistening. "Are you ashamed of us?" he said, and I ran out of the room.

"Come back, you donkey!" he said.

"No!" I shouted from the living room area.

I ran out of the trailer, over to the yard, flung myself dramatically onto the grass, stretched my mind's arm to the stereo in my head, and pressed PLAY. I listened to Ab-Halim and cried. No one here knew who Ab-Halim was, no one knew who I was, and I'd never be like Ab-Halim's neighbor girl, I'd never part, never go away.

I SAT AND waited outside my counselor Ms. Quiff's office, trying not to repeat her name too often in my head—I often got stuck in a giggle fit when I did. I held my midday snack, a shiny red apple, in my hand.

Ms. Quiff called me into her office and I sat in the deep fake-leather chair. She went over my paperwork and announced that I had a 3.9. I told her I knew. She said I'd done very

well. I wanted to tell her that school had been my only constant since I was a child. Mother, homeland, self, that could
all be taken away, but school? School remained. It's why I
loved school.

"What are you thinking of applying in?" she said.

"Writing," I said.

She paused, adjusted her glasses on the bridge of her ugly
warty nose, and looked back down at the paperwork.

"All-righty. There are several colleges and universities, including Texas, of course. Your family has articulated to me their
wish that you study locally. I've been told to focus on campuses
within driving distance."

My stomach folded in on itself. I thought I would have my
counselor on my side. I thought school was my last, my only
hope. I felt betrayed, naked, stripped of all my hopes, and flung
down to earth, with the single bruised apple like forbidden fruit
in my right hand. I began to panic. She could see that.

"Most of your classmates are applying to local campuses as
well. You're not any different."

Oh, but I am. I always have been. And I would use it to my
advantage this time.

"Ms. Quiff, I'd like to apply to one college that is known for
its writing program, preferably on the East Coast. Just for the
hell of it. Like a lotto ticket."

Ms. Quiff adjusted her glasses again and dug around in
a file cabinet. "Here's a reference to most universities," she
said, handing me a book. "It might tell you which have
strong writing departments. Good luck, Nidali," she said,
rhyming my name with Italy. She peered out of the office and
yelled, "Next!"

I put the book in my backpack, hid it like a porno magazine. I rode off campus, skipped the rest of the day since I had study periods anyway. I rode past the small creek and stopped at Big Molly Park, splayed out on the grass, and fingered the book. I ignored the kids screaming at the top of their lungs, the parents screaming back: the drama that is family.

I lay in the grass and stared up at the big oak's branches above me. I thought about what Baba had said: Was I ashamed of my family? Of course I wasn't. As cool and open-minded as my baba claimed to be, he wanted me to stay a virgin, to stay "good." He didn't ever use the word virgin, he used the word "girl." He wanted me to stay a girl because he didn't want me to be a woman. Why didn't he ever want me to be a woman? I pictured him at St. Elizabeth's in Boston, wishing that by calling me Nidal I'd turn out male.

I got up, picked grass out of my curls, and looked over at the park. I watched a dad push his kids on the swings. "Higher, Daddy!" the kids yelled. "Higher!" The dad obliged and swung them hard so that they squealed and pretended to be in space.

I wondered if Baba never wanted me to be a woman because he never wanted me to struggle. It's funny that he called me "My Struggle": for a long time, I thought he meant I was *his* struggle.

So now, did Baba want me to stay a girl because he didn't want me to struggle, because he wanted to be there to help me when I did? Or was it because he loved me and didn't want me to go away from him? I decided that that was the root of his desire to keep me in Texas, at a college "up the street." He just loved me. And his love for me would remain, even if I decided to leave.

I went through the reference book, my "porno," hungrily, searching for the perfect place, like a fourteen-year-old boy searching for the perfect brunette. By sunset, I'd found her: a small college in Boston.

EIGHTEEN

DICTATIONS

• • •

IN PREPARATION FOR MY STATEMENT OF PURPOSE BABA ordered me to write essays, every day, preferably in both English and Arabic, about something purely Arab, or relating to my Arabness, or to a famous Arab. During this same period he began to play the lotto. He asked me to bring him a sheaf of the red-numbered tickets and dictated numbers to me while he lay on the faux-hardwood floor, his eyes shut, his money-making meditation in action. I filled in the circles with black pencil and he gave me fifty dollars, telling me he was glad I was around because he believed he would jinx the numbers if he paid for the bet himself.

Baba was terrified of taking a chance on his own writing and preferred to play the lotto and gamble that way.

He said there was no getting out of the compositions, which he pronounced "combozishans," and so I spent every weekend morning trying to come up with some bullshit so he'd leave me alone for a night.

COMBOZISHAN #3
I Come from Crazy Stubborn,
Mad Lovin' Hoes

. . .

I come from a great line of crazy hoes. My great-great-grand-mother Ibtisam grew up in a village in the Upper Nile valley and fought off rapists from the age of nine. She narrowly escaped getting circumcised by chaining her left ankle to a rail and telling my great-great-great-grandmother that she would not perform any of her required duties on the land unless she got to keep her clitoris—the first known clit-labor-strike in history—and so when all the girls went down to the Nile and threw their clits in it, as was the tradition, she was spared the sight of her own floating on the river's surface like the button of a fisherman's vest that had been scrubbed too hard and come loose.

Her great-great-great-great-grandmother had been returning from a morning washing her two sons' clothes at that very river when Napoleon's army entered Egypt and one of his soldiers thought she was fly.

Barely eighteen years old, she gave birth to her first daughter, a result of the rape, who carried blue eyes in her milky face, and four legitimate children followed.

The blue-eyed one grew up to be a baby machine, ancestor to 19.2 percent of the blue-eyed citizens of current-day Egypt.

The one who got to keep her clit was not blue-eyed, so when she gave birth to a blue-eyed girl everyone wailed that she must have slept around with the English and should have gotten her clit cut off to begin with, but her father defended her, remind-

ing everyone of his blue-eyed ancestor, and everyone relented, the way all small villages quickly make celebrities and abandon them.

Ibtisam's daughter gave birth to many sons, and the eldest married a painfully shy and passive woman, who gave birth to a painfully shy and blue-eyed son, who married a shamelessly loud and aggressive Greek woman, who gave birth to my dirty-green–eyed mama.

Mama married Baba, whose mama's mama had deserted his mama, practically selling her off to work for a family that was distantly related to Baba's mama's dead baba.

That deserting mama came from a bull of a mama who had a veranda of a chest which she got from her mama, whose nickname was Sakhra because her bosom was so immense her father made her lie on her back an hour each day beneath the weight of a giant Nablus rock that he had hoped would crush flat the giant tits; it didn't.

Sakhra's daughter's daughter's daughter gave birth to six daughters, three of whom had come with brothers in the womb: twins. The boys died within hours of their birth, so quickly that nobody sent for certificates of their births or their deaths, so that they were like light dreams that evaporate at the moment of awakening. The daughters grew to be plump and big-titted by the age of ten; even the ones who were left without covers in Nablus winters and the ones who were deliberately unfed for hours while the deserted daughter chanted and burned frankincense and prayed for the boys' lives, in vain.

The dead boys' sisters became famous because of their relentless will to live, and inspired a hikayye khuraffiyye—a folktale—that the deserter's daughter had aborted the fifth one in *the fifth month and threw her in the cistern, but the baby had lived anyway, climbing out of the water hole a few years later and demanding square cheese and bread. The fifth daughter always laughed at the story, with hoots and chuckles that were almost as big as her breasts.*

The seventh pregnancy was the most unwanted: the deserter's daughter had had enough of her belly expanding and her back buckling. So when she gave birth to a boy, she instantly sent for his birth certificate (she wanted to name him Waheed; her husband insisted on Said), and all the six sisters gathered around him, and he went from ample bosom to ampler bosom, and he lived.

And twenty-five years later, he married my flat-chested mother, who gave birth to me, a dirty-green–eyed big-titted mad stubborn crazy loving hoe.

COMBOZISHAN #9

East is East and West is West,

or,

Abdel Halim vs. A Tribe Called Quest

· · ·

In this short yet powerful essay I will attempt to delineate the vast differences in culture yet freakish proximity in purpose of the two musical entities. I will do this by quoting the lyrics and placing the words sung by each entity vis-à-vis the other.

(TRIBE)	(AB-HALIM)
Honey check it out you got me mesmerized,	*Dark, dark Goddess*
Witcha black hair and yo fatass thighs.	*who sent you after me?*

Here is another example:

<table>
<tr><td>

If yo moms don't approve
Then we'll just elope,
Let me save the little
man
From inside the boat.

</td><td>

and every
time
I say Mercy
The hands of fate
Toss me overboard.

</td></tr>
</table>

And yet another:

<table>
<tr><td>

Let me hit it from the back, girl,
I won't catch a hernia,
Bust off on your couch,
Now ya got Semen's furniture.

</td><td>

Yes, love has tossed us
And had its way with us.
So the one who hooked us
Must help get us off.

</td></tr>
</table>

COMBOZISHAN #14

Shoes,

or,

We Are Rootless

. . .

When I was only nine months old, I learned to walk. This is not because you taught me to by taking me to tracks and making me watch housewives and gay men walk at 6 A.M. every morning in Boston or because you taught me by example. Basically, I learned to walk because I discovered you were mental and I wanted to run, run as far away from you as possible. So that night when you took me to the fireworks show and you put me down and made me stand, I waited for the first chance I got, when I noticed you were staring at the reds and blues and silvers falling out of the black sky, and I took off. I walked and walked and all I remembered about you was your shoe, the brown one with the tassel. I walked the incredibly long-for-a-nine-month-old distance of fifteen feet when I saw sneakers and flip-flops and mary janes, and I missed your brown tasseled shoe terribly, so I came back.

Mama used to wear a brace on her leg because she was bow-legged and the brace would squeak. She didn't walk without a brace until she was seven. Her first crush was a boy whose left arm was made out of wood and squeaked. They sat in swings at the park and she squeaked her leg and he squeaked his arm and the swing set squeaked.

Every time I see a shoe's sole facing the ceiling I have to turn it around so that it is straight and flat against the ground. This is because the teachers at religion class taught us that leaving a shoe facing upwards was like giving God the shoe, or the finger, and was thus highly offensive to the High and Mighty. I thought it was true then, and even though now I think it's ridiculous I still turn over everyone's shoes whenever I see their soles facing upwards.

Sitto told me a story once of how her shoes used to be made entirely of tires, and once she told me a tale of a girl named Pome-granate Seeds who left her golden slipper in front of the house of an evil religion teacher who ate his students. He hunted the land look-ing for her but she was saved by a prince and it all turned out cool.

Once I heard you tell Gamal that a shoe is the most important part of a man's attire because it's his root. Gamal outgrew his only pair of sneakers last month.

AT THIS POINT, I should stop and say that upon reading these masterpiece essays, Baba promptly ripped them up and forced me to write down his own thoughts on when Arabness and Americanness first met.

This long opus, which was, of course, dictated to me, was entitled *Ibn Battuta in America*. Baba detailed how Ibn Battuta, the traveler who logged more miles than Marco Polo, had been the first outsider to set foot on the Americas, and that when Ibn Battuta had told his scribe Ibn Juzayy the story, Ibn Juzayy hadn't written it down but had instead written the masterpiece *Travels of Ibn Battuta*. When the book came out and everyone went crazy about it, Ibn Battuta was too ashamed to castigate Ibn Juzayy for his (*huge*) liberty, and Ibn Juzayy threatened to tell the world that Ibn Battuta was a loony who'd claimed to have discovered a new land and a new people, among whom he claimed to have lived for all those years. Ibn Battuta deferred to Ibn Juzayy and split his fortune with him, and Ibn Juzayy kept his mouth shut about being the true writer of the (fictitious) tales. Or so Baba dictated to me, every afternoon. Now back to the combozishans.

COMBOZISHAN #31

Ibn Battuta Did Not "Discover" America

• • •

Despite all your efforts to prove otherwise, he just didn't. There's no fucking way.

Why don't you apply to grad school or something and write your own compositions, instead of beating me up and ripping my shit apart?

COMBOZISHAN #56

Dictation Will Be the Cause
of Our Demise

* * *

Mama doesn't record her piano compositions and never has.

You don't write down your poems; you learn them by heart and don't tell them to me, so I'll never know them.

The Koran was memorized for centuries until someone realized that it could disappear, that people might take it with them to the grave, and so he wrote it down.

When you don't know how to write, like Sitto, someone will always write your letters for you. Even though you dictate them, you can never make sure that they won't add their own bullshit to them.

A dictator made us leave our home, and now a dictator rules it.

I WROTE DOZENS of compositions. The compositions I've chosen to share (3, 9, 14, 31, 56) were, I would like to add, not randomly picked: these numbers were the very ones Baba had once dictated to me for the lotto which—one starry and humid night —"won" him three thousand dollars. The numbers floated up, one by one, on the TV screen, and I stood and watched in shock. He matched the numbers on the screen to the ones on his notebook, then jumped up and down in front of the television screen in joy. When he asked me for his ticket I broke the truth to him gently—that I had been pocketing his fifty-dollar lotto money every week and not turning in his tickets. I told him that I viewed this act of money-taking not as a flagrant act of thievery (his opinion) but as my payment for spending every weekend writing a stupid essay that was promptly destroyed before my very eyes and replaced by my very hand and Baba's very tongue with a much more boring and pathetically improbable historical inaccuracy: in short, payment for my dues as a scribe.

Even Ibn Juzayy, I reminded Baba, had cash flow.

NINETEEN

DEMETER'S DAUGHTER FINALLY
GETS SOME SHOES

• • •

OUT OF THE SIX HUNDRED DOLLARS IN UNPAID LOTTO TICKET money I had kept, I used fifty to apply to the forbidden-fruit college in Boston. I filled out the application feverishly, as though writing a letter to a secret lover. I picked my favorite college essay, removed all the cuss words, and attached it. I was proud of all the work I'd done over the past twelve years of schooling, proud of how well I'd done in spite of a war and a huge move. I said this in my statement. I felt hopeful as I licked the big envelope and sealed it shut, put it in my backpack, and headed out the door.

I found Mama planting azaleas in the yard outside. Her black hair fell over her shoulders and her eyes. She looked in my direction when she heard the swinging screen door slam shut behind me.

"Come here and take this hair out of my eyes," she said.

"Do it yourself," I said.

"Come on," she said, "my hands are full of dirt."

I walked over to her and bunched her black hair behind her ears. Her eyes widened. "*Allah*," she said, "that's so much better. May God brighten the world for you." She looked down and saw my packet and looked back up at me. "*Yalla*, were you going somewhere?" To me, it sounded like her blessing, because don't mamas know everything?

I kissed her cheek and it smelled of dirt. I looked down at her hand and saw a slug crawling resolutely west on the mountainous chain of her knuckles. I ran to the bicycle and rode it up the hill to the post office, thinking all the while of Mama, of how Mama would die, of how much I'd cry when we bury her.

TIME PASSED. THERE was nothing to do and not many people to do it with, plus, everyone had senioritis.

Medina from math class began hanging out with Dimi and me; he had a gorgeous girlfriend, a fly *chica* who wore heavy golden triangle earrings and serious drag queen lipstick. Shit hit the fan when he found her fooling around with some white guy and went on a rebound rampage.

Two weeks later, I went over to his trailer to do calculus homework together. I was in some seriously funky sweatpants, a torn T-shirt, no bra, and I hadn't showered or washed my hair in three days; I'd broken up with the tub's faucet. So we were both on the rebound. He walked down the long hallway and I stuck myself in his way.

"Rebound with me," I said.

He laughed and ruffled my hair. "But you're Nidali," he said. "It ain't like that with us."

"Why *not?*" I said. I could feel my bottom lip trembling.

"You're like my little cousin or something."

"Little? I'm sixteen! I'll be seventeen in August! Plus, we're not at all related. We're not even from the same hemisphere!"

"It just ain't like that with us."

"Great," I said. I was so embarrassed. I wanted to get the hell out of there. But I stayed, and we sat outside his trailer in plastic seats with their netting ripped out and smoked a joint. A wasp that had made its home under the seat, on the remaining netting, must have thought I was IDF doing home demolitions because it stung me in the ass.

"Holy shit," I said. "That fucking thing bit me!"

"Shut up," he said. "For real?"

"Yeah, for real. It stings like a motherfucker!" I stood up and rubbed it. My ass was already big enough.

"It bit you *there*?" he said, and laughed.

"Ha ha, not funny. I'm in pain."

"I have aloe vera," he said, "and some buena-drill. You want it?"

I didn't say anything. I couldn't tell if it was the weed or what, but I felt woozy and warm.

"You look funny. You all right?"

"No," I said.

"Come inside."

We walked through the long fake-wooden hallway to his room, and I plopped onto my tummy, on his small mattress. He brought me pills and aloe vera.

"Shit," I said. "I can't move."

"Maybe you're allergic to wasps. Maybe you're dying," he said.

"Don't *say* that," I said, "don't say that."

"Should I call 911 or something?"

He sounded genuinely concerned. About *me*.

"It's too late anyway if I'm dying. They won't be able to help me."

"Oh, you shitting me now. You just messin' with my head."

"It's a very cute head," I said.

"You're faking it."

"I'm not faking it. Maybe your *chica* used to, though."

"Don't be a bitch," he said.

"What if I *am* dying," I said. I was slurring my words. "You wouldn't let me die a virgin, would you?"

"You're a virgin?" he said, faking surprise.

"I hate you," I said.

"Yes, I'd let you die a virgin. 'Cause you're my friend, and I don't feel that way about you."

"E-u-a-i-u-e-i," I said.

"You sound funny," he said. "Maybe you *are* dying. Flip over, let me look at you."

I flipped over, but the pain of being on my ass was so immense that I screamed out.

"Chill out," he said.

"I can't go home like this. I can't sit on my bike seat. My dad's gonna tear me apart."

"Just relax. Here, take this. It's good for you."

I took it.

He went over to his record player and put on something I didn't recognize. I'd pictured being in Medina's room a few times. Okay, a thousand times. I'd kissed my hand and thought about his eyes, his pillows, his bed, his hands on me just so. I'd never pictured it like *this*. *This* . . . sucked. My ass was swelling as I had these thoughts. The sun was setting as though there was a setting race; the sky outside was darkening abnormally fast. Baba would end up punishing me for no reason. Then I would die of the bee sting, a virgin. And people would assume my sweet, sweet Baba killed me just because he was Arab. I remembered that sixteen-year-old girl in Minnesota or was it Michigan or Montana or Minneapolis, someplace that began with M, whose baba had killed her. He was Palestinian and she was dating a black kid and working at a drive-thru, and so her insane baba killed her.

The story had been on the cover of some magazine and my social studies teacher Mrs. Ruben showed it to the class. I felt sad for the girl, as I'm sure everyone else did. Then, out of the blue it seems, Mrs. Ruben, who, up to then, I thought really liked me, asked me to stand up and say a few words about my Palestinian dad. It took me a few moments to register if she was trying to make the class understand that not all Palestinians were bad or if she was simply reducing me to my Palestinian-ness. Either way I hated her. I couldn't imagine her bringing in a statistic about a black or Latino criminal then asking a black or Latino kid to stand up and defend his entire race.

So I said my father was from a village in the West Bank that got completely fucked in '67 and he had to live in a hostel for a year and try to make it across to Egypt to be educated and he succeeded and now he designs houses and is at work patenting a foundation formula, and then I wished the ignorant bitch would die, just keel over. She didn't. But I probably would.

Medina sat on the bed next to me and read me the album jacket's cover. His voice sounded like it was coming from the inside of a shell or an endlessly tall shower stall. I smelled his sheets. You'll never be on his sheets again, I thought, so suck their smell inside your mind. Memorize this. When he was done reading, I propped my chin up and my greasy hair fell over into my face. His fingers moved the hair out of my eyes like a curtain lifter. Then he looked at me for a while. I frowned and said, "What?" He kept staring. Then he kissed me.

I'd imagined his lips, their fullness, but what I got was so much better. It was like having a watermelon for days then finally opening it up and finding out that it tastes sweeter than any candy bar you've ever bought. His lips met mine and seemed to latch on; then they were on my neck on my nipple on my waist on my hip on my other lips. It was as though he'd done it in one swoop, taken me all in at once. His mouth never left my skin. His tongue made the tub faucet seem like such a waste of time. Here was wetness and pressure and human organs rubbing against each other. This was the best machine. I couldn't do anything. I was numb from the medicine and the bite, and the pain from the swelling kept coming back like a persistent wave. My clothes were off. His clothes are almost all off. I managed to move my arms down to his underwear—*boxer shorts*, I thought, I'd *never* seen boxer shorts in real life—and wrapped my fingers around his erection. At that moment, I regretted all the years I'd spent not using tampons for fear that they would take my virginity. I looked at him then, stared first at his toes, his sculpted calves, his buttocks, his belly, the dark, dark hair at the bottom of it, at his cock, his nipples, his neck, his earlobes, his nose—it was a good nose—and his eyes.

I said, "You're probably part Arab," and he laughed. "Seriously," I said, "somewhere up the line, if you think about it,

there was an Arab *abuela* in there. Your last name means 'city.'"
"No it doesn't," he said. "It does in Arabic," I said. "Okay," he
said. "Maybe an Arab *abuelo*." And he lifted me over him. "You
lead," he said. "You have to control how much you can take; I
don't want to hurt you." I sat over him, took his hand and rocked
it back and forth over my clit until I could let go and he could
guess the rhythm himself. "Keep doing that," I said. I spied a
condom on his dresser and tried to unwrap it, but I had no idea
how to, so I tossed it at him. He slipped it on and I grabbed him
and rubbed myself with his tip. Medina, I thought, slowly, as he
made a pilgrimage from my clit to my insides. I took it in small
quantities, and every few seconds the pain from my sting came
back and took away the pain from my insides so I could go further, so I timed it, and then I loved that wasp. I pictured its stinger,
pointed and targeted and sharp and I sat on Medina and rocked
up and down and wriggled and laughed and grunted and bared
my teeth as he pronounced my name perfectly over and over and
over again and I felt my insides spreading and opening up, a
glowing and growing, until I came.

But Medina didn't. He said he could only come when he
loved someone, and then he started to cry. Now *this* was *weird*.
I had to get on my bike and pedal twenty minutes and then
explain my gimpy, virginity-lost, innocence-gone walk. I had
a good alibi on my ass, I repeated to myself; I could always show
Mama the bite and she could get me out of it. Medina kept crying and saying, "I'm sorry." How to tell him that I didn't need
him to be sorry, that I needed him to help me find my underwear? How to haul ass out of this delicate situation? There was
no way around it. I had to let him cry it out, and once he was
assured that he would one day love again or maybe even get

his girl back, who would in turn bear all ten of his children, I was finally off.

No one was waiting at home. Mama, Baba, and Gamal were all out to dinner, and the frogs stood outside on the rim of the pond and made their regular Friday night mating calls. I bathed reluctantly. I always want to smell this day, this experience, but I didn't want Mama or Baba to. In the tub I gently sponged beween my legs until the blood washed away. I dried off and wrapped my hair in a towel. Then I sat, naked, on an ice pack; my entire nether region needed one. I briefly pondered whether I would go to hell. But then I decided that God would not have created beautiful men like Medina, or wasps, or premaritally breakable hymens, if it were God's intention to throw me in hell. I thought about the man my parents and everyone around me always said I would marry: that was the man I was supposed to lose my virginity to. I felt a sense of panic about whether I would be loved now that I was no longer a virgin, then thought of why I would ever want to marry anyone who held that condition over me. I felt free, unburdened, but I was also scared and in pain. The house was so quiet my ears clutched onto the rare silence. My ice pack melted, dripping water loudly onto the wooden floor, and the drips quickened, then poured, so that I heard water everywhere around me, until finally I realized that it was raining, pouring pails and buckets of heaven's rain onto our metal roof above my head.

Sometimes, Mama would wake up in the middle of the night with a start, lean over me, and put her finger under my nose to check for breathing. I'd resist the impulse to bite it or to hold my breath and terrify her. The pianos in the backyard—pianos she'd rescued, bought at Goodwill and the Salvation Army and dried-out yellow yards and wet dank garages and basements— would beckon her. They littered the property like hungry, broken old dogs in their twilight years. She'd attend to each of them until it got too dark to see or her flashlight died. I'd hear the front door bang against the metal frame and her heavy feet drag along the linoleum floors, her body collapsing into bed and her snores, long like sirens. Real sirens from police cars would punctuate her snores until the cars would turn a far away corner and she'd toss in her sleep.

She woke me up one night in the middle of the night. She shook me. "*Ya bint, is-hi ya bint,*" she said.

"*Eh,* what is it?"

"Tell me the truth, you've had sex."

"Don't be silly," I said.

"Tell me the truth. I know you have. You'll always be a princess to me. Just tell me the truth."

My eyelashes felt like they had mini-anvils pinned to them, and I fell back asleep. She shook me again.

"Tell me, *habibti.*"

"OK, OK," I said. I didn't want to tell her, but her fingers encircled my arms, her hand a lasso o' truth, and something *compelled* me. "I'm not a virgin," I said.

"I love you, still," she said. "Good night."

The next morning, I wondered if I'd dreamt it all.

The only thing I could count on was the mail, which came by at two every afternoon. If I missed last period, I could see the

mail woman walking it up to our mailbox, her underarms
stained with sweat. As soon as she'd lift the mailbox's mouth
shut I'd run up to it and check for acceptance letters.

They say the world says no so many times but that one day,
in the wake of all the no's, and as a break from all the no's to
come, the world said a resounding Yes. One momentous afternoon the mailbox was empty save for four things: a thin envelope for Baba from the bank, a fat envelope for Mama from Ed
McMahon, a thin envelope addressed to Baba for the light bill,
and a big envelope for me from Boston. I shoved the letter from
Boston in a bush, to read later, and took the rest of the letters
to Mama and Baba, who were sitting on the patio, sipping
thick coffee.

Mama opened the letters one by one, tossing most of them
into the barbeque pit. Then she opened and read the letter from
the bank.

"Waheed!" she screamed.

"What happened, woman?" Baba shrieked, fearing the worst,
and grabbing the nearest stick to protect himself and Mama.

"What's the stick for?" she said, wrinkling her brow.

"Is there a snake?"

"What? A snake?"

"Why did you scream so loud if there wasn't a rattlesnake?"

"No, not a rattlesnake! A mortgage! Read this," she said, and
handed him the letter.

Baba read the letter and he screamed too, then Mama screamed
again, so I screamed, and Gamal ran out to the patio from his
room to find out what we were all screaming about, and we
hugged and linked arms and jumped up and down as Baba and

Mama screamed, "We will have our home! We will have our home!" Mama and Baba finally had the money to build the house they'd always wanted.

But even as my feet jumped and my eyes smiled, my heart caved in on itself, like the letters in the barbeque pit, as I wondered how long that home would hold us, how long that home would last.

I WENT TO prom by myself, although technically I was with Juman, a fly black junior Dimi threatened to escort me. At the end of the night he kissed my cheek and told me to have fun; it was only 1 A.M. (the dictator was relaxing his grip).

A week later I almost opened the Boston-postmarked letter. I understood what a big letter meant but I wasn't ready to really know yet or to figure out what I would do next, how I would actually break the news to Mama and Baba, how I would go away.

Graduation was a complete letdown. No one had any weed and Baba wanted me home for chocolate cake and an early, fun-free night. Mama bought me a journal. After cake I sat outside in the wet grass and caressed the Boston letter, feeling like I'd get the runs if I dared open it. I thought of Wonder Woman, how she'd have shredded the envelope to pieces by now, read the letter once, and packed. Assuming she'd get in.

I ripped the envelope open and took the letter out quickly like an unsheathed sword. I put the letter in my lap and unfolded it slowly, like a present or a delicate meal. I read the first sentence and yelped out in ecstasy.

* * *

BABA WAS LIVID: about the fact that I'd applied to the program in Boston, about the fact that I did it without consulting him, about my considering going away, so far away, for university "when there is a university right up the street," about his own life. He told me that I was going against his wishes. He asked me to sit on the patio with him and Mama, and they both sat with hands folded in laps and Baba looked at me and asked, "Why do you do this to us?"

"What are you talking about?" I yelled.

"Waheed, ask her a specific question and let's get this over with."

"What do you want?" he said.

"I want to go to a good college, because I deserve to. That's what you've always taught me! I've worked hard and studied all my life to earn it. If it means leaving here, so be it."

"Is that what you want then? To leave here?"

"Yes."

"*Khalas*, Waheed. Let her go," Mama said, fanning herself with sheet music.

"My daughter will not go anywhere!" he shouted. "She will not leave my house."

"But we haven't even built it yet," I said.

"You will not leave my trailer, then."

"Do you know how ridiculous that sounds?" Gamal said, peeking out from behind a bush. He surprised me rarely, but I was shocked just then.

"You shut up," Baba told him. "You," he turned to me, "will stay at home, finish college and get a PhD and whatever other degrees you want. Staying home will help you focus. Who

knows what would happen if you go far away? You may lose
sight of everything I planned for you."

"But I have my own plans. And I'm determined to see them
through, Baba."

"What do you want?" he shouted again.

"I want to be happy," I said, without thinking. "Just like you
do. Just like Mama does. Just like Gamal does," I said.

"But Nidali . . . what is more important?" Baba said, and
paused. "Your happiness or mine?"

Not ours. Mine.

His question was a brick, heavy and real. Knocked me clean
on the head. I could see.

OPERATION RUN AWAY required much stealth. It demanded se-
crecy and a surprise disappearance with all tracks covered.
I didn't leave a note. It wasn't like the time I ran away to be
a vendor; this time the stakes were higher than letters between
a boy and a girl. This time it was just me: my whole life,
my future.

Mama and Baba were out. Gamal was watching TV and there
was no way around him. I didn't want to tell him I was leaving
because I didn't want to implicate him and get him into trouble.

I packed my bag with clothes and music and a book about
Ancient Greece, stuffed the bag through the crank-window, and
threw it onto the burrs and stickers in the yard. I walked out the
door as though I was going to water the plants, an excuse that I
found symbolic. I ran around the trailer to the bag and picked
off the stickers, a couple of which were too stubborn to let go of

the canvas. I left them there and heard Mama noisily pulling into the flea-ridden gravel and soil driveway. I heard her laugh. I told myself it could be the last time I heard her laugh, depending on how this would go down. I ran again, past the previously homeless pianos with their broken teeth and intact cavities, their mouths flapping farewell farewell farewell at me.

Dimi lived in a small house on the prominently Mexican east side. When I got there I heard loud *cojunto* music and I was dying for a glass of water. I knocked on the front door but no one answered, so I followed the music to the back yard. I was greeted by half a dozen men in cowboy hats, Bud Light in hand, two dozen kids jumping on a trampoline, murals of wild animals and tropical settings on corrugated metal sheets against the fence, a makeshift canopy made of blue tarp, a few plastic chairs, some mosquitoes, the smell of fajita chicken and corn tortillas, and Dimi and her aunts.

"Hey, girl! What are you up to?" she said.

I looked at the aunts and gave each of them an "hola," then asked Dimi, "Can I have some water?" and Dimi leaned over a cooler.

"Is this OK?" she said, handing me a Doctor-B, and I nodded.

"Sit!" she said, "and tell me why you look all bent."

Ten days. I lived with Dimi, in Dimi's room, on her floor, for ten days. I ate a single corn tortilla and eggo and beans once a day. I held myself hostage in this way.

While she was at work I lay on her floor and stared at the ceiling, thought about what I was going to do, and left my shoes facing up, at God.

I thought about home, but I thought about the old apartment in Kuwait, the courtyard all brushy with long grass since we left it, because in my mind it had been neglected and uninhabited all this time.

I spent my days reading on Dimi's floor. I read about Atalanta: her father wanted her to be a boy. When he saw that she was a girl, he took her to a mountaintop and left her there to die. She survived because the Goddess sent a beast to nurse her and raise her. At least my fate wasn't that bad. I was more like Athena, born first of Demeter, then a second time of her father's headache.

Mama came to the house on the tenth day. I sensed her like a cat; I knew she was around even before her fist knocked against the front door. Dimi's mama came to the door and smiled; she didn't speak English. Mama kept repeating, "My daughter? Nidali? She is here? My daughter?"

I heard a new urgency in her voice, a tone I'd never heard before. She sounded the way I did when I was a kid, afraid and worried about my mama in the desert with the tall black electric wires, afraid she'd get swallowed up forever.

Dimi took off her headphones.

"Who's that? That your moms?"

"Yeah. Don't tell her I'm here, Dimi! Don't give me up."

She nodded and smiled, told me to get under her bed. I stayed down there and listened as she talked to Mama.

"She's not here. I ain't seen Dolly in like two weeks."

"You are a liar. I know she's here. I've been looking for her every day. Nidali, *ana shayfaaki, ya kalba*! I see you, you bitch! Come home!"

She yelled desperately. She couldn't see me. She couldn't. I stayed where I was: under the bed like a bogeyman.

I heard the door creak shut and stayed where I was until Dimi came back into the room and sat down. She tapped her foot against the linoleum floor and finally said, "You can come out." When I did, she looked away, and said, "Your mami's face was white and pale like a ghost. Ay, Dolly, this is sad. She looked crazed. Her hair was all wild."

Mama was Demeter, come to bring me back home.

We discovered later that day—from Camilla, from Medina (whom I hadn't heard from since the wasp incident), from the guy who worked the door on poetry slam nights, from the dude at the gas station where we got our smokes, and from a few other people—that Mama had gone everywhere I'd ever been, looking for me. She'd done it at least three times each place, throwing fits and yelling.

That night I couldn't sleep. When I closed my eyes I saw flashes from my childhood: Gamal and I dancing while Mama played the piano in Kuwait; Fakhr's nose; Geddo's swimming lessons; the Allenby Bridge. I remembered how I used to believe that when I was forced to run to a new home, the skin of my feet would collect sand and rocks and cactus and seeds and grass until I had shoes made of everything I picked up from running. I always thought that when I got those earth-shoes, I'd be able to stop running and settle down somewhere I'd never have to run away from again. In the morning, I'd be going home. I had to stick up for myself so that when I went away to school I wouldn't be running. Just going. I raised my leg then and looked at the bottom of my foot. It was dark and thick with dirt.

TWENTY

DEPARTURE'S ARRIVAL

. . .

WHEN I APPROACHED OUR TRAILER, NO ONE WAS THERE. IT was eerie; someone was always home. I tried the front door but it was locked, so I went around back and tried the hallway door, but it had always been locked; we'd never even used it once.

I was exhausted. I got in the hammock by the old Bush & Gerts and passed out almost immediately.

When I woke up I thought I was still in a dream because a woman was standing a few yards away from me on the patio, her hands on her hips. She looked like Mama, except she had a lot of white hair. I looked at her some more and decided it was Mama. She nodded and said "*Shayebteeni, ya kalba,*" turned around and walked back into the house. I saw her hair from the back: all white, as I suspected, with dozens of two-inch strands of black hair.

"You made me go gray, you bitch."

I followed her inside. She was in her bedroom, lying in bed. "Pull up all the curtains, and close my door. Don't let anyone wake me up."

"I'm sorry, Mama."

She made a "hmm" sound and pointed at the curtains. I drew them and went to the door. Mama buried her body completely under the blanket.

"Mama, I really am sorry."

"Close the door. We'll talk when I wake up," she said.

I shut the door and got one last glimpse of her head, her white head with the thirty-odd black strands.

My mother's head was a piano.

Gamal slammed the door and lumbered in. I could hear his loud hip-hop through his enormous black earphones. He animatedly slammed the door shut and threw his backpack four feet away from his body, into the corner. He kept his earphones on when he saw me, walked past me to his room and said, "You're in deep shit." He said it loudly because the earphones were still on and he couldn't hear his own voice. His voice was newly manly and made the entire trailer vibrate.

I'm shocked that Mama didn't wake up after that.

She didn't wake up. She slept: she slept through my forty-five-minute shower. She slept through the guys who loudly picked up the trash. She slept through Baba coming home and yelling at me, "I won't hit you this time. I won't hit you! What's the point? What do you want, Nidali? You almost killed your mother! You killed your mother!" She slept through my screams about wanting my own life, and she slept through Gamal blasting music in his room to drown us out.

EVENTUALLY MAMA RECOVERED and went out to tend to her plants and play the piano.

"She stayed awake for ten nights for you," Baba said, now that he'd calmed down. He sat on the couch with me, at ease. "You know, like the Fairuz song."

I remembered that song, remembered listening to it in the old Oldsmobile, on the glittery Gulf Road with Mama and Baba, his pitch-black mustache gleaming at me in the sun then, his young smile as he said, "Sing, sing! *Ghanni, ya binit!*" and my girl voice beaming out in perfectly pitched peals, Mama's eyes closed, her black hair cascading down the torn upholstery, the black electric towers flying past us like giant measurements, calculating the height of our memories. I was a child; I had no worries about where I belonged. We were a family with a short history then; my parents were making my memories.

It must be strange to be a parent, to be like a filmmaker who is always on, always rolling one memory or another for your child.

I pitied my mama, who stayed up like the little girl in the Fairuz song, waiting for the moon to come down for her love. And I didn't spend too much time wondering who the moon was and who her love was.

I'd spent all my life wondering whom Mama loved more: Baba or me. Who would she choose? It seemed she always chose him. It seemed she only wanted him. Now it didn't matter. Now I saw her heart wasn't perfectly divided into keys. She loved us both. She wanted us both. And this fact was probably the cause of much struggle, much joy, for her.

Baba stroked his mustache and looked at me. "So, this is your decision?" he said, finally.

"Baba . . . even if I went to college here, I wouldn't want to commute from the house. Do you know why? Because I don't want to be different. I know I *am* different, I know it, but I don't want to feel like an outsider. I want to do college right, because . . . it means a lot to me."

I pitied my Baba in his suit, his brow furrowed, his heart broken.

I reached out to hug him; I rested my face in the cloth of his suit; I breathed in the fabric and heard my father's heart, and Baba said, "I remember the way you used to breathe against my neck when you were a baby. I'd rock you to sleep and you would breathe . . . two tiny columns of breath against me, here," he gestured with his hand. "I can still feel it."

THE NIGHT BEFORE I left for Boston, as I was dreaming in bed, Mama hovered over me. I woke with a start because at first I thought she was a ghost. I told her this, that I felt like there were spirits riding me. She smiled like a spirit.

"I wanted to give you these," she said, and handed me a heart-shaped box.

"What the fuck is that?" I said, shocked at the box.

She slapped my mouth gently, "Why 'fuck'? Always 'fuck.' Fuck this, fuck them, fuck her, fucking A, fuck that, fucking stupid, fuck me, fuck you."

"Whoa," I said, "that was cool. Can you say it again?"

"Fuck you," she said.

"No," I said, "the whole thing."

She gently slapped my mouth again. "I bring you treasure and you want to hear me say vulgar words. Maybe I take back." She put the heart box in her lap and stood up to go. I reached out and fixed my grip on her skinny arm.

"What it is?" I said. "Is it your jewelry?" She shook her head. "It's your letters to Baba and vice versa?"

"Just open the fucking thing," she said, and I laughed. I untied the leather ribbons and broke knots with my teeth. I opened it up and I saw them. Folded up pages. I said, "So they *are* the letters." Mama's letters to Baba when they were in lust.

Mama shook her head. "No. I'm not that sentimental. You are the sentimental one. Here. Proof." She unfolded the letters' square shapes and showed me my compositions from fifth grade, seventh grade, eighth grade. She saved every single thing I'd written for *imla* or composition, every single thing I thought Baba had discarded. "I told you I save things for you," she said.

"But I thought you meant mementos . . ." I said, "you know, like earrings and plastic nametags on umbilical cords."

"These are your writings," she said. "These are your words. You will be a writer, no? You must keep all of this for posterity. I want you to write."

I hugged her hard against myself. I smelled her burnt hair. I smelled her goodness. I heard Chopin.

"Don't you ever, ever, in your life, *umrik*, ever, ever . . ."

"Spit it out," I said.

". . . ever forget us."

THE PEN IS a *sura* in the Koran that starts: "*Nun*. By the pen, and what they write, you are not mad: thanks to the favor of your Lord! A lasting recompense awaits you, for yours is a sublime nature. You shall before long see, as they will see, which of you is mad."

One afternoon, shortly after we'd moved to America, I found
Mama and Baba fighting about a pen a woman had given him
twenty years ago on a flight from Amman to Kuwait. Baba said
the woman had insisted he keep the pen. I assumed that Mama
was just jealous about the woman, but it became clear after a
few minutes that she believed this pen to be a spy pen. I went
to their room and tried to calm her down. "Look at it," she said,
"feel how heavy it is." And she was right. "I can't get the top
part to open," she said. "That's where the microphone is." Baba
told her to calm down. She wouldn't. "Our lives have been
recorded," she said. "Someone out there knows everything
that's gone on inside our house."

Baba tried to open the pen, to show her there was nothing
inside. But it wouldn't open.

Gamal ran over the pen with his bike. It remained intact.

I got a hammer from the toolbox and started hammering into
the pen. I hammered for minutes, then, it seemed, for hours.

Nothing.

That's when we knew Mama was right and we all piled into
the old car, drove out to the back roads, and took the pen
with us.

Baba recited from *Luqman*, "If all the trees of the earth were
pens, and the sea, replenished by seven more seas, were ink,
the words of God could not be finished still."

Mama reached over and threw the pen out the window.

I catch the pen now and listen to all our stories.

ACKNOWLEDGMENTS

My deepest gratitude to the following:

My fairy godmama, Leslie Marmon Silko, who encouraged this project and went above and beyond to support it. Jin Auh for her unwavering faith and perseverance. Kathryn Lewis for her efforts and dedication, and Mindy Okura-Marszycki for her insightful suggestions. Judith Gurewich for her belief in the book and her eagerness to share it with the world.

My friends who read earlier drafts and listened over the years, supplying advice, coffee, wisdom, comfort, encouragement, and, in some cases, babysitting services and rent money: Michalle Gould, Erika Kane, Hayan Charara, Zeina El-Azzi, Michelle Detorie, Laila Lalami, Jamie Allen, Elka Karl, Kim Jackson, Selina Keilani, Wendy Mitchell, Ahmad Aidy, Muhammad Aladdin, Leila Abu-Saba, Karen Olsson, Jim Lewis, Nirvana Tanoukhi, Christine Lee Zilka, Taiyaba Husain, and Laura Wetherington.

Russell Mulvey, for his love and support.

Naomi Shihab Nye, Khaled Mattawa, and Anton Shammas for their example and their encouragement.

Jo Glanville and Lee Klein for publishing early excerpts. Hedgebrook, for its magical residency in 2006, and the Million Writers Award, the Avery Hopwood and Jules Hopwood Award, and the Geoffrey James Gosling Prize for their support and celebration of the manuscript.

Much love and many thanks to my son, Angelo, for his daily inspiration and encouragement, and to my siblings, Raed and Donia, for all the love and comfort they've given me. Finally, I am eternally grateful to my mother and father who for many years supported and believed in my writing in general and this novel in particular: their faith, love, and generosity were crucial to its completion. Thank you.

• • •

I owe some of the historical information in this novel to *A History of the Arab Peoples*, by Albert Hourani (New York: Warner Books, 1992). Some of the ideas in chapter eleven were gleaned from *Rule of Experts: Egypt, Techno-politics, Modernity*, by Timothy Mitchell (Berkeley: UC Press, 2002). I first read the folktale told by Sitto in chapter six in *Speak, Bird, Speak Again*, by Ibrahim Muhawi and Sharif Kanaana (Berkeley: UC Press, 1989). All quotes from the Koran are from the NJ Dawood Penguin edition. Also, I acknowledge the few historical inaccuracies in the novel. For example, I am aware that Jay-Z's "Big Pimpin'" did not appear until 1999.